A DETECTIVE INSPECTO

MURDER OF ANGELS

NEW YORK TIMES #1 BESTSELLER **TONY LEE** WRITING AS

JACK GATLAND

Hooded Man
MEDIA

Published by Hooded Man Media

First Edition: January 2021
Second Edition: July 2023

PRAISE FOR JACK GATLAND

'This is one of those books that will keep you up past your bedtime, as each chapter lures you into reading just one more.'

'This book was excellent! A great plot which kept you guessing until the end.'

'Couldn't put it down, fast paced with twists and turns.'

'The story was captivating, good plot, twists you never saw and really likeable characters. Can't wait for the next one!'

'I got sucked into this book from the very first page, thoroughly enjoyed it, can't wait for the next one.'

'Totally addictive. Thoroughly recommend.'

'Moves at a fast pace and carries you along with it.'

'Just couldn't put this book down, from the first page to the last one it kept you wondering what would happen next.'

Before LETTER FROM THE DEAD...
There was

LIQUIDATE
THE PROFITS

Learn the story of what *really* happened to DI Declan Walsh,
while at Mile End!

An EXCLUSIVE PREQUEL, completely free to anyone who
joins the Declan Walsh Reader's Club!

Join at bit.ly/jackgatlandVIP

COVERT ACTION

COUNTER ATTACK

STEALTH STRIKE

DAMIAN LUCAS BOOKS

THE LIONHEART CURSE

STANDALONE BOOKS

THE BOARDROOM

.

For Mum, who inspired me to write.

For Tracy, who inspires me to write.

CONTENTS

PROLOGUE

THE MORNINGS ALWAYS STARTED WITH A COUGHING FIT.

Derek Salmon leaned over the side of his bed, violently coughing into a small clear Tupperware container that he'd left there for such situations. He'd found out the hard way that coughing blood onto a carpet first thing in the morning destroyed the weave in it and, as he'd spent a lot of money on having the entire house re-carpeted a few years back, this wasn't on. Now Derek started his mornings leaning to the side and racking up phlegm and blood into a small plastic box; one that used to hold his packed lunch back in the days when he used to have a job.

Cancer was a bastard.

Getting to his feet, Derek stretched his arms and opened out his chest, trying to shake away the morning sluggishness. This was an important day. He needed to be at the top of his game today, although he had been nowhere near the top of anything in quite a while.

After a quick shower, Derek stared at himself in the bathroom mirror. The chemotherapy had turned his once dark-brown hair white, but it hadn't fully fallen out yet, and this now made it nothing more than a collection of random white threads of hair that damply flattened out over his scalp.

This wouldn't do.

Grabbing a cordless shaver, Derek ran it over his head, allowing the shaver to remove the wispy white hair, leaving the scalp with nothing more than a small amount of stubble. This done, he used the shaver on his beard scruff; he needed a full shave for the day ahead.

With a closely cropped head and a clean jawline, Derek felt he looked a little more respectable. He pulled at his skin as he stared in the mirror; his face was drawn and haggard, the skin from his rapid weight loss gathering around his jowls. But he expected this, and there was nothing that he could do about it.

Not even makeup would hide the fact that he was dying.

Next was dressing. For the last month he'd worn jogging bottoms and an old tee-shirt as his daily clothing, with maybe a hoodie placed over it when he got a little colder, which was increasingly more common these days. He wasn't going out anywhere, and it seemed churlish and vain to tidy himself up to wear his better clothes for pottering around the house. But today was a day that he needed to be taken seriously. And so, it was a shirt, tie, and suit day for Derek Salmon. It was the first time he'd worn such a sartorial combination in months.

He didn't have any breakfast as he didn't know when he'd eat next, and he also knew that there was a very strong chance that he'd throw it back up anyway, most likely in a holding cell. No, it was better to risk hunger than shame. And, if he was finding himself peckish later, he was sure that some old friends would help him out, maybe with a few biscuits or a sandwich.

Pulling his scarf on, Derek looked over to the sideboard in his living room. On it were photos of two women, both in their own respective frames. The older of the two was his ex-wife, Amanda. They'd been separated for over ten years now and barely spoke these days, but he liked the photo and had kept it up. As far as Derek knew, Amanda didn't know about his illness and the terminal diagnosis; that was unless the woman in the second photo, his daughter Evie, nineteen years old and starting her second year in University right now, had told her. Derek had decided early on that no matter what happened with Amanda, Evie had to be a part of this, had to be *aware* of this, if only to cope with the administration nightmare that would occur once he died.

Now ready for the day ahead, opening his front door and walking out into the brisk North London air, Derek smiled to himself. For the first time in a long while he had a purpose, a reason to *do* something. It might not be something that he wanted or even expected to do, but he could still do it. The doors were closing on him, but this door was still wide open and beckoning.

He didn't have a car anymore, but the walk to the Tottenham North Command Unit where he once worked wasn't that far a stroll. That said, by the time he reached the entrance he was already woefully out of breath, forced to lean against the door to get his breath back before entering.

The reception to the Unit was the same as any other London Police Station: the floor was a strange linoleum swash of lines and squares, the walls were a mixture of salmon and cream as if they had once been lighter but years of constant crime passing through the doors had darkened them, while the doors themselves were a pale-blue. And, at the front was a glass window above a white counter where the Desk Sergeant sat, waiting for people to come in and most likely ruin her day. Today, the reception was empty, and the Desk Sergeant looked up as Derek entered the Command Unit, her face paling as she saw the horrific changes to the once Detective Inspector. She hid it well with a fake smile, though. Derek knew it was a fake smile. He'd seen so many of them over the last six months.

'DI Salmon!' she exclaimed. 'Good to see you up on your feet.'

'It's just Derek these days, Maisie.'

'You'll always be DI here, sir.'

Derek smiled back. Unlike the Desk Sergeant's nervous one, his was genuine. Derek genuinely appreciated the sentiment, even if he was going to destroy every piece of goodwill that he'd built up there over years in the next few minutes.

'Did you want to go through?' the Desk Sergeant continued, indicating one of the pale-blue doors to the side. 'I can call ahead, let them know?'

'It's not really that sort of visit today,' Derek replied. 'I need you to call DCI Farrow down. Or, if he's not about, call for anyone in serious crimes.'

The Desk Sergeant's face broke into a frown. 'Are you alright?' she asked, the concern obvious in her voice.

And it was the concern that finally broke ex-DI Derek Salmon's patience.

'*Of course I'm not bloody well alright!*' he snapped. Then, composing himself, he continued. 'Look, Maisie, we've known each other for years, and you're a lovely person, but I have terminal pancreatic cancer. I'm absolutely riddled with the bloody thing. I've been told I have weeks left to live. Every pain-ridden moment is now important to me, and I can't waste the minimal time I have left.'

He leaned closer to the screen now, his voice rising.

'So, if I say I need to speak to DCI Farrow or the serious crimes unit, I suggest that rather than having a nice little chat about it, you *do your bloody job and call them down here!*' The last part of this was shouted, and Derek felt light-headed, his legs giving way.

No, goddammit.

Forcing himself to straighten, he looked to the Desk Sergeant, already on the phone. After a moment, she looked back to him, the warm, sympathetic smile now gone.

'DCI Farrow will be down in a bit, *sir*,' she said, her tone now cold and expressionless. Derek nodded at this. He understood why she'd feel that way. At the same time though, after he'd said to Farrow what he was there to say, nobody would smile at him again, so she was ahead of the curve there.

A minute later, DCI Farrow opened the pale-blue door beside the counter, emerging cautiously into the reception area, already aware of Derek's outburst. With his wire-rimmed glasses and tufty hair sticking out to the sides, Farrow was often likened to a rather irritated owl by the detectives who worked under him. He'd transferred into Tottenham North around six months before Derek had started his treatments, so Derek hadn't really worked with Farrow much in the time they'd both been in the Crime Unit, and he had known little about the man except for Declan's occasional updates.

But he'd known enough to know that DCI Farrow was a jobsworth.

'Derek,' Farrow said, holding out his hand. Derek didn't

shake it, so Farrow let it fall back to his side. 'What can we do for you?'

'I need to speak to DI Walsh,' Derek replied.

'You need to keep up a little,' Farrow smiled. 'Declan Walsh no longer works here. He was transferred—'

'I know, to Alex Monroe's team,' Derek nodded. 'But I need you to bring him here. He needs to lead this case.'

Farrow frowned at this, as if worried that Derek was having some kind of episode, one where he thought he was still a DI himself.

'Case?' he asked.

'Yes,' Derek said. 'And yeah, I know you're thinking *what's the old bugger playing at now*, but it's important to me.' He pointed to the Desk Sergeant. 'Promise me, in front of this witness, that after I've explained, you'll bring Declan Walsh in to run the case.'

Farrow sighed. 'Or you could just toddle off down to Temple Inn, find him there and leave us out of whatever this is.'

'I can't,' Derek shook his head. 'I have to confess here. It's part of the agreement.'

'Fine,' DCI Farrow held up his hands. 'You do whatever it is, explain whatever it is you need to explain, I'll get Walsh and his friends to come here and play with you, and you can bugger off with them, okay?'

Derek thought about this for a moment.

'I needed a legal witness,' he explained. 'You might change your mind. I wanted to ensure you can't. If you don't bring Walsh in now, a court can take my confession as under duress. I could call for a mistrial.'

'What bloody confession?' Farrow was getting exasperated at the theatrics now.

'You know I'm terminal, right?' Derek asked.

'Of course.'

'Then you'll understand that because of this, I've gone beyond the British personality disorder of caring what people think about me,' Derek continued. 'You're an obnoxious little shit, Farrow, and I've hated you since you took over. And yes, I know, I stepped down because of all this,' he pointed to his white stubble, 'but there's something just wrong with you. I can't pinpoint it. I know it's like my cancer, but this time it's affecting everyone here.'

'Is this the explanation?' Farrow asked, bored now. 'Because I really need to—'

'For one bloody second just listen!'

The reception area was silent.

Stone faced, and silent now, Farrow motioned for Derek to continue.

'You remember the Angela Martin case?' Derek asked. 'Was right before I stepped down fully from duties.'

Farrow nodded, now all business, as if the mention of actual police work had brought his interest back. 'Of course. Seventeen years old. Went missing while out with her boyfriend in Walthamstow.'

'That's the one,' Derek said. 'Never found a body, never found a witness. She could be out there under another name as far as we know.'

'So, what's this got to do with this minor scene you're making?' Farrow asked. Derek shrugged.

'I killed her,' he replied. 'I killed her, and I hid the body in Epping Forest.'

Neither Farrow nor the Desk Sergeant spoke for a good few seconds.

'That's not funny,' Farrow's tone had grown dark now. 'I'll

give you the benefit of the doubt, that your condition has given you a gallows humour ...'

'*Do I look like a damned comedian?*' Derek screamed. '*I killed her! I confess! And when Declan Walsh takes over the case, I'll take you to where the body's buried!*'

He paused, a smile now on his lips, the anger fading.

'But until then, how about a cuppa for old times?' he asked. 'I'm gasping.'

1

PAYING A DEBT

DECLAN WALSH LEANED NERVOUSLY AGAINST THE WALL OF THE cottage and looked down at his rifle. A *Heckler & Koch MP5*, it was a semi-automatic carbine with a torch augmented onto the fore grip, currently aiming out of the window at the approaching Armed Response Vehicle, or ARV, that was making its way cautiously up the mud and gravel path that led towards Declan.

This was not how the day was supposed to start, he thought to himself.

Nervously, he let the MP5 hang down on its strap as he pulled out his gun, a *Glock 17*, examining it in his gloved hand, ensuring that the first bullet was in the chamber. The seconds wasted if it wasn't could mean life or death right now. Happy that it was ready for whatever was to come, he slotted it back into the holster and watched out of the window again.

He wore black overalls, and with the lights in the cottage not working, he hoped that this would help him blend into the shadows. His bulletproof vest was sparse; usually it would have a taser, cuffs, a radio and a ton of other things Velcro'd onto it; but that was for *police*. And currently Declan Walsh and his team were as far from police as you could get right now.

Can't be pissed at that, he thought to himself. *This was all on us. And bloody Monroe.*

On his face was a black balaclava hiding his identity, and a helmet and goggles covered his head and eyes. It felt like overkill to Declan. When he had been in the Military Police, he'd never bothered with the headwear, preferring the simpler ballistic glasses over his eyes. That said, he was glad for the extra protection. The lack of visual appearance gave him plausible deniability in what he was about to do. And, as the enemy clambered out of the ARV, cocking their weapons and moving into positions, Declan could see that they wanted blood. His blood.

DCI Monroe – no, now just Alex Monroe – emerged from a side room, dressed the same as Declan, although he wasn't wearing his balaclava yet, holding both it and the helmet in his hands. Monroe was slim with a runner's frame due to his ongoing obsession with park running, and the black overalls that he wore seemed too large for him, giving him the appearance of a young boy trying on his father's clothes. White hair, thinning at the parting, framed a face with clear, blue eyes above a well-cropped white beard under them.

'They're here?' he asked. Declan nodded.

Monroe grimaced. 'Christ, how did we get into this mess?' he muttered, checking his own carbine.

'We listened to you,' Declan said. 'You should put the helmet on.'

'It's too big,' Monroe complained. 'It's all too big.'

'Don't worry,' Declan grinned, still monitoring the activity outside. 'You'll grow into it one day.'

Monroe didn't reply, instead raising up two fingers in a V sign before pulling on the balaclava.

'Where are the others?' Declan asked, still watching the enemy outside as they moved around the building, and resisting the urge to remind Monroe once more that this total mess was because of him. 'We need to watch out. They're trying to flank us.'

'Marcos and Davey are trying to board up the kitchen, and Anjli and Billy are upstairs with the hostages,' Monroe replied.

'Why do you do that, Guv?' Declan asked. 'Anjli and Billy by their first names, Marcos and Davey by their surnames?'

Monroe thought for a moment. 'I have no idea,' he said. 'Probably because forensics have scared me since I was a small child. Is that really the conversation you want to have now?'

Declan shrugged. 'Just passing the time.'

'Well, pass it by killing a few of those bastards out there, soldier,' Monroe snapped, before glancing nervously out of the window at the opposing force. Monroe had never been in the military. This was a new situation for him. 'They're going to hit hard, aren't they?'

'Yeah,' Declan said. 'You'd better find somewhere to gain cover.'

'What about you?' Monroe asked. Declan forced a smile, but it wasn't a happy one.

'I've been here before, and I know what to do,' he said as he rammed the carbine of the MP5 through the pane of glass, firing out at the approaching enemy, wincing at the sudden noise while seeing them dive for cover as the bullets zinged past them.

'Well, there goes the negotiation option,' Monroe

adjusted his balaclava when Declan finished, pulling back from the window in case they returned fire.

'They would never negotiate,' Declan said. 'They want to kill us.'

There was the sound of an explosion in the back room; the gunmen who had flanked to the left had most likely found the kitchen door and had blown it in. Semi-automatic gunfire could be heard, most likely Rosanna Marcos and Joanne Davey trying to hold them off. Monroe looked nervously back.

'Should I help?' he asked. Declan nodded.

'I can hold the buggers here,' he said. 'All we have to do is keep them off us long enough for Anjli and Billy to get the hostages to talk.'

Monroe sighed and with a *ka-chick* of his MP5 left the room. Declan looked out of the window, firing wildly again, keeping the gunmen outside pinned. Pulling another magazine out, he quickly reloaded, reminding himself that unlike the enemy, he only had limited bullets.

Best to stop pretending he was John Rambo.

Bullets smacked into the wall of the cottage and Declan backed away, watching the door and finding a position in the room where he could defend himself. It was a small room with minimal furniture; stairs led up at the back to where Billy and Anjli were, while the door to the left-hand side led to the kitchen where gunfire and screams of anger and rage could now be heard. Beside Declan was a fireplace with a sofa, a hideous red and pink one with flowery patterns on it next to the mantlepiece. But neither of those could save him right now. To his right, however, was a dining table made of solid oak, something chunky and heavy that could save him from the oncoming attack. He ran over to it, overturning the heavy table with a sizeable amount of effort and setting up a position behind it.

He'd only just settled into some sort of loose defending position when the door exploded in. A CS gas canister rolled in, filling the room with smoke as three SCO19 officers entered it, guns at the ready.

Screw this. They were just police. He was military trained.

Declan quickly rose, firing his MP5 at the officers before dropping as the bullets slammed into the table. He'd seen one officer go down; he hoped it was a kill shot. He needed to remove the others quickly, force them to back out so he could retreat upstairs and help his colleagues. The gunfire from the kitchen area had already ended; he didn't know if that was a good thing or a bad omen for the day. Although, as nobody was entering from the side door, he hoped this meant that Monroe and the others had forced the issue there.

'I don't care how you do it, just shoot that bugger!' the SCO Team Leader shouted. 'We need to save the hostages!'

The table protecting Declan was hit again with multiple shots, and Declan slid backwards towards the stairs. He had a gas canister of his own and he tossed it into the midst of the officers, using the explosion and the confusion to run up the stairs, feeling the zing of bullets hit the wall as they followed him up.

Billy Fitzwarren was at the top of the stairs, nervously watching.

'The others?' he asked.

Declan shook his head. 'I think they're already dead.'

Billy cursed and looked back to the bedroom doorway where Anjli Kapoor currently stood. They were in the same armour as Declan was, but Anjli had removed her rifle and held the Glock instead.

'Where's your weapon?' Declan asked. Anjli shrugged.

'Feel more badass with a Glock,' she said, bringing it up and firing past Declan as he ducked; the SCO officers that were already making their way up the stairs dropped back as Anjli's bullets pinged around them. Billy turned to continue fire, but the SCO officers were ready this time, had moved back up quickly and Billy slammed back into the wall as four bullets slammed into his chest.

'Billy!' Anjli screamed.

'Billy's dead!' Declan pushed Anjli into the bedroom, passing her his own Glock. 'We need to—'

He didn't continue, as the force of three bullets slammed into his back, sending him stumbling into the corner of the hallway. As he spun, ignoring the pain up his spine, he went to fire a last round at the SCO team, but two more bullets struck him in the chest, with another striking his helmet.

Declan's body slumped to the floor as the SCO officers moved in.

'Targets one and two dead!' the lead officer shouted. 'One more to—'

He didn't finish as Anjli dived out of the door, guns in both hands firing wildly, the Glocks pumping out bullets *John Woo* style as she crashed to the ground. Two of the SCOs were struck by these, but their brother officers had blocked the ones behind and now, with Anjli on the floor, they raised their weapons and shot her.

Repeatedly.

'All hostiles down!' the Team Leader shouted from the stairs, watching the scene from behind. 'Cease fire!'

All gunfire stopped. There was a long silence.

And then, the SCO19 officers applauded.

Declan, pulling off his helmet and balaclava winced as he moved.

'Jesus, those bullets really hurt!' he said as Specialist Firearms Officer Andrews helped him up. 'That's not a bloody paintball bullet.'

'Never said they were,' Andrews grinned. 'They're *Simunition* rounds. Paintball's for little children.' He looked to Anjli, now clambering to her feet. 'What was that?'

'John McClane, *Die Hard*,' she explained. 'Always wanted to try it.'

'And how did that work out for you?' Declan was pulling his bulletproof armour off now, wincing at the bruising on his back. Anjli looked down at her own armour, now covered in red paint.

'Not great,' she said.

'At least you fired a shot,' Billy walked over now, a gloomy expression on his face. 'I went out like a bitch.'

Anjli looked to Declan. Neither of them spoke. Billy saw this.

'Oh, so you think that too?' he groaned.

SFO Andrews entered the bedroom. 'Did you gain anything from the hostages?' he asked.

'They're dummies,' Anjli said. 'They weren't really conversational.'

SFO Andrews walked over to the two dummies, both dressed in suits, and pulled a sheet of folded paper out from the inside pocket of the dummy to the left.

'Christ,' Declan muttered. 'You didn't check them?'

'I was too busy stopping Billy soiling himself and worrying about his oncoming death,' Anjli replied indignantly. Billy shrugged.

'Never been a baddie before,' he said.

Walking down the stairs, Declan found Monroe, Doctor Marcos and DC Davey waiting. All were covered in paint, although Doctor Marcos was currently tying some small baubles to her tactical vest.

'What are they?' he asked.

Doctor Marcos smiled and held one out to him to see. It was a 3D printed SCO19 helmet with goggles, spray-painted black.

'Trophies,' she said. 'One for each officer I killed.'

SFO Andrews looked to Monroe with an expression that seemed to combine a small amount of amusement with a far larger element of horror. 'She's one of yours, right?'

Monroe smiled. 'In a loose kind of way,' he said. 'Did we at least fulfil our side of the debt?'

'Well, my boys and girls needed a less disciplined force to go against, so definitely yes to that,' he said. 'But we killed you all rather quickly. Maybe we could have a second round?'

'Oh definitely,' Billy nodded. 'And this time I want to be behind that table. With a bigger gun.'

Monroe however was now taking a call on his phone, frowning as he listened.

'I'm afraid we're going to have to take a rain check,' he eventually said as he disconnected. 'Maybe next week?'

'Problem?' Declan asked. Monroe looked to him.

'New case,' he said. 'You've been asked for personally, laddie. Seems an old friend of yours has been accused of murder. Well, more admitted to it. Or, rather, walked into the Command Unit in Tottenham North and told everyone, very loudly that he did it, before demanding that you take the case on. And by you, I mean us. All of us.'

'Who's the friend?' Anjli asked, pulling off her helmet.

'Declan's old mentor, and an old colleague of mine,' Monroe said. 'DI Derek Salmon.'

'Derek?' Declan exclaimed. 'He's terminally ill!'

'Aye,' Monroe replied, already passing his equipment over to one of the SCO19 officers. 'Which means that we have a lot less time than we thought to find out what the hell is going on, and either save your friend, or convict him.'

And, with that, the team of the Last Chance Saloon stopped being terrorist insurgents for the day and returned to their usual roles, while Declan wondered how the hell Derek Salmon had found himself tied up in murder.

———

2

THE PICK UP

THE NAME BIRMINGHAM CAME FROM THE OLD ENGLISH WORD *Beormingahām,* which was the name given to the home or settlement of the *Beormingas*, a tribe whose name literally meant *'Beorma's People'*. And, as for the man himself, Beorma was a 7th Century Anglo Saxon leader who settled his tribe beside the River Rea, to the East of what would one day become Birmingham City Centre.

Stripe didn't know if this was true; he didn't learn it at school and nobody that he knew discussed Anglo-Saxon tribes that much these days, but every day for the last week he would return from school at around 4pm and stand on Gooch Street Bridge beside an ornate brass message that spanned the brick wall.

BEORMA INGHAS HAM
HOME OF THE PEOPLE OF BEORMA

UNDERNEATH IT WAS A PLAQUE THAT TALKED ABOUT ALL OF this history rubbish, and across the road was another brass message that read:

NEAR THIS RIVER CROSSING AN ANGLIAN TRIBE
LED BY BEORMA FOUNDED BIRMINGHAM

He'd often re-read both brass signs while the bridge was quiet, inventing stories of the mighty Beorma, who in his mind spoke in the Black Country *Yam Yam* accent and wielded a mighty broadsword. He'd even drawn Beorma once, but Macca Byrne had laughed at it, said it was shit and set fire to it with his lighter.

Stripe had said nothing. He never did. He simply returned to his post and re-read the plaque on the side of the Gooch Street Bridge.

But later in the day, especially into the evening, Stripe would stop examining the walls, he'd stop imagining the adventures of Beorma and would instead spend his time watching the road, keeping an eye out for cars slowing down. When a car slowed down on the bridge, seeing the boy in the school uniform standing alone, there was usually only one thing they wanted.

Stripe knew it was dangerous, but at fourteen years old, he was the smallest and fastest in the gang. He could run from anyone. However, the point of his waiting wasn't to run. It was to wait.

To wait for one particular car.

Stripe had an actual name, Alfie. But nobody ever used it; they all called him *Stripe* because of the inch wide stripe of white hair that streaked through his fringe, contrasting with his normal auburn colouring. Nobody knew why it grew that way; it just always had. His mum had said once that there was an accident when he was tiny, and the trauma had caused it. Stripe didn't ask more than that as it was never wise to get into a conversation with his mum, or else she'd sober up, remember she had a son, and then the arguments would begin again.

Besides, he liked the nickname Stripe. It made him sound cool.

Standing in the rain wasn't cool though. It wasn't heavy rain, but it was irritating. That light fall, only a mist that still drenched you throughout. They'd said that he couldn't wear his parka, that he had to have his face visible. And that meant no hood, which meant that his white stripe was now plastered to his head in the rain.

Waiting for the car.

It had passed him twice over the last few days; a jet-black Mercedes A-Class, a quality motor which probably cost more than his parents made in a year, if not several years. Each time, he'd watched from the shadows, noting the registration number, checking when it slowed, when it sped up, working out the best place to stand for maximum exposure when the time was needed. Stripe liked this part; it made him feel like a spy. The part that he didn't like was the part he was playing now. Standing in the rain, exposed, waiting to see the car one last time.

And then he did.

Driving up Conybere Street and approaching the small, three-way roundabout that was barely more than a bump in the road, the Mercedes A-Class was crawling towards him in the early evening rush-hour traffic. Seeing this, Stripe turned north up Gooch Street, trudging along, his hand out as if thumbing for a lift. He'd walked about twenty yards before he risked looking behind; the Mercedes had just turned on the roundabout, and was passing across the bridge, the two brass signs on either side of it.

Stripe turned to face the oncoming car now, walking backwards, holding out his left hand, the thumb extended in the international sign of hitch-hiking. He wanted the driver of the car to see his face.

To see how young he was.

He'd been told that this part was important. He was walking alongside a series of blue railings now, shivering with the cold. This wasn't make believe; he was genuinely cold now; the lack of his parka coat now being felt.

The Mercedes drove past him.

It didn't stop.

Stripe fought the urge to turn, to watch after it, but he was playing the part of a hitchhiker. Maybe the driver had seen him, but was suspicious? Maybe he was being careful?

It turned out that it was more likely the latter, because as Stripe eventually turned to continue walking, he saw that the Mercedes had pulled to the side of the road about ten yards further on, now in a parking bay as the other cars passed by.

Stripe pretended that he hadn't realised that the car was waiting, instead pretending that he was still watching the cars as they drove past. Inside there was a mixture of excitement and fear running through him; excitement that he'd succeeded in his mission, that he'd caught the prey, but fear as to what would happen next. He was still a long way from the target.

As he passed the car, the passenger window wound down, and the driver leaned across to call out.

'You need a lift?'

Stripe looked into the car and, for the first time, he saw

the driver clearly. He was old, like maybe forty or so. He had short-cropped light-brown hair and wore a Pea coat over a pale, textured sweatshirt. Swallowing, suddenly regretting his rash decision to agree to this in the first place, Stripe nodded.

'Please,' he said. 'Are you heading towards Digbeth?'

'I can be,' the driver said, leaning over the passenger seat and opened the door. 'Get in. You look half drowned.'

Quickly, Stripe climbed into the passenger seat. 'Thanks,' he said. The inside of the Mercedes smelt like new leather. Stripe had never been in such an expensive car and wondered if this was the new car smell that everyone always talked about in the adverts.

The driver smiled.

'Not a problem,' he replied. 'I've been caught in the rain before. Why didn't you catch a bus?'

'Bullies stole my money,' Stripe lied. The driver shook his head.

'Bastards,' he said, believing the story. 'I'm Dave. What's your name?'

'Matthew,' Stripe lied again. The last thing he wanted was for the target to know his *actual* name.

'So, where to, Matthew?' Dave asked, already indicating into the traffic and preparing to pull out.

'Next right, please,' Stripe replied. 'I can guide you.'

Dave continued to drive down Gooch Street, turning right into Vaughton Street South. If he knew the area, he didn't say.

'You shouldn't allow strangers to pick you up,' he said. 'You never know who you'll meet.'

'*You* picked me up.'

Dave grinned. 'Exactly,' he laughed, as if making a joke, before returning to a more serious and concerned expression. 'How much did the bullies steal from you?'

'Ten pounds,' Stripe replied. In answer to this, Dave reached into his pocket, one hand on the wheel, and pulled out a crisp fifty-pound note.

'Here,' he said. 'I don't like bullies. Take this.'

'I can't take that,' Stripe shook his head, his eyes already widening at the sight of the note. 'It's too much.'

'It's nothing, really,' Dave replied, throwing the note onto Stripe's lap. 'Buy your girlfriend something nice. You do have a girlfriend?'

'Not really,' Stripe replied, noting the subtle way that Dave had thrown the question into the conversation. Macca had taught him what to say if he'd been asked that, too.

Dave tutted. 'Good-looking boy like you? You must have loads of girls after you.'

Stripe shook his head again.

'I'm not really into girls,' he admitted softly, another lie coached to him by Macca. 'Oh, it's right here.'

The car turned into Adelaide Street, now an area of warehouses and car parks. Dave smiled again. 'That's okay, Matt,' he said. 'It's okay to not be into girls. You're young. You should try everything at your age.'

By now they were turning onto Lombard Street, and the buildings were turning into a mixture of warehouses, red brick car sales frontages and small accountancy firms. It was an industrial district, and the streets were almost empty for the time of day, many of the offices long closed, or out of business.

'We're almost there,' Stripe said, waving over to a gated entrance on the right. 'Could you pull over in that car park? I don't want my dad seeing me pull up in this car. He's told me off before for taking lifts.'

'Sure.' Dave turned into a small warehouse car park,

pulling up in one of the bays. Like the other buildings around, it was shuttered up. 'I wouldn't want to meet your dad like that.'

Stripe forced a smile as he pocketed the fifty-pound note. 'Thanks for the money, Mister,' he said. 'It's a lot.'

'It's nothing, and it's Dave, not Mister,' Dave replied as he pulled out a roll of twenties from his pocket. There was probably two, three hundred pounds there. 'And don't worry about it. I have enough.'

'Wow!' Stripe said in admiration. 'What did you do to get that? Rob a bank?'

Dave smiled, but the smile wasn't a friendly one anymore.

Now it was a hungry one.

'The question isn't what *I* did to get it,' he said. 'It's what *you'd* do to get it.'

Stripe shivered, and it wasn't just the rain sliding down his neck. Again, he'd been warned about this by Macca, that Dave was known for this, had form for getting young boys to do bad things. Macca had promised, sworn even that Stripe wouldn't get to this point.

So, where was he?

Luckily, Dave was so engrossed in his new, young friend that he didn't notice the tall, blond man in the hoodie who walked up to the driver's side of the car and, with one fluid motion opened the door and yanked him out into the car park.

'What the hell! I'll cut you, bitch!' Dave stumbled to the car park floor and rose quickly to his feet, spinning to face the man now stepping back from him, but paused as he saw the other four teenagers walking up behind his attacker. He looked back to the car where Stripe was already getting out, backing away from the upcoming encounter.

'You knew about this, you little shit!'

'You've been a hard man to find, Dave,' a voice interrupted the rant. It was a calm, self-assured voice with the hint of a Black Country twang. Dave spun to respond to it but stopped as he saw the voice's owner. 'It's almost like you've been evading my calls, forcing me to take a more extreme approach in gaining your attention.'

Macca Byrne was only nineteen, but in the last couple of years he'd built up a tiny empire for himself between the areas of Digbeth, Bordesley and Deritend, all to the east of Birmingham, stealing the scraps from his father's far larger and more lucrative table. There were rumours that he was making his move into the clubland area of Five Ways and Broad Street to the north, which was ironic as he wasn't yet old enough to even drink in half of the clubs, although to do that would definitely bring him up against George Byrne, and Macca the son would likely lose that battle. Unlike the others surrounding him in their jogging bottoms and hoodies, Macca was well dressed in a three-quarter-length All Saints wool coat over an equally expensive jumper and torn black jeans and Chelsea boots, also black. In fact, everything was black, even his dyed-black hair; short and spiked out, framing a clear, intelligent face with an old scar that ran down the left side from the temple to the cheek.

'Mackenzie,' Dave said, his voice changing from anger to a more disdainful tone.

'Never call me that,' Macca replied. 'My friends call me Macca. Everyone else calls me Mister Byrne.'

'Whatever, *Mackenzie*,' Dave squared up to face Macca. 'I don't talk with monkeys; I talk with organ grinders. Does your dad know that you're hanging around in car parks?'

'What my dad knows about me could be written on the

back of a fag packet and still have space for chapter two.'
Macca moved in closer now, only a foot away. What he lost in
height to the older man, he gained back in attitude. 'And as
for why I'm here? Well, I'm just doing my civic duty, ain't I?
Saw you about to molest this poor lad, had to step in.'

'I was giving him a lift home,' Dave said, the indignant
attitude mixing with alarm now, as if finally realising that
they had set him up.

'Parking in an abandoned car park? That's not quite a lift
home now, is it?' Macca grinned. 'And there you were, in your
shiny car with a strange child. Know what I think? I think you
were offering money to this poor, innocent boy for services
rendered.'

'Cut the shit, Byrne,' Dave was tiring of this. 'What do you
want?'

'What I want is for you to send a message to the Seven
Sisters,' Macca turned and walked away a little at this, as if
not wanting Dave to see his face. 'I want you to tell them I
know that they killed her.'

Dave choked back a laugh. 'Is this what all this is?' he
exclaimed. 'You're blaming my bosses for your junkie girlfriend dumping you a year ago?' He shook his head. 'She
found someone better. Get over it.'

Macca turned back and across the car; Stripe stepped back
in fear. Macca was a vicious man, a psychotic man, but his
expression was one Stripe had never seen in such a situation.

Macca Byrne was ice cold calm.

'Maybe your dad killed her?' Dave suggested. 'Maybe he
was shagging her too? I heard that she'd get on her knees for
a small bag of meth.'

'Let me tell you what I know,' Macca said calmly, ignoring

the jibe as he walked back to Dave. 'I know that Gabby was killed a year ago in North London, I know that she's buried somewhere in Epping Forest, and I know that those bitches called the hit. I want them to know that I know this, and that I will gain retribution for this.'

'You'd better run this past your dad first,' Dave continued, keeping up his unconcerned bluff. 'You're talking about fighting other gangs. Bigger gangs. Better gangs. And that's a little above your pay grade, isn't it? You're more the *dime bag junkies* and the *tween twinks* world, right?'

Ignoring the insult, Macca looked over to the blond man in his early twenties who'd pulled Dave out of the car. 'I don't need to ask my dad to send a message. Harrison here is going to ensure that it's sent.'

'What, you want this prick to babysit me while I tell Janelle Delcourt you're wearing your tinfoil hat again?' Dave laughed. 'This is a joke. That junkie bitch made you into a joke. Jesus, George must be so disappointed in you. I'm Janelle's right-hand man, not some kind of postman!'

Macca thought about this. And then he reached into his pocket, pulling out some black leather gloves.

'Yeah, you're right, you *are* some sort of big shot gangster paedo,' he said. 'And I know that right now you want your shot at me, don't you?'

Dave shook his head. 'Not my scene. I'm more a numbers kind of guy.'

'You got a blade on you?' Macca asked.

Licking his lips nervously, Dave shook his head.

'But I clearly heard you saying to my friend you'd cut him.'

'Banter, nothing more.'

Macca nodded at this and reached into his own jacket, pulling out a hunting knife in a sheath.

'This is a nice knife,' he said, offering it to Dave. 'Take it.'

Dave took the offered knife by the hilt but didn't remove it from the sheath.

'I don't want to fight,' he said, tossing it to the floor. 'And you don't want any of this coming back onto you.'

Macca faced Dave, currently standing defiantly and, with a quick motion, pulled the roll of twenties out of Dave's jacket pocket. Turning to Stripe, Macca tossed the roll over.

'Services rendered,' he said to the small boy. 'Now bugger off, before you become a witness to what we're about to do.'

'Wait, wait, wait!' Dave had his hands up now, realising that he may have gone too far, and was now surrounded by angry teens in a deserted car park. 'You can't do anything to me if you want me to pass a message!'

Macca laughed. 'Jesus, you really are stupid,' he said. 'I didn't say that you were taking a message to the Sisters, I said that you *were* the message.'

And with that, he rammed a small butterfly knife into Dave's gut.

As Dave screamed out, falling to the floor and clutching at his bleeding stomach, the others in Macca's gang, led by Harrison moved in, kicking and punching. Stripe, having seen enough, ran from the car park, running north towards Digbeth and safety.

Macca Byrne and his dad scared him, but it was Harrison that filled his heart with terror. Because no matter what Macca said, Stripe knew that Gabrielle Chapman, Macca's girlfriend, hadn't been killed in London and buried down south. He knew this because a year ago he'd had a massive row with his mum and dad and had run away for a week, hiding out in the Lickey Hills Country Park, about ten miles south of Birmingham. It had been a hot summer, and Stripe knew that he could easily hide out there until his parents had calmed down, or until the heroin had caused them to forget why they were angry in the first place.

And it was there, deep in the Lickey Hills, that Stripe had seen Macca Byrne's right-hand man Harrison drive up late one night with someone else and bury the dead body of Gabrielle Chapman.

3

RETURNING HOME

It felt strange returning to Tottenham North's Command Unit, especially when the last time that Declan had been there he had been told to leave on an indefinite suspension. But he was no longer suspended and, with Monroe beside him, he pulled his Audi into a free space in the police car park.

Before he turned the engine off, he looked to Monroe.

'I still don't get why Derek would say such a thing,' he said. Monroe shrugged.

'He's on some strong meds,' he replied. 'Perhaps he's having hallucinations.'

'He took me in, you know,' Declan climbed out of the car, looking around the car park. 'When I left the Military Police and started as a Detective Constable, he was the one that mentored me.'

'On your father's recommendation.'

Declan thought back for a moment.

'In the cottage after the call, you kept saying "your friend" when talking about Derek. Not "our friend". But you worked with him too.'

'Aye, I did. But not everyone you work with is your friend,' Monroe was already walking towards the back entrance to the Command Unit. 'Let's see what he says before we pass sentence.'

Declan nodded, following Monroe into the Command Unit. 'Are you saying you're not my friend, Guv?'

'Christ no, laddie. I only help you out because of some sad Stockholm Syndrome level devotion to your late father. Didn't I already tell you that?'

Declan laughed, but the smile soon faded as the weight of what was about to happen struck him. Although Derek Salmon had helped Declan when he first joined the police, and although in the eight or so years that they'd worked together he'd never seen Derek perform any kind of illegal act, his recent worldview had been shaken by the discovery of his late father's secret study in his Hurley-Upon-Thames house: a small, hidden room that held a crime wall, covered in images.

One that held a picture of Derek Salmon upon it.

Added to that, Declan's most recent case had shaken his belief in his own father when one suspect had hinted that the officers on a case twenty years ago may have been less than clean; officers that had included then-DC Salmon and then-DS Monroe, now staring at him from the open doorway.

'Are you coming, laddie, or shall I just hold the bloody door open all day for you?' he asked. Declan smiled apologetically, entering the building. Monroe stopped him though, pulling out a handkerchief and dabbing it at Declan's auburn hair.

'What are you doing, Mum?' Declan asked.

'You've got paint in your hair, you bampot,' Monroe folded the handkerchief up and stuffed it back in his pocket. 'Can't have you looking like an eejit when we see your old boss, now.'

If it felt strange pulling up in the car park, it felt damn-right unnatural entering the actual offices of Tottenham North. Even though Declan had spoken to DCI Farrow since the suspension, the last time he'd actually stood in his office was shortly before he placed his items into a stationery box and left after being effectively fired from the police over a month earlier.

'Good to see you looking healthy,' Farrow said, emerging from his office and shaking Declan's hand. 'You've lost weight since I last saw you.'

'More toned up what I had,' Declan replied. In actual fact, all he'd really added to his routine was running along the Thames when he could, although he'd noticed that there was a distinct lack of burger vans and kebab shops around Temple Inn, which restricted his lunch-time options far more than Tottenham ever did.

'Well, whatever it is, keep it up,' Farrow added. 'Sorry to hear about Patrick.'

He looked to Monroe, shaking his hand as well. 'Glad you're looking after this reprobate.'

'Well, after you threw him on the scrap heap, someone had to help the poor wee bugger,' Monroe replied conversationally, his Glaswegian accent seeming to deepen as they entered Farrow's office. Farrow winced a little at this as he returned to his desk.

'There was nothing I could do about the suspension,' he said as he sat back down, indicating for the others to join him. 'Higher voices were demanding it.'

'All the way to Heaven, I hear,' Monroe continued. As much as he wanted to join in, Declan kept his mouth shut. Monroe and Farrow were both DCIs, but Monroe had a slight seniority advantage.

'So, Derek Salmon,' Farrow changed the topic. 'He's all yours. Please take him off my hands.'

'What happened?' Monroe asked. 'I mean, we've heard he admitted to murder, but what the hell?'

'I thought the same too,' Farrow admitted, opening a folder on his desk. 'I even said I felt the joke was in poor taste. He damn near took my head off for suggesting he was lying. But then I only knew him for a few months. The pair of you have known him for years.'

'And he called for DI Walsh by name?' Monroe was already pulling out his notebook. 'Mighty strange. I wouldn't call for Walsh if my life depended on it. Tell me about Angela Martin.'

'Wasn't my case, so I knew little I'm afraid,' Farrow said, indicating Declan. 'Maybe ...'

Declan spoke now. 'She's Danny Martin's daughter.'

'Jesus!' Monroe exclaimed, almost rising from his seat. 'And you thought you'd wait until *now* to tell me that?'

'Yeah. Sorry.'

'Who's Danny Martin?' Farrow asked.

'Danny Martin was, well maybe still *is,* an enforcer for Johnny and Jackie Lucas,' Monroe muttered. 'I knew he had a kid, but I didn't put the two together.'

'The East End gangsters?' Farrow nodded. 'Now that makes a little more sense. You think this could have been a gangland killing then?'

'We didn't think of any kind of killing,' Declan shook his head. 'DI Salmon and I worked the case, but it was nothing more than a missing person. Angela simply disappeared. There was talk that she had a secret second boyfriend in the Midlands, and she dabbled in a ton of dodgy shit as well, so we assumed she was running away from her father's life of crime. Either that or she was making a run from some serious debt collectors.'

'And there was no suspicion of foul play?'

'Well, she hung around with some seriously dodgy people so everything she did hinted of foul play, but not regarding the missing person's report,' Declan looked to the floor. 'But then I suppose that if Derek had done this, he'd ensure that there wouldn't be.'

'Don't sentence the man until we know the crime,' Monroe muttered, looking back to Farrow. 'I understand that he's asked for us to take this case on, but Temple Inn doesn't have custody cells. Can we ask for Mister Salmon to stay here for the moment? And if possible, could we question him now?'

'Of course,' Farrow picked up a phone, tapping a number on it. 'I'll have him placed in Interview Room Three right now. And, as long as I don't have to talk to him, you can keep him as long as you want here.'

Monroe and Declan rose from their chairs.

'Thanks, Alan,' Monroe said.

Farrow nodded, indicating to Declan.

'He might be a pain in the arse to deal with, but Walsh there is a damn good investigator,' he replied. 'If anyone can work out what the hell's going on here, it's him.'

Declan nodded once to show thanks for the compliment, but as he left Farrow's office with Monroe, he couldn't help but visualise his father's crime board; a board that had links to both Johnny and Jackie Lucas on it.

Danny Martin worked for The Twins.

Derek Salmon had confessed to his daughter's murder.

What if it was true?

DEREK WAS WAITING FOR THEM IN INTERVIEW ROOM THREE. Alone, he'd waived his right for a solicitor, sitting on one side of the table as Declan and Monroe walked in and sat down at the other. The room itself was unlike the glass-walled Interview Room at Temple Inn. For a start the walls were an off-white, green colour and, as the room was slightly below ground level, there was a window high up on the right-hand wall looking out towards the street, too high to see through. Declan had sat in this same room, on this same chair many times over the last decade and, during most of those interactions, Derek had sat next to him, rather than across from him.

'Alright Declan?' Derek asked, looking to Monroe. 'Guv?'

Declan couldn't reply, shocked at how ravaged Derek's face was. The weight loss was visible and turned him speechless for a moment.

'Sorry,' he eventually said, realising how rude he must seem. Derek smiled sadly.

'I know,' he replied. 'I feel that way every morning when I look in the mirror.'

Monroe leaned forwards, as if scared that someone would overhear in the empty room.

'What's going on, Derek?' he asked. 'This is bullshit. Is someone making you say this?'

'Turn the tape on.'

'Derek, seriously.' Now it was Declan's turn to talk. 'You can talk to us.'

'Turn the tape on.'

Sighing, Declan leaned over to the recording device at the edge of the table, pressing record.

There was a long beep; Declan leaned back while he waited for it to stop. Eventually it did and Monroe, as the senior detective in the room, spoke.

'Tottenham North Interview with DI Derek Salmon, retired. No solicitor or Federation Rep attending. In the presence of DCI Monroe, DI Walsh.' He looked to Derek. 'Are you sure you don't want a rep here? A solicitor?'

'I'm confessing, Alex,' Derek replied. 'I don't need someone telling me what words to say.'

Declan pulled out his notebook. 'I understand that you're confessing to the murder of Angela Martin, aged seventeen and four months at the time of her disappearance eleven months ago.'

Derek nodded and then, remembering that the interview was being recorded, simply said 'yes.'

Declan reached over to the tape recorder. 'Pausing recording for a toilet break,' he said as he clicked the pause button, looking back to Derek.

'What the bloody hell are you playing at, you dopey bastard? Are your meds making you screwy? You think neither of us know you, know what you're capable of? Tell us who's doing this—'

'Declan,' Monroe's voice was soft and sad as he leaned over and held his finger over the pause button. 'We need to hear his statement.'

And, with that, Monroe restarted the recording.

'Interview continued, Derek Salmon, DI Walsh and DCI Monroe in the room,' he whispered, looking at Declan as if daring him to say something. Declan just leaned back, angry.

'So, tell us how it happened,' Monroe said. Derek nodded.

'I killed her,' he replied. 'I killed her and then I buried her in Epping Forest, near Jack's Hill.'

'Why?' Monroe asked.

'Why what?' Derek looked surprised at the question.

'Why kill her?'

'No reason,' Derek said, looking from Monroe to Declan as he answered. 'She was there at the wrong time. Wrong place.'

'Convenient,' Declan shook his head, still unable to accept this. 'That you just so happened to kill the daughter of a man you'd repeatedly nicked ten years earlier.'

'I didn't know she was Danny Martin's daughter.'

'How did you do it?' Monroe returned to the questioning.

'I strangled her,' Derek replied. 'With some rope.'

'What sort of rope?' Monroe continued. 'Twine? Ship's rope? You used to be a rock climber, right? Was it Paracord? What did you use?'

'I don't remember.'

'You don't remember what you used to kill a teenage girl with?' Declan almost laughed at this. 'Come on, Derek. If you're going to create some kind of murder fantasy, you could at least—'

'*This isn't a fantasy!*' Derek screamed out, slamming his hands upon the table. 'You don't believe me? I'll take you to the body! How would I know where it was if I didn't bury it, eh?'

Monroe looked to Declan for a moment before speaking to Derek. 'You'll take us to the body?'

'I agreed to do that before Farrow called you,' Derek said. 'But Declan takes me there. You hear me? You can all meet us at the forest, but Declan alone takes me there.'

Monroe went to answer this, but then stopped, as if deciding that this was the only option. Reluctantly, he nodded.

'Fine,' he said. 'I'll cadge a lift with Doctor Marcos and her team.'

'Fine,' Derek mocked as he leaned back in the chair. 'Then this little chat is over. I've confessed, I'm showing you the body and then you can charge me.'

'Interview ends at ...' Monroe looked to his watch, 'At twelve-forty pm.' He turned off the tape, looking at Derek.

'I don't know what's going on here, but you're ending your life for something that isn't connected to you,' he said.

Derek shrugged.

'You got the first part right,' he said. 'Now, let's go dig up a body.'

4

GRAVE SECRETS

THE JOURNEY FROM TOTTENHAM NORTH HAD BEEN SIMPLE FOR the time of day; Declan had taken the North Circular towards Walthamstow North, turning left into Woodford, driving north through the small suburban village as Woodford New Road turned into Woodford Green Road.

As he drove past a statue of Winston Churchill on the green itself, erected during Churchill's time as MP for Woodford in the forties, fifties and sixties, veering left into Epping New Road, he glanced to Derek Salmon currently sitting handcuffed in the passenger seat.

'Okay, we're alone now,' he said. 'Can we drop all the lies and discuss what's actually going on?'

Derek nodded slowly, looking to Declan.

'I'm not able to tell you what's happening, and they're listening to everything I do when I'm out there,' he replied. 'If I didn't do what they wanted, I would have lost everything.'

'What do you mean, lost everything?' Declan overtook a cyclist, keeping his eyes on the road.

'I mean, I made a deal,' Derek explained. 'With the Seven Sisters.'

Declan almost slammed the brakes on at this.

'Are you mad?' he shouted.

'No, Declan, I'm dying!' Derek shouted back. 'Amanda and I might not speak much, but Evie's just starting University! How am I supposed to look after her once this takes me? A police force pension? Do me a favour!'

'So what, you said you'd take one for the Sisters?'

Derek nodded.

'Pretty much, yeah.'

Declan thought about this for a moment. 'The deal you made. You were to confess to Angela's murder, show the body and then take the hit. Why bring me in?'

'Because they didn't say someone could prove me innocent,' Derek replied. 'I just had to admit to the murder. If someone showed that I was lying, and if I hadn't helped them come to that conclusion, then that wasn't my fault. When I die, Amanda would still get the house paid off. Evie would still have her student debt paid.'

'You're relying on me to solve this murder and clear you,' Declan whistled. 'That's a big expectation.'

'Not really,' Derek grinned, and for the first time Declan saw his old mentor in the car. 'You just closed a case that even your father failed to solve. You're one of the best detectives I know.'

Declan sighed. Compliments from an old mentor were always going to strike home.

'I'm guessing I can't tell people I know about this,' he said. 'Outside of people I trust.'

'If you trust them, sure, but if it gets back to the Sisters that I'm trying to find a loophole? I'm toast. All I care about is that my ex-wife and daughter are looked after.'

Derek looked out of the window, watching the woodland as it sped past. 'Do you know how insulting it is to go to people I've actively hated, actively hunted all these years, asking for a payout? It killed me, Declan. More than this bloody cancer.' He turned back.

'The chances are you won't solve this before I die. And if that happens, they'll get the payout anyway.'

Declan didn't answer. He knew that Derek Salmon must have been desperate if he'd turned to the Seven Sisters for help. They were to the North of London what The Twins were to the East: seven women, all from different backgrounds and ethnicities who'd come together as a group to take over the streets that their husbands had failed to win. A powerful, matriarchal unit; when one sister died or left, another would replace her.

Seven voices, all equal.

Of course, in the same way that the 'twins' were just one rather mad gangster with a multiple personality disorder, the Seven Sisters weren't a collective. They were a way of giving plausible deniability to Janelle Delcourt, who'd run North London's under-city for over twenty years now.

'How do you know where the body is?' Declan asked. 'I mean, you didn't kill Angela Martin no matter what you claim, So, how do you know there's even a body there for us?'

'I was told,' Derek replied. 'They showed me on a map.'

'Who showed you?'

Derek shook his head. 'Sorry buddy, that's something you're going to have to find out on your own. Even giving you a hint could cause you to cut corners, and that'd reveal me as helping you.'

'Do you know who really killed her?'

'No.'

'Do you know why she died?'

'No. All I know was that it wasn't to do with her father, but more who she was dating.'

'Who was she dating?' Declan took the third exit on a roundabout, turning down a country lane. They were nearing Jack's Hill now.

'Moses Delcourt,' Derek replied. 'But there was some kind of drama going on with a gang up in Birmingham. Seems that she was seen up there too.'

'With who?'

'Macca Byrne. George Byrne's kid.'

Declan shook his head. 'Never heard of either of them,' he said. Derek nodded.

'You will, boy. You will.' He pointed at a car park to the right of the lane. 'Turn in there.'

Following Derek's directions, Declan arrived at the northern car park for Jack's Hill, in Epping Forest. It was calm, peaceful even, the type of place you'd walk a dog or go for a run. It reminded him very much of the woods around Hurley.

Declan sighed.

And soon it would be a circus.

DECLAN HADN'T BEEN WRONG; ONLY HALF AN HOUR AFTER HE'D arrived with Derek Salmon, the car park had filled with police vehicles, the rest now across the road in the southern car park. Many of them had been vehicles from nearby Epping, but there were some familiar faces in the crowd.

Monroe had gained a lift with DC Billy Fitzwarren and DS Anjli Kapoor, while Doctor Rosanna Marcos and DC Joanna Davey had arrived in a CSI van, handing out white PPE suits, latex gloves and blue booties as if it was a carnival. Doctor Marcos's wild black hair fell over her olive skin as she tried to pull it back under the PPE suit's hood, while DC Davey's frizzy ginger hair was poking out through the sides of the opening. The local police had cordoned off the exits at all ends; difficult to do when you were in a woodland that covered a few square miles and sided onto several main roads. But the Duty Officer, a grizzled old Epping Police Sergeant who gave the impression of a man who'd done many of these in the past was doing his best, now stopped local journalists from trying to learn what was going on in their woodlands.

'I used to mountain bike through here,' Billy said as he walked with Declan along the wooded path, towards the Iron Age fort known as Ambresbury Banks. Now out of his overalls, Billy once more wore an expensive and well-tailored three-piece suit, his blond hair styled immaculately.

'Of course you did,' Declan replied. 'Did your butler cycle beside you?'

'That's uncalled for,' Billy said. 'You know they're called manservants these days.'

'Aren't you worried about the mud on your trousers?' Declan asked, looking down at Billy's feet before pausing. 'Ah.'

Billy grinned, waggling one of his olive-coloured Hunter boots. 'Always keep these on hand,' he explained, looking down at Declan's shoes. 'I'd have thought you'd have got some too by now.'

'Why?' Declan replied, avoiding a mud puddle. 'I'm a city boy.'

'Who lives in a country village,' Billy added. 'You should look around. You probably have some of your father's boots in the house.'

'I'll check for some. You know, for when you take me grouse shooting next.'

Billy shook his head. 'I'm afraid my family wouldn't allow that to happen,' he replied. 'You don't have a tweed suit.'

The two of them chuckled for a moment. That Billy came from one of the richest families in England but was cut off from all funds because of his police loyalties was a constant source of jokes and comments. Billy welcomed it, to be honest. He wasn't a fan of his family either.

'Anyway,' Billy continued once he was sure Declan had finished. 'This is quite a historic place.'

'Yeah? How so?' Declan was now painfully aware that his shoes were about to get destroyed by the mud and was making a mental note that after this and the crime scene a few weeks back in Savernake Forest, he really needed to hunt around and see if his father had any wellies for days like this.

Billy meanwhile was still in the middle of his history lecture.

'The road you most likely drove up to get here? Epping New Road? Dick Turpin used to hold up coaches on it when it was the primary route to Cambridge. Had a place known as *Turpin's Cave* a few miles south near Loughton Iron Age Camp,' he waved ahead. 'And up here is Ambresbury Banks fort. Legend says that Queen Boudica died here while fighting the Romans.'

'I thought she died at King's Cross?' Declan raised an eyebrow at this. 'Under platform three or something?'

'There's about a dozen places that claim her death,' Billy shrugged. 'I didn't say it was fact. Just commenting that there's a lot of legends and ghosts around here.'

And there was one more ghost to be unearthed, Declan thought to himself. Ahead of them and arriving at a turn to the right in the path, Derek had stopped.

'Here,' he said, keeping straight on, moving off the path and across the fallen leaves, towards the raised mound of the hillfort. Declan watched his one-time mentor carefully, noting the silent movement of Derek's lips as he counted steps, turning left, and then right again before stopping deep in some scrubland.

'Here,' he said, the uncertain tone clear in his voice. 'I'm sure it was around here, give or take a few steps.'

A couple of PCSOs with shovels moved towards him, their white PPE suits rustling as they made their way into the small clearing. Declan pulled Derek aside.

'You sure?' he whispered. Derek shrugged.

'We'll see in a minute.'

The forest was quiet; the only sound heard was the crunch of shovel against dirt as the police officers carefully tested the ground, digging into it, looking for any kind of evidence.

Then, with a cry, one of them raised a shovel.

'We have a black bag,' he said.

At this point Doctor Marcos, DC Davey and some Essex-based forensics officers moved in, a crime scene tent already being constructed at the side, ready to be placed over the scrubland. Declan knew that there was nothing more to be done here, so he walked Derek back to Monroe, who watched the grisly scene with a stoney expression.

'Guv, we need to talk later,' Declan said. 'When we're back.'

Monroe glanced at Derek. 'So, you finally told him what bloody mad plan you're playing at here?' he asked. 'I hope so for your sake.'

Declan glanced across the forest at Anjli, who was staring at Derek with a mixture of horror and fear while trying to force another, calmer expression on her face. Indian and in her thirties, Anjli's dark hair was now free of an SCO19 helmet, and styled into a trendy bob, while her navy suit was shop-bought and off the peg, contrasting with Billy's. Leaving Derek with Monroe and another uniformed officer, Declan walked over to her.

'You okay?' he asked. Anjli went to reply, but then stopped.

'No,' she said. 'Not really.'

'This can't be your first body.'

Anjli shook her head. 'Christ, Walsh, I'm from Mile End. I was seeing bodies before I joined the plod.' She indicated Derek. 'It's your friend. The cancer. It's his appearance ...' Her entire body language changed as she seemed to deflate a little.

'My mum has breast cancer,' she explained. 'We're going private for treatment and they're optimistic, but then I ...'

'You see someone like Derek and the mortality of it all hammers in,' Declan nodded. 'I get it. I really do. But Derek? His cancer is different to your mum's. Don't compare them.'

Anjli forced a smile as Doctor Marcos emerged from the crime scene, walking over to Monroe.

'Early days and she's not dug up yet, but from a preliminary visual examination it's a woman, possibly late teens, and from a quick viewing the decomposition seems to match about a year in the ground.'

'Is it Angela Martin?' Monroe asked. Doctor Marcos sniffed, looking around.

'I won't know until we examine the body, but with it being where your man there said? I'd say it's likely. We still need to dig her out and check through everything. It's going to take a few hours, to be honest. I'll give you an update tomorrow morning.'

Monroe and Declan looked to Derek, who was staring up at the sky, as if waiting for God to strike him down.

'We won't find out anything standing around in a wood,' Monroe muttered. 'And I so wanted this to be some kind of excessive medication episode on that man there's part.'

He looked to Billy and Anjli.

'Billy? Find out everything you can on the victim. Anjli? Danny Martin lived near where you grew up. Have a root about, see if you can learn anything about who wanted him or his daughter dead a year or two back.'

'I thought DI Salmon killed her?' Billy looked confused now.

'He's a suspect,' Declan chimed in. 'But I want to know whether there are any other possibilities out there first.' He looked to Monroe.

'What do you want me to do?'

Monroe pointed to Derek Salmon, now kneeling on the floor, praying openly.

'Take him back to the custody cells at Tottenham North and find out whether he needs any medication brought in,' he said. 'There's no way Mister Salmon here will return home for quite a while.'

With their orders given, the team of the Last Chance Saloon left the crime scene and the probable body of Angela Martin, each with their own mission to find out what really happened in an old Iron Age hillfort almost a year earlier.

5

PERSONAL CRISIS

ONCE DECLAN SETTLED DEREK SALMON BACK INTO HIS custody cell and ensured that the Desk Sergeant would arrange for the right medication to be brought in, the time had moved on past six pm and so he made the rush hour drive back to Hurley, hoping that some kind of normality might help him right now. The drive back from Epping had been silent, as if Derek Salmon had finally realised the severity of the situation and had resigned himself to it. Even when Declan had uncuffed him, leaving him in the hands of the Desk Sergeant, Derek hadn't spoken a word, silent tears streaming down his face.

Declan wanted to cry too; tears of frustration and anger. This wasn't on Derek, but on Janelle Delcourt and the Seven Sisters. He needed to link them to this without using what he already knew.

And that was going to be difficult.

His phone rang as he was driving; the screen on the car audio switched to Bluetooth phone mode, the display reading 'LIZZIE'. Declan tapped it, connecting the call to the car audio.

'Everything alright?' he asked. The voice of his ex-wife came through the speakers.

'Yes and no,' she said. 'You remember how we said that even though we're apart, we'd still make life or death decisions together about Jess?'

Declan didn't like how this was going. 'Go on.'

'She's been asked to a milkshake diner.'

'She's fifteen, Liz. She's allowed to—'

'On a date.'

There was a silence as Declan took this in. 'With a boy?'

'Of course with a boy! What else did you ...' the voice on the phone trailed off. 'Oh, yeah. No, it's a boy. His name is Owen Peterson.'

'Have you met him?'

'No. but I will. And I wanted to know whether you wanted to be here too when I do.'

'When?'

'Tomorrow. After school.'

Declan thought for a moment. He'd been on dates when he was fifteen, but that was in Hurley, a sleepy little village, and it had been a million years ago. Now the world was different, scarier ... but at the same time, he couldn't stop Jessica dating purely because he was overprotective.

Could he?

'Sure,' he said into the phone. 'I'll be there. And thanks.'

Lizzie ended the call, and Declan continued the drive in silence, jumping when the phone rang again. A different name was on the screen this time. He answered it.

'How old were we when we started dating?' he asked.

There was a pause, and then the voice of Kendis Taylor spoke.

'Well, hello to you too, Dec,' she said. 'I was fourteen, I think. Why?'

'Jess is going on her first date,' Declan explained, but was surprised to hear Kendis laugh down the line. 'What?'

'Buddy, this isn't her first date,' Kendis said. 'This is the first date that *you* know of. Come on, we were going out for a good month before I even told my parents about you!'

'I told my dad immediately,' Declan admitted.

'Yeah, but your dad was a super detective,' Kendis laughed. 'He would have worked it out straight away, anyway. And Jess is like you. She probably keeps bigger secrets than this from you and her mum.'

Declan thought about this for a moment. He knew this to be true, as for the last couple of weeks Jessica had been helping him work through his late father's notes, trying to help Declan work out who could have killed him. And part of this involved keeping everything secret from Lizzie.

'Damn,' he muttered, before realising something. 'Sorry, why are you calling?'

'Journo hat on,' Kendis said. 'Hearing that Derek Salmon is in custody for the murder of Angela Martin.'

'No comment,' Declan grit his teeth. *Who'd told her?* 'And I'd like to know where you gained such fantastical news.'

'I tell you, and you tell me,' Kendis replied.

'Off the record.'

'Of course.'

Declan sighed. 'It's true,' he said. 'But I don't think he did it. He's taking the blame for something.'

'That fits,' Kendis agreed. 'My source heard it from

someone in the Sisters. Which means they're getting it out there for some reason. And if I know ...'

'Then everyone else knows,' Declan slammed his palm on the steering wheel in frustration. 'Thanks for this, I owe you.'

'Buy me dinner when it's done,' Kendis finished. 'And give me the exclusive during it.' She disconnected the call.

Declan drove for a while, thinking about what Kendis had said. If Janelle Delcourt was sending the news out, she wanted this known publicly. But why? What did she gain from ensuring that the world knew that a dying police officer caused a murder, when it was most likely connected to her? Tapping the dashboard again, Declan phoned Monroe.

'Guv, the case is getting leaked to the press,' he said when the call connected. 'I just had a reporter—'

'I know,' Monroe replied, cutting Declan off. 'Someone's told the news outlets everything. Angela Martin's photo was just on the TV. I need to know everything that Derek said to you when you were both alone, laddie.'

'Want me to come back now and brief everyone?'

'Don't bother,' Monroe said. 'The cat's out of the bag, so we'll wait until Doctor Marcos has done her magic. But you need to tell us everything tomorrow, okay? And stop talking to Kendis bloody Taylor.'

And with that the phone disconnected.

Declan carried on down the motorway. He needed to find a link between the murder of Angela Martin and the Seven Sisters fast, because there were a lot of questions for Delcourt to answer, and an actual murderer to find.

THE SIX O'CLOCK NEWS WAS ON WHEN THE POLICE RAIDED Stripe's house.

It wasn't Stripe that they were looking for; he was a child. They didn't raid houses of children. They were after his parents.

'Alfie!' his mother screamed as the door was smashed in by a police battering ram. 'Get upstairs and flush!'

Before Stripe could move though, the house filled with police officers, all moving as one, pushing Stripe's mother to the wall of the living room and turning her to face it as they handcuffed her.

'Trisha Mullville, I'm arresting you for Class A narcotics dealing!' the police officer shouted. 'Anything that you say—'

He didn't finish because at that moment Stripe's father, currently tripping on a sizeable amount of ingested medications came screaming down the stairs like a deranged banshee, a large and vicious looking machete in his hands. He didn't do anything with it though, as he tripped on one stair, crashing to the floor and cutting into his own arm with the blade, screaming as it bit into the flesh. The police ran in and restrained him before he could rise, taking the machete away and stemming the blood flow with a tea towel.

And then, just like that, it was over. Trish slumped against the door now, crying while her husband, Stripe's father, was screaming incoherently as the police tried to stop him from swallowing his own tongue.

As Stripe sat beside the television, a woman made her way over to him. She wasn't in uniform, and because of this Stripe knew she was probably the Vice Officer in charge of the case. In her late fifties or early sixties, her short blonde hair mixed with grey, and a smart blue suit worn over a cream blouse, she knelt beside him.

'Alfie, is it?' she asked. Stripe nodded. 'I'm Detective Chief Inspector Bullman. We're going to get a social worker in to stay with you, okay?'

'What's going to happen to them?' Stripe asked, looking to his parents. Bullman followed his gaze.

'They've done some bad things, and they'll be dealing with that for the moment,' she said. 'But they're low on the ladder, so the chances are they can make a deal.'

Stripe looked back to the news on the television. There was footage of a police crime tent in a woodland clearing, and the image of a girl, a school end-of-year photo was shown over it. A young girl, smiling, her entire life ahead of her.

A girl that Stripe recognised.

'What's this about?' he asked. Bullman looked to the screen.

'They found a body in Essex,' she said. 'That's a photo of her.'

'That's not her,' Stripe replied, looking back to Bullman, a plan suddenly forming in his head. 'She's not buried in Essex.'

'What do you mean?' Bullman waved for another plain-clothed officer, a stocky, white male with greying hair to join her. 'Who's not buried there?'

'That girl,' Stripe said. 'Gabby Chapman. She's not buried down south. I saw her buried.'

Bullman looked to the other detective for a moment before turning back. 'Can you show me where she's buried?' she asked. Stripe smiled.

'You said you could make a deal with my parents, right?' he asked. 'So, I want the same thing. You let my parents go, and I'll show you where the girl on the TV is really buried.'

Bullman looked to DI White, he of the greying hair. White looked to the television and then shrugged.

'If it pans out, we can talk,' he said. Bullman looked back to Stripe.

'Did you see who killed her?' she asked. 'Was it a man? An old man? A police officer?'

Stripe knew who killed Gabby. He'd seen them put the body into the ground and bury it. But even though he wanted to save his parents from prison, there was no way that he was going to rat out Macca Byrne or his right-hand man Harrison. Instead, he simply shook his head.

'It was dark, and it was in the Lickeys,' he said.

DI White was on a radio, talking to someone just out of earshot. Eventually he walked back.

'We're taking your parents in for questioning,' he explained. 'And while we do this, you're going to take us to where you saw the body being buried, okay? And if you're not talking shit, then we can sort out some kind of reduced—'

'No,' Stripe folded his arms. 'Amnesty.' He looked over to his mother, who stared at him. She didn't know that Stripe hung out with Macca Byrne, and her expression was one of stunned betrayal.

And Stripe knew that even if he showed the police the body, even if he did free his parents, life at home would never be the same.

6

NIGHT TERRORS

Ricky Johnston knew he'd screwed up the moment the bouncer kept staring at him.

He rarely drove down to London; the M40 was a boring motorway, and it was always a pain to drive back, especially if he wanted to toot some gak or have a few shots. Nine times out of ten he'd end up crashed on some tart's floor, waking up with a killer headache and leaving before dawn. Somehow, he'd never worked out how to upgrade this into waking up in some tart's *bed*.

But tonight was different. Although Ricky lived in Sparkhill in Birmingham, he'd been born and raised in North London, and a lot of his friends still lived in the area. So, when one of his oldest friends had announced her twenty-first birthday piss-up, he knew that he couldn't miss it. The only problem was that it was being held in Islington, upstairs in a trendy pub called The Old Queen's Head, half-a-mile north of the Angel Underground Station. And, although Islington was now a very nice, middle-class and gentrified area – you knew an area was gentrified when bakers were called *boulangeries* and loaves were now called *artisan bread* – it was also North London, right beside Hoxton and the Coleville Estate.

And that was Seven Sisters territory.

But he wasn't there on business, he wasn't there to start a fight; it was purely a social visit. And although Moses and Macca had been at each other's throats for the last year while the Sisters and George Byrne had tried to rein each of them back, Ricky knew that they'd once been as thick as thieves. He knew he could gain some aggro from going south, especially after Macca and his gang beat the shit out of some Delcourt gang Paedo goon recently, but he could deal with aggro. Maybe even talk his way out of it.

And so, Ricky Johnston had driven down to Islington, parking a couple of streets east and, once in The Old Queen's Head, had found himself a safe spot to base himself in upstairs. Staying sober and drug free for a change he was constantly aware of the entrance to the function room, and always keeping one eye on the other partygoers, worried that any of them could have connections to Moses and his psycho mum.

The problem for Ricky though, was that this made him stand out in the crowd, and the pub's bouncer, watching a ton of early twenty-somethings party like there was no tomorrow couldn't help but notice the one guy who sat by the window in his loud shirt and leather bomber jacket, watching everyone with great interest. In fact, the bouncer wondered if the guy was simply a hired bodyguard himself, until he heard the birthday girl call out his name, and demand that he stopped worrying and had a drink; he could drive back to Birmingham tomorrow.

Walking over to the birthday girl – now utterly wasted,

her sparkly silver dress stained with red wine and the two floating, helium-filled balloons attached to her slowly deflating – he pointed to Ricky.

'Who is he?' he asked. 'He looks like he wants to start a fight.'

'Nah, that's Ricky Johnston,' the birthday girl laughed. 'Known him for years. He's actually trying to keep out of one!' And with that the music changed to a *Spice Girls* song and the birthday girl danced off, belting out the first verse.

The bouncer walked back to the door, typing a message on his phone, sending it.

> Got a Birmingham lad called Ricky Johnston here. Looks nervous. Any good to you?

He carried on watching the crowd while keeping a weather eye on the sober young man by the window. After a couple of minutes, his phone dinged.

> Keep him there. On way. M

The bouncer looked at Ricky, suddenly feeling sorry for the little bugger. But, Moses Delcourt would appreciate this. And that was far bigger than some Brummie getting a beating.

Leaning back against the doorframe and nodding his head to the music, the bouncer found that he was enjoying the night.

RICKY WASN'T FEELING THE PARTY, SO, AFTER A COUPLE OF hours of sitting by the window feeling anxious, he decided to get back to his car and drive back to Sparkhill. He was feeling a little paranoid too; for the last twenty minutes, he was utterly convinced that the bouncer on the door had been eyeballing him. Which meant that he either wanted to fight Ricky or shag him. And Ricky wasn't into either of those right now.

And so, deciding just to slip out of the party without saying goodbye, Ricky asked where the toilets were and walked down the stairs, slipping out of the back entrance to the pub. He made his way quietly down the street towards his car, breathing in the night air and allowing his heart rate to calm down as he did so. Once he was in the car, he could lock the doors. He could drive. He could ...

He wasn't going anywhere.

Ahead, Ricky saw some men turn into view from Cruden Street. They could have been anyone, but the moment they saw him they picked up their pace as they approached. Looking back to the pub, Ricky saw the bouncer outside now, watching him.

Turncoat bastard. Ricky knew that he had been eyeballed.

Now, with nowhere to retreat and the enemy approaching from the front, Ricky looked to his right and saw that he was beside the entrance to Raleigh Mews, a small apartment complex. Turning and making his way to the door, he started pressing the buttons on the keypad, buzzing as many people as he could. It was early, not even nine pm; there was a chance that someone in there would expect friends or a fast-food delivery and would buzz him in without checking. Once through the door, he could make a run for it.

He was about to try again when a hand grabbed his shoulder and spun him around to face his pursuers. There were four of them in total: three wearing a combination of puffer jackets and hoodies, while the one at the front wore an expensive leather jacket. Ricky immediately recognised him.

Moses Delcourt.

'I'm leaving,' Ricky said. 'I was born in London. I was seeing some friends. I swear to you, I wasn't working.'

The three men beside Moses grabbed Ricky, turning him around and backing him against the opposite wall, next to the gated garage entrance to the apartments.

'You work for Macca Byrne though, yeah?' Moses asked. Quietly and nervously, Ricky nodded.

'I work for George, not Macca,' he said. 'But that sometimes means that I'm with him.'

'Good that you didn't lie to me,' Moses moved in closer. 'That would have been bad.'

'I got no beef with you, Mister Delcourt,' Ricky continued, cursing his stupidity for coming down to London in the first place. He looked to his side; there was a window leading into one of the ground floor apartments, a television visible through the net curtains. The news was on.

Surely they can't do anything around witnesses, he thought to himself.

Moses was considering this. One of his gang was getting antsy, pacing back and forth. Ricky realised that he was obviously high on something, and that never made for rational decisions.

'We should muck him up,' the gang member snapped. 'We should do to him what they did to Dave Ewan, man.'

'Dave was an idiot,' Moses replied calmly. 'He was cruising for boys and he got punished. He deserved that beating.'

He was watching Ricky carefully.

'Have we met before?'

'We were at school together,' Ricky said. 'I was Year Three, you were Year Five.'

'Nah man, that's not what I meant.' Moses was thinking now. 'You were here when Macca came, weren't you?'

'Macca's been here a few times, Mister Delcourt. So has his dad. That could have been any of them, as I was here twice with them.'

'You anything to do with what happened with Dave?' one of the gang asked. Ricky hadn't been, but he'd heard what had happened. He shook his head.

'George Byrne and the Sisters have an arrangement,' he said. 'I don't know why Macca tried to break it.'

But Moses wasn't listening now. Instead, he was staring through the window at the television. Risking a glance, Ricky saw that the news was now showing a photo of a girl. One he recognised.

Gabby Chapman. Macca's ex-girlfriend.

Moses returned his gaze onto Ricky.

'I'm not gonna do to you what you did to Dave, 'cos he was a nonce and deserved a kicking. But I want you to pass a message back to your bosses, yeah?'

'Y-yeah, sure,' Ricky stammered, realising there was a chance at getting out of this.

'You tell Macca that we're coming up to the endgame, I've seen the news and I'm gonna be calling in my chits soon. Get it?'

'Yeah, yeah, I get it.' Ricky was nodding now, desperate for these four men to see that he wasn't a threat and should be allowed on his way. 'I'll tell him.'

'Good,' Moses said, looking back to the television in the room as he waved his men off. 'Let the little white man go, boys. Let him swim home to Daddy.'

Ricky almost breathed out a sigh of relief as he turned to leave, but Moses' next words froze him to the spot.

'Wait.'

Ricky turned to see Moses still watching the television. On the screen now was a CSI tent in a forest. Moses seemed to think, making some kind of decision.

'I'm worried that you didn't take in the full message.'

'No, I got it, I swear.'

'Tell it to me,' Moses was now staring back at Ricky.

'You wanted me to tell Macca that you're coming up to an endgame, you've seen the news,' Ricky paused, trying to remember, 'and that you'll be calling in your favours soon.'

'*Chits*.' Moses whispered the word. 'The term I said to pass was chits. C, H, I, T and S. Chits.'

'Yeah, sorry. I'll get it right.'

Moses looked to his men who suddenly surrounded Ricky, grabbing his arms. Moses pulled out a wicked-looking butterfly knife, opening it up.

'I'm gonna need more than a promise,' Moses said, using the blade to cut the buttons off Ricky's shirt, opening it up and exposing Ricky's pale chest. 'I'm gonna need your full attention. C—'

Three quick cuts to Ricky's chest carved a rough 'C' on the left. Ricky went to scream in pain, but the third member of Moses' gang held his hand over Ricky's mouth, muffling him.

'H—' Three more cuts on the chest.

'I—' One long slow, carving downwards. By now the blood was flowing down Ricky's chest and the tears were in his eyes as he tried to free himself.

'T—' Two vicious slashes.

'And S.' Three final slashes with the butterfly knife and

Moses stepped back, observing his handiwork: a rough spelling of CHITS on Ricky's chest.

'Let him go,' Moses said to his men. 'I think he'll remember it this time.'

And with that Moses Delcourt and his men walked off, leaving Ricky Johnston slumped against the wall crying in pain while the inhabitants of Raleigh Mews watched the news on television.

7

FATHERS

THE *JAM HOUSE*, JUST TO THE EAST OF THE JEWELLERY Quarter in Birmingham was a bit of an oddity. Nestled into a row of terraced eighteenth-century houses on St Paul's Square, the last thing you expected to find on the other side of the white Georgian door with the two small pillars either side was a three-storey jazz and blues club, complete with stages, bars and a busy kitchen that took up three houses worth of the street, book-ended either side with a solicitor and the University of Birmingham Jewellery Department. In between these, an arched mews led through into the more exclusive car park while the regular punters and music goers were forced to find parking around St Paul's Church, an equally Georgian place of worship built around the same time as the buildings that surrounded it on all four sides.

Entering the event venue led you into a large, open area to the right, a mixture of deep, vibrant oak and green and cream painted walls, surrounding a stage and a dance floor. On the left was a well-stocked bar and kitchen, while stairs to the right led you to an upper balcony level where, at the back was a slightly raised VIP section.

And it was here that Macca Byrne sat with his friends, listening to a blues band play a live set.

There was a dress code in the Jam House – no sportswear and no trainers – but Macca didn't dress like that on a day-to-day basis anyway, and he was enjoying the music in his usual black attire. His companions, however, including Harrison, dressed more smart casual than usual, ensuring that they didn't cause any problems for Macca while he listened to the live music, surrounded by plates of exquisite food. Macca knew though that even if one of them had worn trainers, the bouncers would probably have let them through or found them a pair of shoes to wear, purely because they were with Macca.

And the rules were created to be broken; there was a strict Under-21 policy here, and Macca was two years away from that milestone.

As the band played, Macca leaned back in the chair and watched the other diners in the club. This was the world he wanted to live in; one that was more respectable, that was more refined than the world that he came from. He didn't want to stay where he was, a gallery of prostitutes and dealers, but that was the portfolio that his dad, George Byrne, didn't want to touch, and so Macca had been given it, to "make his own" way in the business.

That he'd done very well in his little area was a definite concern to the older people in George's crew, and Macca knew that he was being watched, that any move he made against his old man would be seen by them way before he made it. In fact, Wesley O'Brien, one of George's long-term generals and actually one of Macca's godfathers, had once told Macca in no uncertain terms, that going for the King would leave him dead or exiled, as Macca's world was full of football players, while George's world was populated by Chess Masters.

But Macca didn't need to play chess to understand strategy. Football was full of it.

It was true that Macca was reckless; his handling of Dave Ewan showed that. But Macca knew that the dinosaurs of his dad's organisation couldn't see the big picture, couldn't see the endgame.

They would, though. And soon.

Harrison, wearing a bomber jacket, white shirt and tan chinos leaned over, half-eating an onion ring.

'Do you think they know yet?'

'Yeah,' Macca replied. 'Ewan will have called the bitch the moment we left, before the ambulance even arrived.'

'Should we have stopped Ricky going into London?' Harrison started on his fries now. Macca shrugged.

'Ricky was always sucking up to Dad when he should have been working for me. And hey, what happens in London stays in London,' he laughed, but then his smile dropped.

Because walking up the stairs, moving through the dining tables towards them was Wesley O'Brien, an expression of utter fury on his face. He wore a camel jacket, grey sweater and black jeans over trainers, and Macca knew that the only reason they had allowed him in was because he was there to pass a message to George's wayward son.

'Right, Wes?' he asked. 'Grab a chair, we've got more food coming.'

'You need to come with me,' Wesley ordered, ignoring Macca's crew. 'Your dad's out back. He's spitting bullets.'

Macca groaned at this. 'I'll see him—'

'You'll see him now, you cocky little bastard,' Wesley snapped, noting that some nearby diners had glanced in his direction. 'What? Piss off and watch the show.'

Macca nodded to his crew and rose. The last thing he wanted was Wesley making a scene, and he'd known that this conversation would be coming. Following Wesley down the stairs and out into the back carpark, Macca noted that George Byrne was alone as he stood beside his silver Range Rover. Usually he was surrounded by more muscle than Stallone, so this wasn't a good sign. That said, he spent his former life as a bare-knuckle fighter, his frame short and muscled, like a power lifter. If anyone attacked him, he'd most likely snap them like twigs.

'You little shit,' George said, storming over to meet Macca. 'What the hell were you thinking?'

'I need a little more than that, Dad,' Macca couldn't help the smile. 'I mean, I'm real busy right now. It could be any number—'

He didn't finish, as George Byrne viciously backhanded him, rocking Macca's head back and splitting his lip.

'Richard Johnston just called in,' George snapped. 'He's in hospital. Moses Delcourt just slashed his chest up, all because of what you did with Dave Ewan.'

'Dave Ewan was a nonce,' Macca glared defiantly at his father. 'He had a teenage boy in his car.'

'This issue that you have with Moses Delcourt ends now,' George grabbed Macca by the throat, pulling him close. 'And you will apologise to the Sisters for escalating it. Do you hear me?'

'Yes, Dad,' Macca croaked as George Byrne's hand tightened.

'You might think you're ready to replace me, but you're a child,' George Byrne hissed into his son's ear. 'That junkie bitch weakened you. That priest confuses you. And if you try for me you'd better not miss because son or not, I will bloody well end you.' He tapped the scar on Macca's face.

'I can always give you another one of these.'

And with that George Byrne released his hold on Macca's neck, pushing him back as he turned and walked back to his Range Rover. Wesley replaced him, passing Macca a tissue for his cut lip.

'And clean yourself up,' he said. 'This is a respectable place. Not for gutter scum like your mates.'

The Range Rover started up and drove out, leaving Macca in the car park. He stared balefully after it as the Range Rover indicated left onto the street and turned out of sight.

Now alone, Macca dabbed at his cut lip, while tracing the faint line of the scar on his face, a wound given to him five years earlier by his dad, a reminder that not mowing the lawn when asked was a punishable offence.

And then he smiled.

'Check and mate,' he whispered as he returned to the Jam House and his friends.

———

FATHER BARRY LAWSON LIT A CANDLE IN THE LADY'S CHAPEL, spoke a silent prayer of thanks and walked out into the nave of *Our Lady of the Sea* Church, an old place of worship nestled between the new high-rise buildings beside the Thames in Deptford. Now in his early fifties, Father Lawson looked a good decade younger. His hair was still dark brown, with barely a silver hair showing. His beard was trimmed and thick, and his frame was lean and muscled. He was a good-looking man; he knew this because of the messages he received from lonely wives, mistaking his friendly manner as flirtation, and the approving looks that he received when travelling to his other churches in Birmingham and Beachampton. But these compliments and lustful gazes slid off him like water off a duck's back.

He had no interest in women.

He'd lost that lust a long time ago, through penance and pain.

If you'd looked into Father Barry Lawson's history, you would have seen a varied career. In his thirties, they had placed him in charge of Saint Etheldreda's Mission House in Poplar, while also spending a lot of time working with missionaries abroad, often disappearing for months at a time in third world countries. It was outstanding work. It was God's work.

It was profitable work.

And, while he did this, Father Lawson had also taken up his second residence in Birmingham, and a third, occasional one just outside of Milton Keynes. There were too many churches and not enough priests; many had to 'double up' these days. And besides, Saint Etheldreda's had a secondary Nunnery in Alum Rock, so it had made sense to take on light duties at Saint Wilfred's Church, in Saltley. Father Lawson took confessions there, and occasional services.

But this had all ended five years ago, when Father Lawson had left Saint Ethelreda's church in Poplar, moving to Our Lady of the Sea in Deptford, and hopefully a quieter life.

None quieter than what he has now, Father Lawson thought to himself.

The church was still empty; he had recently been playing

with the idea of staying open until ten pm to gather in some of the Deptford community who worked long hours, but the middle of the week was always quiet, so he took this opportunity to wander down into the crypt, strolling casually and almost reverently along the passage to the back of the crypt where the mausoleums lined in rows on the walls. There hadn't been a coffin placed down here in decades, although one stone frontage, proclaiming that the family MARLOWE were buried behind it, seemed to have been shifted recently, a not small amount of car air fresheners hanging around it.

Father Lawson paused beside the stone, stroking it. His hand was calloused, with small dots tattooed onto it. He stared at them for a moment, mesmerised by the patterns; a series of five dots and a second series of three, the latter of which he called his *Father, Son and Holy Ghost*.

'Hello, brother,' he said, softly. 'It's been a while. Will you hear my confession?'

The crypt was silent, so Father Lawson pulled out his Rosary Bead; it comprised black acrylic beads, held together with strong, knotted cord. At the end was a silver Christ on his cross. The company that made it had based the design on the Dominicans. They used Type Three Paracord instead of the usual weaker metal parts, and the link that held the cross into place could withstand over three hundred pounds of pulling power.

Father Lawson knew this because he had tested this, immediately after taking it.

'I know, you can't take my confession because you're family. But family doesn't do what you did. Family doesn't betray family,' Father Lawson smiled now. 'You almost ended your calling a dozen times. Or, rather, *my* calling. I was better than you, after all. I've always been better at this than you.'

There was a faint noise; someone had entered upstairs; most likely a late night parishioner needing guidance. Gathering his composure, Father Lawson patted the stone once more.

'I'll catch you later, brother,' he whispered. 'It's time to go see God again. It's time to apologise to him for what I did.'

He chuckled.

'But then you've probably had to apologise for what *you* did, too.'

And with that Father Barry Lawson adjusted his dog collar and walked back up the stairs into the nave.

———

8

VILLAGE LIFE

DECLAN PULLED UP TO HIS HOUSE (IT STILL FELT WEIRD thinking of it that way) and got out of the Audi. Looking around the street, he felt his tensions finally slipping away, as if the sleepy village of Hurley was simply taking them from him. He knew that it was more likely a case of the house being the one he grew up in, a safe place to be in a time of change and confusion than some magical *Brigadoon*-esque power, but for a moment he stood in the cool evening air, allowing the day to quietly flow away from him.

Looking around, he saw a couple of curtains down the street twitch; people watched his home like a hawk these days, more so since he'd had a stand-off with armed police outside it a few weeks earlier. He'd tried to explain that they weren't *real* police, or more likely they *were* real police, but they'd been convinced to attend his house by a man who *wasn't* ... but it was just confusing for them. All they knew was that the son of Patrick Walsh had moved into Patrick's old house, and within a couple of days they had more police cars and blue lights flashing in the village than in probably the last year put together.

Not exactly the easiest of entrances back into the community.

Opening the door, Declan entered the house. He couldn't explain it, but even after living full time in it for the last couple of weeks, the house still smelled of his father; it was almost as if Patrick was still in the living room, smoking his bloody pipe, even though Declan knew that he only smoked it outside. But then Declan still hadn't really ventured into the back garden as yet, so maybe the ghost of Patrick Walsh preferred to smoke his ghost tobacco in the living room now.

He picked up the letters on the floor, noticing with a slight hint of amusement that the bills may now have been in his name, but they still read MR WALSH, so he didn't know whether the billing companies were now contacting Declan or Patrick still. He'd called as many as he could find to have the details changed, but there was a lot of red tape involved, and several of the companies had demanded things, from a solicitor's letter confirming the change of ownership all the way to an actual scan of the death certificate. And to be brutally honest, there wasn't enough time in the day to do all of this and solve crimes.

Placing the bills on the side table, Declan walked over to the phone, the little red "message" symbol on it currently flashing. Pressing the "play" button, he then moved towards the drinks cabinet as a voice spoke through the speaker. It was Karl Schnitter's, his mechanic neighbour whose house backed onto his, and an old friend of the family.

'Declan,' the voice said, the slight German accent still audible. 'Karl here. Look, I know you are still moving in and busy, but some of us are raising a glass tonight for dear Patrick in The Olde Bell. I thought you might like to join us.

We will be here from eight until around ten.' The phone beeped to show that it had ended the message as Declan considered it. The last time he'd been in the village pub was when Monroe had offered him a job. It had also been the day of his father's wake. Declan wasn't sure if he was up for a drink with the village yet, so instead he turned back to the cabinet and started pouring himself a small whisky. This wasn't something that he'd done while living in the small apartment in Tottenham, the apartment that he still paid rent on for the next two months because of his three-month exit clause; this was very much a new habit, and Declan knew exactly why he did it.

Patrick Walsh had the same ritual when Declan was growing up, and this was a subconscious way for Declan to feel closer to his father again. That and the fact that his father had always had a great taste in Irish Malts, and the cabinet had been stocked well when he passed away.

When he was murdered.

The thought sparked across Declan's mind for the briefest of moments, but it was enough to kill any relaxation that Declan had. He believed without a doubt that someone had murdered his father, but he still needed to work out why and by whom. Luckily, there was a whole crime board of suspects for Declan to work through, and for the last couple of weeks he'd been doing that with the help of Jessica, although without her mother knowing. One day Jessica wanted to be a police detective like her father, grandfather and even great-grandfather; to her, this was more a simple case of *helping Dad get closure while learning some wild police skills.*

Declan turned and looked across the living room; since moving in, he'd barely touched the place, and he knew exactly why. The ghost of Patrick Walsh was strong here, as was the ghost of Declan's mother, Christine Walsh, who had passed away four years previously, leaving a widower in the house. The furniture, the random ornaments on the shelves, the book choices, these were once chosen and bought by his parents, many of which had been purchased and placed in their locations on sideboards and shelves while he lived here both as a child and as a teenager. It felt almost heretical to remove them.

He would though; just not right now.

Declan wanted to finish the case, to find who killed his father first and then, having honoured him in death, Declan would start remodelling this small village house. And he knew that he would start with removing the small, secret room upstairs.

Taking the tumbler of whisky, Declan made his way up to his father's secret study; a small, hidden priest hole of a room that was obstructed by an empty bookcase. It was a room that had been built for some unknown bloody reason that Declan had never been told about. In this secret hideaway was a crime board covered in photos, notes and news clippings, all linked by yards of red string, some kind of unofficial investigation that Declan's father had been working on before he died, an investigation that he'd not left any information on. On that board were faces Declan didn't recognise, but others stood out to him; a recent photo of Johnny Lucas, one of the "twins" of the East End, well-built and in his early sixties, his salt and peppered hair blow-dried back, giving him a little quiff at the front; a picture of Jackie beside him, exactly the same as Johnny, but with a white shirt on and a parting to the side the only differences; and an old photo of DI Derek Salmon, taken from the time that he worked under DI (or even the later promoted DCI) Patrick Walsh.

Placing the tumbler of whisky down, Declan checked through his father's folders, looking for something that could explain why Derek was on the board. His father was a known hoarder; every case he worked on had been copied out into duplicate folders and then filed in the large metal filing cabinet in the room's corner. It was how Declan had learned that someone had doctored the official copies of the Victoria Davies murder, when the copies that Declan had worked through in the Temple Inn Crime Unit simply didn't match up. It held decades of crimes in brown foolscap folders; many solved, some still outstanding. His father had retired six months before he passed away, and Declan knew that this blot on his copybook, this failure to have a hundred percent close ratio had caused Patrick Walsh to write his own memoirs, and most likely caused his death.

The problem was that Declan had read the manuscript several times now, and found it watered down, even censored. He'd unlocked the old iMac downstairs with a password given to him by Monroe and even Jessica – she of the generation that understood technology better than anyone – couldn't find anything of worth on it. It was as if the true book, the true *story,* had been hidden away and they had placed a forgery on display for all to see. Maybe Kendis could help here? She'd written it for Patrick, or with Patrick, or something along those lines.

Maybe tomorrow.

Declan had searched the cabinet from top to bottom, still unsure why Derek Salmon's picture was on the crime wall. In all the time that Declan had known Derek, he'd not once seen him perform any kind of criminal act. And his father had even vouched for Derek when Declan started working under him. Surely you didn't do that when you had no faith in someone. Yet a conversation that Declan had in this same house several weeks ago with Shaun Donnal, then a suspect in another murder, came to mind. Donnal had come to Declan's father's house for help, unaware of Patrick Walsh's death. He had explained that he'd learned of a book, written five years earlier by Michael Davies and based around a crime that then-DI Patrick Walsh had solved; a solved case that Declan had proven invalid by the time that he had solved it and found the true murderer himself. According to Donnal, in the book it had been stated that the detectives on the Davies murder had been bought off. When questioned about this, and when Declan had angrily shouted that *his father wasn't a bent copper*, Shaun had replied one simple phrase.

'I didn't say your father, I said detectives. Plural.'

There were only a handful of detectives on that case. Patrick Walsh had been one of them. Then-DS Alexander Monroe had been another.

And then-DC Derek Salmon had been on the team as well.

Was *this* why he was on the wall? Was this one reason that the Seven Sisters agreed to let him take the fall? What else did he have hidden with those skeletons in the wardrobe?

Sitting in his father's desk chair, Declan slowly turned in it, taking in every one of the study's four walls. There was nothing that gave him any inspiration here.

Wait.

In the study's corner, on the highest shelf of a bookshelf, Declan saw a battered-looking hardback book amongst a random grouping of old police procedural handbooks.

THE HOUND OF THE BASKERVILLES

Sir Arthur Conan Doyle

For some reason this felt out of place there, probably because it was the only fictional novel in the room. Declan also knew that as a fan of the Great Detective, his father owned this in two other editions.

Why would you keep a cheap-looking book on the shelf when you had better copies to show?

Rising from the chair and pulling it from the shelf, Declan realised that it felt stiff, more solid than it should. Even hardbacks had a little give where the paper would shift when held. Turning it around in his hands, he realised this was because the book's pages had been glued together to create an effective box and, when he opened the cover of the book he saw that it had been converted into a keep-safe, with a small recess cut into the middle. In the recess was a USB flash drive and a post-it note stuck to it that simply said:

Wintergreen

Declan stared down at the flash drive for a moment. There wasn't anything in the study that could explain what this was, so he placed the keep-safe on the desk and, taking the flash drive, he left the study and made his way to the iMac downstairs. Turning it on and logging in, Declan placed the flash drive into the back of the iMac, slotting it into an available USB slot, watching a folder named WALSH appear on the desktop.

Opening it however proved to be a problem as a box flashed up onto the screen the moment that he clicked onto it.

Enter password

Declan tried *wintergreen* with no success; he tried a variation of versions of the word, even trying the password that unlocked the iMac, but none of these opened the folder. Until he could open it, the flash drive would be yet another puzzle for him to solve, along with what a Wintergreen was.

The clock on the wall chimed nine pm; Declan ran his hand through his hair and rotated his shoulders in a circular motion, trying to ease the stress and tension within them.

It didn't work.

He sighed, looking to the clock. *Maybe a drink around actual people would help.*

Grabbing his coat, Declan left his house, heading for The Olde Bell.

———

THE BAR WAS QUIET WHEN DECLAN ARRIVED, A YOUNG GIRL working behind the bar.

The Olde Bell was a tourist destination in the summer; almost nine hundred years old, it had once been the hostelry of Hurley Priory, which made it one of the oldest hotels in the world. It was also a pilgrim point for war afficionados, as the British Army used it as a meeting place between Churchill and Eisenhower during the war. But this wasn't tourist season; this was late autumn and the tourist trade had left for the year. Now the bar was almost empty, the hotel that backed onto it equally so.

Looking around, Declan saw Karl sitting alone at a booth beside the wall, a pint of what looked like lager in his hand. He nodded to Declan.

'This is it?' Declan asked as he walked over. Karl shrugged.

'There were more, but it is getting late for them,' he said. 'I waited in case you came.'

'Thank you,' Declan nodded to the drink. 'Can I buy you one?'

'I would like that,' Karl smiled. 'Any pilsners.'

Declan ordered a drink for Karl and a Guinness for himself, taking the drinks and walking back to the booth. As he sat down, he realised with a small amount of amusement that it was the same one that he'd sat at with Monroe, when the canny old Scot had recruited him into the Last Chance Saloon.

Karl raised his own half-empty glass.

'To Patrick,' he said. Declan raised his own glass, clinking with Karl's before taking a sip. His father had taught him from an early age never to toast without clinking glasses. It was something to do with bad luck, but he couldn't remember the whole superstition.

'So,' Karl smiled, 'when are you allowing me to fix your poor battered car?'

Declan chuckled. 'When the police pay me money to do so.'

'Such a shame,' Karl lamented. 'Audis are such good cars. German built is always good.'

Declan paused while sipping, observing his drinking companion. A tall, tanned, robust German in his mid-sixties, Karl had lived in the village since Declan was a small boy. After the fall of the Berlin Wall, during the early nineties Karl had moved to England, and had embraced the life of the "country squire" ever since.

Karl stopped mid-drink, as if remembering something. Slowly and deliberately, he raised his glass again.

'And to Christine,' he said.

Declan paused at the mention of his mother, but Karl just smiled.

'They are together in Heaven now,' he continued.

Declan nodded, clinking his pint glass to Karl's. He wasn't a deeply religious man, but he hoped that his mother and father were now somewhere better, and more importantly, together.

'He never got over her loss,' Karl said into the glass. 'He was never the same after her murder.'

Declan almost spilled the glass. 'What?'

Karl looked to him, as if realising he'd spoken out of term.

'Her death. He was never the same after her death.'

'You said murder.'

Karl shook his head. 'Apologies, sometimes words for me merge when speaking in another tongue. Death and murder, they are very similar in German.'

Declan nodded, placing his glass on the table and rubbing at his eyes. His mother had passed away after an illness, so there was nothing suspicious there. However, since examining his father's death, he'd seen conspiracies in every corner.

'Don't apologise,' he forced a smile. 'You at least speak a second language. I have trouble speaking my own.'

Karl laughed at this. 'When in Rome,' he said.

Declan took a mouthful of Guinness, taking the time to consider his next line.

'Can I ask you a question?' he eventually asked. 'You back onto my father's–I mean *my* house. Before he died, did you see anything strange?'

'What do you mean, strange?' Karl seemed confused by this.

'I don't know. Visitors, perhaps?'

'No more than usual,' Karl thought for a moment. 'Your woman, she was there—'

'My woman?'

'Sorry, again with language. I believe you would say your ex?'

Declan nodded at this. 'Ah yeah, you mean Kendis.' Karl had been around since Declan was a small boy and had seen the trials and tribulations of Kendis Taylor firsthand. And Kendis had already admitted to helping Patrick with his memoirs. But Karl shook his head at this.

'No, I mean yes ... she was there, Kendis, but I mean your other ex.'

'Lizzie?'

Karl nodded. 'She visited your father often.'

'With Jessica?'

'No, more alone,' Karl sipped at his drink. 'And there was an older woman. At other times that is, not with Elizabeth.'

'A local?'

'No. She was ...' Karl fought for the words. 'Helen Mirren. You know the actress? Very good actress. Exquisite.'

'I know Helen Mirren,' Declan frowned. 'The woman looked like her?'

'Yes. Short white hair, very slim. Beautiful.'

Declan couldn't picture anyone that he knew looking like that, and he was pretty sure that Helen Mirren herself had never visited his father, but Karl hadn't finished.

'I never learned her name,' he said. 'Although I asked Patrick about her. I wondered whether she was a lover, and if not, whether I might contact her.'

'And what did my father say?' The thought of Patrick Walsh having someone after Declan's mother was unnerving to Declan. Karl shrugged.

'He said I was mistaken,' he finished. 'That there was never such a woman visiting his house.'

Declan leaned back in his chair. If this was true, then his father had been meeting someone in secret before his death, someone who wasn't on the crime wall, or in his memoirs.

The question was who though?

9

EARLY DAYS

DECLAN ARRIVED IN TEMPLE INN, AND THE COMMAND UNIT OF DCI Monroe's Major Crimes Investigation Unit just before nine o'clock the following morning. He hadn't slept well; partly because even after a couple of weeks, he still felt that he was intruding in his late father's house; partly because he was worrying about Jessica and this stranger she was seemingly dating and telling no one; and the revelations from Karl Schnitter about his own father's meeting habits. But more because of the actions of the previous day, and the revelation of Derek Salmon as a potential murder suspect still weighing heavily on his mind.

Entering the building, Declan saw that the examination table was empty in the downstairs morgue; the chances were that Doctor Marcos had finished her post-mortem examination of the body believed to be Angela Martin earlier that morning, or even the previous night. Declan didn't know where the bodies went after that, or even if there was some kind of cold storage in the building; he couldn't see the owners of Temple Inn, where the police leased the property from, being happy with bodies being held on site. Hell, they hadn't even allowed custody cells.

Entering the upstairs office, Declan saw that it was currently empty, as Monroe had already called everyone into the briefing room to the side, the glass wall revealing Anjli, Billy, Doctor Marcos and DC Davey as they faced Monroe, currently standing by the enormous plasma screen that he'd somehow wrangled from the police funds. Monroe meanwhile was watching for Declan.

'Come on in, son,' he said. 'The gate guards alerted me you were driving in, so I called all the soldiers together. Let's get this show on the road.'

Declan entered the briefing room, sitting at a space next to Anjli. 'Have we swept this room recently?' he asked.

Hearing this, DC Davey nodded, pushing her glasses back up her nose as they slipped down slightly. 'Do it every day now,' she replied, a hint of pride in her voice. It was a strange thing to expect; the sweeping for bugs in a police Crime Unit, but recently the Last Chance Saloon had found a mole in their ranks who had bugged all the rooms on the upper level, mainly to gain intelligence for a suspect in a murder case.

It was only paranoia if they weren't out to get you. And there was already a long list of powerful enemies that would go to extreme measures to get revenge on Monroe's team, following the outcome of that case.

'DI Walsh, would you care to update us on what happened with Mister Salmon while alone in your car yesterday?' Monroe asked. Declan nodded, looking to the others.

'So as the Guv rightly guessed, while I drove to the crime scene yesterday, Derek Salmon spoke alone, coming clean with me about the confession. But what he said was taken as confidential and doesn't leave this room. If it does, then I think it's pretty much confirmed that it could only be one of us that spread it, you understand?'

There was a silent assent by nodding from the others, so Declan continued.

'Derek told me he didn't do it,' he started. 'And yeah, I know that everyone says that, but he also told me he's being paid a ton of money to take the fall.'

'Why?' Billy asked. 'I mean, am I the only one here not seeing this right? He's staining his career, his reputation by doing this, even if he's freed.'

'Because he's dying,' Monroe added. 'And dying men don't care about reputation.'

Declan nodded. 'Exactly,' he said. 'Derek knows he's dying, and he also knows the police pension isn't worth that much. His daughter's started university, and his wife, estranged as she is, will end up shouldering a ton of debts when he goes. So, he made a deal with the Seven Sisters.'

'They killed Angela Martin?' Monroe was surprised at this. 'Didn't see that coming.'

'We don't know that,' Declan interrupted, shaking his head. 'Derek said that they showed him the location of the body on a map and was told by whoever showed him it wasn't anything to do with her father, but more who she was dating. Apparently Angela Martin was seen with both Moses Delcourt, son of the Matriarch of the Seven Sisters, and some Birmingham gangster wannabe called Macca Byrne.'

Billy was already typing on a laptop. After a moment photos of Macca Byrne and Moses Delcourt appeared. Macca was in his traditional all-black clothing, his black hair hidden under a peaked cap, the wicked-looking scar on his face visible. Moses meanwhile was in a hooded top, his head almost shaved, the slightest hint of a goatee on his face. He looked no older than eighteen.

'Considers himself a bit of a Peaky Blinder,' Anjli muttered, looking at the image of Macca.

'Mackenzie Byrne,' Billy read from the laptop. 'Got quite a jacket for a lad his age. Been in and out of detention centres since he was nine. His father is George Byrne.' Another photo appeared on the screen. A vicious-looking thug of a man, his black hair cropped short as he glared at the camera on a police line-up. 'George runs Birmingham, and it looks like Macca is some kind of criminal sub-contractor.'

Monroe nodded. 'And Moses?'

'Clean sheet,' Billy looked up from his laptop's screen. 'Almost like someone powerful has his back.'

'Must be great when Mummy is a crime boss,' Doctor Marcos said. 'No, really. Mine was a cashier.'

'I'm guessing Mackenzie, or Macca, or whatever he's called is priming himself to take on the family business when darling Daddy dies?' Monroe stared at the images on the screen. 'They look familiar. And his dad. When you get a chance, check if we had any issues with either Mister Byrne down here.'

'So what do we know about the body?' Declan asked. Doctor Marcos moved to the front, now tapping the plasma screen, bringing up images of the forest crime scene.

'Salmon wasn't lying when he said the body was there,' she said. 'Although watching him at the burial location, it was almost as if he was counting out the steps on a pirate map, which makes sense if he didn't bury the body. The body however is definitely that of Angela Martin. We gained her identity from dental records and fingerprints.'

'She was printed?' Declan raised an eyebrow.

'She was Danny Martin's daughter,' Anjli said, looking at the screen. 'They might have named her after an angel, but she sure as hell wasn't one. Of course she was printed.'

'Sounds like you knew her,' Monroe looked at Anjli. She shrugged.

'I worked the Mile End beat before taking the DS exam, and after that worked for DCI Ford there,' she said. 'We had a lot of occasions to get into it with the Lucas gang. And I saw the Martins, father and daughter around the place. They were local to the area, and she wasn't a shy, retiring flower in any sense of the word. She was worse than her old man half the time.' She sighed. 'If she'd stayed alive, she might even have given The Twins a run for their money down the line.'

Doctor Marcos coughed to regain everyone's attention.

'We also found two identifying marks on the body,' she explained. 'The first was a broken arm. Well, an old break, that is. Angela broke it on a school skiing trip a year before her disappearance, and the repaired bone was clear on the X-ray. Also, there was a small tattoo on the right shoulder in the shape and colour of a red rose.'

She tapped the screen and another photo, this one showing a younger, smiling Angela Martin appeared on the screen. She wore a vest top and was dancing with friends, possibly at a school disco.

'We took this from her social media. It shows the tattoo clear enough to identify and confirm.' She indicated a tattoo on Angela's shoulder. Another tap and the same tattoo was seen on another image; this time though it was faded, on leathery, year-dead skin.

'Thank you, Doctor,' Monroe said. 'Did you learn the cause of death?'

Another tap, and now the image was a closeup of the dead body's neck, the rounded bruises clearly visible.

'Strangulation,' Doctor Marcos read through her notes. 'Either by a rope or a cord pulled around her neck, or by hanging, As you can see here, there were faint bruises and ligature marks on the skin.'

'Type of cord?'

'Unknown as yet,' Doctor Marcos admitted. 'We found some synthetic threads and we're examining those. Also, the ligature marks seemed to indicate small knots in the cord, all spaced regularly along it. We're looking into that, too.'

'So a knotted rope?' Declan wrote this down.

'Or something with bumps in it,' Doctor Marcos pointed at the windows to the briefing room. On the blinds were rope pull cords, designed as beaded strings. 'Something like that, for example.'

'So Angela Martin was hanging out with the wrong crowd, twice,' Anjli mused. 'Either Daddy's friends or the North London crowd.'

'Three times,' DC Davey interrupted. 'Birmingham too.'

Anjli nodded. 'Thanks. Yeah, so three times then. Something happens, she's killed. Buried. And then a year later Janelle Delcourt's band of happy woman gangsters pay Derek Salmon to take the hit? Why? And why now?'

'Because they needed it out in the open,' Declan suggested. 'They had to have someone waiting near the body to call the press when we arrived. They timed this. For what, I have no idea.'

'Something like this screams gang war,' Monroe suggested. 'They're about to do something bad, and this gives them the opportunity and reason to. Angela was seeing Moses, and they killed her. Now the body's been found,

Moses and his mother can blame one of the other gangs Angela hung around with.'

'Then why make Derek do it?' Declan asked.

'Because there's more to Derek Salmon than we're seeing here,' Monroe mused. 'I reckon they'll use him as the patsy but claim he did it on someone's orders.'

'That'd do it,' Anjli nodded.

'We need to find out what's going on, but we need to do it correctly and by the book if we're going to free our current suspect,' Monroe continued. 'We need to find a link to the Sisters before we go near them. Find some details on Moses and Angela being seen together. See if Danny Martin knows anything.'

His fingers tapped on the wall beside the screen and Declan could see he was irritated about something here. 'There are too many things we don't know. Who killed her, why she was killed, how she was killed and where she was killed. What were her activities leading up to her disappearance, and what's the connection with Birmingham?'

'Romeo and Juliet with gang wars,' Billy muttered, looking up, suddenly aware that he was being watched. 'You know, Montagues and Capulets?'

'Indeed,' Monroe nodded. 'But which of these young people is Romeo, and which is Juliet?

There was a strange tune suddenly echoing around the room.

'Is that the theme to *Quincey, MD*?' Declan asked as, with an apologetic look to Monroe, Doctor Marcos pulled out her phone and left the briefing room, taking the call.

'Looks like it was,' Anjli smiled. 'Did you expect anything less from our medical examiner?'

'Right then,' Monroe turned back to the team, all business. 'We have little more than we ended yesterday with, and we already have a prime suspect that we currently know didn't do it.'

'Do we?' Declan asked. Monroe looked to him, surprised.

'He was your mentor for years,' he said. 'You think he could have done this?'

'I can't help thinking about Shaun Donnal,' Declan continued. 'He said that there were corrupt detectives on the original Michael Davies case. Derek was on it.'

'As was I, laddie, so tread carefully.'

'And so was my father,' Declan replied. 'But you just said there's more to Derek Salmon than we're seeing here, and you're not in a picture on my father's crime board.'

There was a silence at this revelation.

Declan silently cursed his own stupidity and quick-talking mouth. He hadn't wanted Monroe to know this yet.

'Patrick had a crime board?' Monroe asked carefully.

'Of sorts,' Declan answered equally carefully. 'I think it was for his memoirs. But Derek's on it and linked to Johnny Lucas and a couple of other people.' He forced a smile. 'If it makes you feel better, you're not on it.'

'I'd bloody well hope not,' Monroe snapped, visibly rattled by this news. 'We shall have a long talk about this crime board later, DI Walsh.'

Doctor Marcos walked back into the briefing room, and for the first time, Declan saw that she seemed to be shaken by something.

'Problem?' Monroe asked her, seeing the same thing. Doctor Marcos nodded.

'That was a colleague of mine. A West Midlands CSI,' she said. 'They dug up a body last night in the Lickey Hills, just south of Birmingham.'

'Whose body?' Billy asked, already typing into his laptop, pulling a map of the Lickey Hills up and casting it onto the plasma screen. Doctor Marcos paused for a moment, as if still trying to comprehend the call she had just taken.

'They were calling me for a comparison,' she continued, ignoring Billy's question. 'They had some identifying marks and DNA results on the body and they were a little confused.'

'Confused about what?' Declan asked. Doctor Marcos looked around the room again, as if hunting for the correct words.

'They were confused because what they had shouldn't exist,' she said. 'You see, they've just dug up the body of Angela Martin, complete with matching strangulation ligature marks, a DNA match, a broken arm, and a faded rose tattoo.'

The line hung in the air for a moment as the officers in the briefing room tried to understand what Doctor Marcos had just implied.

'If they've dug up Angela Martin, then who did *we* dig up?' Anjli had stopped writing in her notebook, the pen just hanging there.

'That's the problem,' Doctor Marcos replied. 'We dug up Angela Martin. The data proves it. The historical injuries prove it. The identifying marks, the fingerprints and the DNA prove it.' She sighed, looking to the ceiling before turning her attention back to the team. 'It's just that it looks like they *also* dug Angela Martin up in Birmingham.'

'We have two identical bodies, and one victim.'

10

THE WORST CONVERSATION

THE BRIEFING OVER, AND THE TEAM NOW UNSURE WHAT WAS truly going on, Monroe decided that the best course of action was to ignore this second, identical body for the moment and to work on what they already knew. This meant however that someone had to be labelled Family Liaison Officer and tell Danny Martin that his daughter was definitely dead.

Monroe decided that Declan and Anjli should speak to Danny Martin while Billy used the *HOLMES2* system to find out whatever he could on Angela's movements before her death. That she had been rumoured to be in Birmingham, only a few miles from where this second body had been found, had not been lost on the team, and it was a confused and sombre Declan and Anjli that made their way into Bethnal Green.

'Twins,' Anjli muttered as they climbed out of the Audi and stood outside a row of identical looking terraced houses on Cyprus Street. Every house on either side of the road had arched doors and windows, each painted cream to contrast against the tan bricks, while curved royal-blue wooden shutters framed the downstairs windows, matching the royal-blue doors of every house on the street. 'It has to be. Or clones.'

'I don't think we're in the latter's realm yet,' Declan was turning around, staring at the houses as he spoke. 'But Danny must have known, right? You can't miss a second baby. And the pre-natal ultrasound stuff that Billy pulled up only showed one baby ... Why are all the houses identical here?'

'Housing association rules,' Anjli walked up to one door and hammered on the black metal door knocker. 'They love their uniformity.'

After a moment the door opened, and a man stared at them through the crack. He was in his early forties but looked artificially younger. Tall, muscled and with his jeans and a Ted Baker polo shirt with his blond hair swept back, his teeth looking like they'd been veneered and his forehead looking suspiciously smooth and wrinkle free for a man his age. Danny Martin looked like a reality TV star trying desperately to knock a few years off his age.

'Alright, Danny,' Anjli said.

'DS Kapoor,' Danny Martin replied. 'You here to tell me what BBC sodding News already informed me?'

'I'm afraid so,' Anjli nodded. 'Can we come in?'

Danny looked to Declan who held up his warrant card.

'DI Walsh.'

Danny nodded. 'I remember you from a year ago. Did a piss-poor job finding her then, didn't you? Still, better late than never. You're Paddy's kid, too, aren't you?' And with that he opened the door, allowing the two of them to enter. Declan paused for a moment, thrown by the apparent familiarity that Danny Martin had for his father but followed Anjli into the house, closing the door behind them.

The house was small, but clean. A three-bedroom terrace,

the entrance hallway led to the stairs, while a door to the right took them into the living room. It was minimalistic and clean. The wall was a mixture of white shelves and art deco paintings, the fireplace filled up with wooden logs like some kind of bricked-off irony. The floor was hardwood, with a grey rug covering most of it. To the left were doors into the kitchen, and a patio door to the back garden while to the right were two sofas, both matching white leather, placed around a mahogany coffee table. One sofa faced the front window while the other faced a fifty-five-inch television attached to the wall over another log-filled fireplace.

As Declan sat on one sofa, Anjli beside him, he noted that behind him was an artistic screen print of Ronnie and Reggie Kray, the only thing in the entire room that even remotely screamed 'gangster'. The other thing in the room that screamed out anything was the collection of ornate crosses that seemed to populate the windowsills and shelves around him. Declan hadn't been in here before, although he had been the one to interview Danny back when Angela had gone missing, but he had never mentioned in any reports that Danny Martin was overtly religious.

'Nice house,' Declan said. Danny nodded.

'Should be for the money I paid,' he growled. 'Bloody place is worth more than a million now, but alone I just rattle around it.' He looked to Anjli. 'Go on then, give us the worst conversation.'

'Worst conversation?' Anjli frowned.

'The one where you tell me that the body was Angela and yes, she's dead,' Danny replied. 'I've had to do the same myself a couple of times, so I'd rather we just ripped the plaster off. I've been expecting this call for a year now, it's not new to me.'

Declan nodded to this. As an enforcer to Jackie and Johnny Lucas, Danny Martin had probably had to tell many people that their sons and daughters were dead.

'A body was discovered in Epping yesterday,' he said before Anjli could reply. 'Forensic examination has identified it as that of Angela Martin.'

He glanced at Anjli, who had looked at him sharply, slightly shaking his head. He didn't want to mention the second body yet. Missing this silent exchange, Danny just nodded.

'You know who did it?' he asked.

'We have a suspect in questioning, but we have several lines of investigation,' Anjli replied.

'Who?' Danny asked, his tone rising slightly. 'Who've you got in?'

'You know we can't tell you that,' Declan leaned forward, ensuring that he took Danny's attention from Anjli. 'Just know that we're going to find her killer and bring them to justice.'

Danny chuckled. 'I bet I find them and bring them to justice first,' he growled.

'Not what I'd expect from a man that seems to have taken the word of God in so strongly,' Declan replied, indicating the crosses.

Danny shrugged. 'I'm Catholic,' he said. 'We very much believe in guilt and original sin, but we also believe in an eye for an eye. What do you need to know?'

'What you can tell us about Angela. Did she have any enemies? Boyfriends?' Anjli asked, opening her notebook. 'People who would have seen her in her last days?'

'We weren't talking at the end,' Danny admitted. 'We were always rowing. Well, until about a year or two before her death, that was. Then she kept disappearing for weeks on end, which made things a little easier.' He thought for a moment. 'She was seeing some lad. Black kid; didn't know the name. From North London. The rest of the time she was God knows where. She was a serious crackhead at the end, too. I tried to get her off it, but she kept finding more, the cunning little mare.'

Declan pulled up the photo of Moses Delcourt on his phone, turning it to show Danny. 'This the kid?'

Danny nodded. 'That's the one,' he said. 'Never knew his name. Who is he?'

'You don't recognise him?' Declan looked surprised at this. 'I thought you knew all the gangs around London.'

'I know the players, not their children.'

'Fair point,' Anjli replied. 'Did your daughter ever visit Birmingham?'

'Yeah, she was arrested there twice. God knows why she chose there of all bloody places,' Danny replied. 'Why would you ask that?'

'Lines of enquiry, nothing more.' Declan wrote in his notebook. 'Angela was an only child?'

'Yeah,' Danny's face wrinkled as he spoke, and Declan realised that Danny was trying hard not to cry. 'She was everything to me. Her mum, my Cheryl ... she died in childbirth. There was nothing the nuns could do.'

'Nuns?' Declan glanced at Anjli before looking back to Danny. 'You didn't give birth in a hospital?'

'Well, yeah, and also no,' Danny said, failing to explain anything. 'Cheryl was a proper Eastender, you know? Wanted to keep the traditions of her family going. She was born in Saint Etheldreda's Mission House in Poplar, and we were both devout Catholics, so we went there for the birth.'

'I thought that closed down?' Anjli asked Danny before turning to Declan. 'There were a few Missions like this in the fifties and sixties in the East End of London. They used one for that BBC show on midwifes. Lots of people around here, mainly Catholics, would choose Missions over the local maternity ward. Probably because they felt more secure having "God" watching over them.' She turned back to Danny. 'But I thought they moved on in the seventies?'

'They did,' Danny replied. 'But this was eighteen years back. They still had a presence there and still took in a few hereditary family cases. One of them was us. Both me and Cheryl were born there.'

'So the midwife nuns looked after you during the birth?' Declan asked. 'Were you allowed to attend it?'

'Again, yes and no,' Danny said. 'I wasn't there at the start, but once they felt the baby's – Angela's – head, Father Lawson called me in.'

'And Father Lawson was ...' Declan was writing in the notebook, glancing up.

'I dunno. He was the vicar there or something. Cheryl seemed to know him; I think he was part of the church beside the Mission. Anyway, he stayed with us. But then it all went wrong. They knew something had gone pear shaped. They called for an ambulance, but it was too late. Just after Angela was born, my Cheryl ...' Danny paused, tears streaming down his face, '... she left me.'

'I'm sorry,' Anjli said. 'I remember your wife from when I was a kid around here. She was a firebrand.'

Danny chuckled, wiping his eyes. 'She was that,' he smiled. 'Anyway, the nuns passed me Angela, and I took her and Cheryl to the hospital.'

'Sorry to ask, but do you remember anything else from that day?' Declan asked.

'They were a small Mission House, and it was a busy time,' Danny explained. 'There was another family there, come from the other house to have their baby.'

'Other house?'

'I dunno. Apparently a lot of the nuns had gone to Saltley or Alum Rock or something, but they didn't do midwifery there. These guys had driven to have the baby there and then drove to London once they realised. Traveller family, I think. Didn't want the hospital involved. Your dad passed a month back, didn't he?' Danny changed the subject, calm again. 'He was a prick. I liked him.'

Declan bristled at the insult but accepted the back-handed compliment.

'We may have some more questions for you,' he said as he rose, Anjli rising with him. 'You know, getting a better picture of what was going on, that sort of thing.'

'Sure,' Danny said. 'And when I find the killer and cut his balls off, I'll be the first to phone you.'

Declan rose. 'Did you keep her room?' he asked. Danny frowned.

'What do you mean?' he asked. 'I didn't rent it out, if that's what you're insinuating.'

'I mean that often when we have missing person cases, or ones where the victim isn't found for ages, we find that the parents leave the victim's room alone, almost like a shrine. As if hoping that they'll return,' Declan explained, looking towards the door and the stairs outside. 'I wondered if you did the same thing.'

Danny nodded. 'What if I did?' he asked. Declan shrugged.

'I was hoping we could have a look at it before we left,' he said softly. 'Maybe we could find something that was missed.'

'Nobody's been in there for a year,' Danny growled. 'Even I haven't gone in there.'

'Danny,' Anjli placed a hand on Danny's shoulder. 'It might help us find out who did this.'

Danny nodded, showing the door with his head. 'You know where it is,' he said. 'And you'll understand if I don't join you.'

Declan nodded in return. 'Of course.'

And, with that, Declan and Anjli left Danny Martin to his memories and went upstairs to examine a dead woman's room.

———————

11

HIDDEN THINGS

THE ROOM WAS ON THE LEFT OF THE STAIRS AS DECLAN AND Anjli made their way up them; obvious by a faded piece of A4 paper stuck onto the door that said *Angela's Room*. It was coloured in with pencils and drawn images of unicorns and wizards stood either side of it. It looked like a very young Angela had drawn it and had been stuck on to the door for over a decade.

Opening the door, the first thing that struck Declan was the smell. It was musty, old smelling, as if the air hadn't properly flowed through this part of the house in a very long time. Entering the bedroom, Declan glanced at Anjli before reaching into his pockets and pulling out a pair of blue latex gloves in a packet. Opening it, he removed the gloves from the wrapping, pulling them on, noting that Anjli was doing the same.

The bedroom was painted a deep blue; an interesting and unconventional choice for a girl's bedroom, but then Angela Martin looked to have been an interesting and unconventional girl. There was a single bed against one wall, a flowered duvet pattern on it. Beside it was a small white sideboard with two drawers, and next to that was a writing desk, a lamp and an old iPad the only two things on it. Declan tapped the iPad and wasn't surprised to see that nothing happened. After a year, the battery would have been drained.

Anjli was walking to the third wall of the bedroom, to the large built-in wardrobe. Painted white with a full-length mirror on it, the doors slid open to reveal a comprehensive collection of teenage clothing, with a long shelf along the top filled with boxes. The last wall, the one where the door was, had a white side-cabinet with a small television on.

Anjli was already examining the wardrobe, so Declan opened the first of the drawers. It was filled with underwear, and Declan almost pushed it straight back in, already feeling awkward for breaking this memorial's silence. Also, this was the room of a girl only a couple of years older than Jessica, and that made him think about his own daughter, to wonder how he'd react if something like this had happened to her.

Forcing himself, he rummaged into the drawer. When he had been a teenager, he'd hidden his secret items in his own underwear drawer, and then in a small keep-safe he'd made behind the extraction vent. He wondered if Angela had attempted the same thing.

Anjli had plugged the iPad into the charger and was trying to boot it up.

'Maybe we should see if we can take this for a check over,' she said. 'Billy could probably get this open.'

'It needs a fingerprint lock,' Declan replied before grimacing. 'And don't reply that we have her fingers in the morgue. That's just ... well, you know.'

Anjli nodded. 'Yeah.'

Declan's latex fingers brushed against something and he pulled out a small travel wallet. Opening it up, he withdrew a couple of used train tickets.

'Euston to Birmingham New Street,' he said, reading them. 'So she was definitely there. Doesn't give us anything more.' He flipped through the wallet, pausing as he pulled out a small photo. It had been taken in a photo booth, and was one of four, the other three missing. Angela sat in the booth, but two other boys were in it as well. The first was a familiar face, Macca Byrne. The other one though was unknown, a blond boy, half out of the photo because of the crowding. Declan replaced it into the wallet.

'Nothing here says anything more than a teenage girl hanging out with friends,' he said. 'You wouldn't think that she had any secrets.'

'She had one,' Anjli said, currently going through a box from the wardrobe. She tilted it so that Declan could see what was inside. A collection of small crosses, statues of the Virgin Mary and old, broken Rosaries were cluttered inside, surrounding a small cigar box. 'You saw downstairs. If your dad is such a Catholic, why would you hide it?' She pulled out the cigar box, opening it, revealing a syringe and a burnt spoon among other drug-related paraphernalia.

'And why would you stick it all in a box with your drug stuff?' she continued.

Declan's phone rang, and he answered it.

'Walsh.'

He paused for a moment as he listened. Anjli, putting the box back into the wardrobe, turned and watched his face; it darkened as he heard the voice down the phone. Eventually, with a curt "thanks" he disconnected the call, staring down at it.

'Everything okay?' she asked. Declan looked to her.

'We have to end this search, I'm afraid, and I'll have to drop you off at Temple Inn,' he replied. 'I need to go to Hurley.'

'Why?' Anjli was closing up the wardrobe as Declan replaced the wallet into the drawer.

'Because someone broke into my house.'

'Then we'd better hurry,' Anjli said. 'We can make it in an hour if you use the lights.'

Declan looked to her in surprise, and she smiled.

'You don't seriously believe I'm going to turn down an opportunity to see your father's secret crime board, do you?' she asked. Declan smiled in return, grateful for Anjli's candour as they left the room, closing the door behind them, taking a last look at the child's drawing on the door before returning downstairs.

Danny Martin was still in the living room when Declan and Anjli entered it.

'You find what you were looking for?' he asked.

'No, but we will,' Declan replied. 'I promise you.'

Danny nodded, saying nothing more as he followed Declan and Anjli to the door, closing it behind them, leaving them once more in the uniform street. Declan looked at the house one last time, but then his expression changed as he pulled his phone out once more.

'What?' Anjli asked, looking at Declan.

Declan was already walking to his car, staring down at his phone. 'Hold on, I'm googling,' he said as they both climbed into the car. 'Wait, now this is interesting,' he muttered, reading the screen.

'What's interesting?' Anjli was fit to burst now. 'What did you just realise?'

Declan looked to her. 'We were so busy looking at the bedroom, we forgot to check on what Danny said to us,' he replied. 'Saint Etheldreda's Mission House in Poplar, where Danny and Cheryl had Angela. They built it in 1892. Although they stopped officially doing midwifery there in the mid-seventies and moved to Alum Rock, there were a few nuns who stayed, working independently for the local community.'

'Well yeah,' Anjli replied. 'Danny said that. So what?'

'So, we're not looking at one murder anymore,' Declan said. 'We're looking at two, if the call Doctor Marcos took was correct. Two identical bodies, one in Epping who we know links to Danny Martin, and one found in Birmingham, that likely links to Macca Byrne somehow.'

He tapped on his phone, bringing up a map image, and turning it to show Anjli across the car.

'Alum Rock, where half of the nuns went,' he explained. 'As you can see, it's just over a mile outside Birmingham. That's where the other couple, having a baby the same time as Cheryl and Danny Martin came from, and it's smack bang in the middle of George and Macca Byrne's home turf.'

'Jesus,' Anjli said, looking back to the house. 'That's too much of a coincidence.'

'Yeah,' Declan replied. 'But it'll have to wait.'

And, with that, Declan started the car and headed to Berkshire.

THE DRIVE TO HURLEY FROM CYPRUS STREET WOULD USUALLY have taken an hour and a half, but Declan's Audi was a police issue one, and had all the lights and sirens you'd need for a high-speed chase. Declan and Anjli arrived at the house in less than an hour.

A police officer was waiting outside for them, his car parked on the road outside the house. An officer of colour, he looked no older than twelve, but was more likely to be in his mid-twenties and had a young earnestness on his face as they emerged from the car and walked over.

'You local police?' Declan asked. The police officer shook his head.

'PC Monteith, sir. From the Henley station,' he replied. 'They said I should wait for you to turn up.' He showed the door currently open. 'They came in through the back, but we opened this from the inside. Hope you don't mind.'

Declan shook his head, moving past the police officer and into the house.

'I think someone disturbed them,' PC Monteith continued. 'Your TV, video, stuff like that is still here, and they didn't take the jewellery from the bedroom.'

'I didn't realise I had jewellery in the bedroom,' Declan muttered, smiling at the police officer's confused expression. 'I recently inherited the house from my father,' he explained. PC Monteith nodded in relief.

'That makes sense,' he said, although Declan felt that PC Monteith would have said that even if he'd stated that he wore the jewellery in a drag act.

Looking around the living room, Declan stopped.

'They took my father's iMac,' he said. 'It was there on that desk.'

PC Monteith noted this down. 'Anything else visible?' he asked. Declan shook his head.

'As you said, they probably ran the moment someone came to the front door,' he replied. 'Who called it in?'

'Your neighbour, Mrs Thickett,' PC Monteith pointed through the wall, presumably at a house matching the direction. 'She saw movement through the window when passing.'

Declan made a mental note to thank Mrs Thickett at his first opportunity and, after examining the broken window at the back of the house where the thieves had most likely gained entrance, Declan thanked PC Monteith for waiting around. As soon as he'd left, Declan called for a glazier to come and fix the window.

Walking around the house, Declan couldn't see anything else missing.

'They came for the computer,' he said. 'They weren't opportunistic, this was deliberate.'

By now they were in the study, and Declan looked to Anjli.

'Welcome to my father's world,' he said as he pushed the bookshelf to the side. Anjli whistled as she entered the small room, looking around.

'Jesus,' she said, looking at the wall. 'You weren't kidding.'

'Recognise any of the faces?' Declan asked. Anjli was already examining the images.

'You mean apart from the obvious ones?' she replied. 'Not really. Is anything missing in here?'

Declan opened the cabinet, flipping through the files. Everything was as he left it.

'Now I understand why Dad had this,' he said, waving around the room. 'They didn't even consider that he might have this.'

'What?' Anjli asked as Declan's face fell. He shook his head.

'It's stupid,' he said. 'When I first saw this board, and when Shaun Donnal was here, I wondered if Monroe was something to do with all this. I even thought he could be the person who betrayed my location to the man with the rimless glasses. When he wasn't, I kind of put it on the back burner.'

'But?' Anjli was helping Declan move the bookcase back now, covering the door. Declan shrugged.

'But I still know that he has secrets, and it just seems suspicious that an hour after he learns that Dad had a crime board, someone breaks into my house.'

'True,' Anjli replied as they walked down the stairs. 'But, he could have simply turned up at the door, and you would have shown him the board without him having to break in.'

Declan thought about this. 'Then who did this?' he asked.

'It could simply be kids, thinking the house was empty after Patrick's death,' Anjli replied. 'It might mean nothing.'

Declan nodded, staring at the empty spot where the iMac had been.

'Well, good luck to them if they were after anything on that,' he said. 'Jess and I went through all of it and found nothing.'

There was the sound of a van pulling up outside. Looking out of the window, Declan saw that it was a glazer. With him was Karl Schnitter, marching quickly to the door as Declan opened it.

'Ryan told me what happened,' he said, showing the glazier, now following up behind. 'Are you okay?'

'Yeah, nothing stolen, it seems,' Declan replied, deciding to omit the loss of the iMac. 'Mrs Thickett saw them and called the police.'

'I have a Wi-Fi camera on my back door,' Karl said. 'I'll check it, see what was recorded.'

'Thanks,' Declan replied, already walking Ryan the glazier to the window. 'How bad?'

Ryan examined the broken pane of glass. 'Well, they're old and you should upgrade them to some double glazing, but it's a half hour job.'

Declan looked at Anjli. Karl saw this, offering his hand.

'Karl Schnitter,' he said. 'I am Declan's neighbour.'

'DS Anjli Kapoor,' Anjli replied. 'I work with him.'

'Should you not be hunting criminals?' Karl asked. Declan shrugged.

'Kind of got distracted,' he said. Karl nodded.

'Go hunt criminals,' he replied. 'I will stay with Ryan and close the door behind me. You can call him later and pay over the phone.'

'Do you mind?' Declan seemed surprised by this. Karl laughed.

'Again, you forget the generosity of village people,' he said.

'Thanks, Karl,' Declan gratefully replied, patting the German on the shoulder. 'I'll return the favour one day.' Nodding to Ryan, already getting to work on the window, Declan and Anjli walked back to his Audi.

'Have you decided if you're selling or staying yet?' Anjli asked as they climbed into it.

'Staying, I think. Why?'

Anjli smiled. 'Because if you ever need a housemate, let me know. I feel like I've fallen into Midsomer Murders here.'

Declan chuckled.

'People die each week in Midsomer,' he said as his phone beeped. He looked down at the screen.

'Monroe?' Anjli asked. Declan shook his head.

'Just a friend, asking if we can have a lunchtime catchup,' he said. 'I'll drop you off at Temple Inn first, though.'

'Actually, could you drop me back off in Globe Town?' Anjli asked. 'I thought I'd check about, see if I can use my history there to chase up some leads.'

Declan nodded and, gunning the engine, started back towards London.

12

SECRET RENDEZVOUS

IT TOOK ANOTHER HOUR AND FIFTEEN MINUTES TO GET BACK TO Bethnal Green and Globe Town; by now it was past twelve, so Anjli promised to take no more than an hour and meet Declan back at the Crime Unit, watching him drive off to wherever his lunch date was.

Regardless of what she'd told Declan, the last thing Anjli wanted to do was walk around her own stomping grounds though so, after sending a quick text message, she made her way down the Roman Road, eastwards to the Angel & Crown Pub. It had a white and blue frontage, freshly painted because of new owners, and had received a complete over-haul in design. Anjli liked it, but felt a little wistful for the older look, the one she'd grown up with, with battered red (previously green) paint on the outside walls and half the letters stolen or torn off. It was a real "spit and sawdust" pub; a term used for pubs that used to place sawdust on the floors of their public bars to soak up the inevitable beer (when they really meant blood) that would fall, and a few years earlier had received the notorious reputation of one of the "worst pubs in London", with the then Landlord selling up and leaving after complaints. Now it was more of a gentrified gastro pub, though with a stronger community feel to it. Which, although fitting with Bethnal Green's gentrification, still felt a little out of place for Globe Town.

The inside had also received a spruce up; they'd painted the walls with white and blue to match the outside, the wooden bar had been stripped and sanded and rather than hard wooden benches, you could instead sit in a comfy leather sofa. Ordering a lemonade, a gin and tonic and a large red wine, Anjli found a place by the window and sat down, waiting. She knew that this was once one of the main meeting spots for Johnny or Jackie Lucas, and she hoped that by picking it, she would gain some kind of nostalgic interest from them. The text she'd sent was to an old friend who now worked next to the boxing club, suggesting that they meet for a drink. She hoped that the message would get through to the right destination and, sure enough, ten minutes later the door to the bar opened and Johnny Lucas walked in, immediately wrinkling his nose. He saw Anjli and walked over.

'This better be important,' he said, sitting beside her on the sofa. 'I haven't been in here since ... well, let's just say in a while.'

'You should,' Anjli took a sip of her lemonade. 'You could do with a bit of gentrification too.'

'Sass, DS Kapoor? From you?' Johnny raised an eyebrow. 'Someone in as much debt to me shouldn't throw sass.'

'I paid my debt to you a long time back, Johnny,' Anjli snapped. 'You're the only one who seems to think I owe you anything. I've been nothing but grateful.'

'And yet here you sit, calling me like a lapdog.' Johnny leaned back into the sofa. 'This is comfy. You shouldn't feel comfy in here. Not with the history this place has.' He looked to the two drinks. 'For me?'

'Wasn't sure whether I'd be meeting you or Jackie, so I bought both,' Anjli explained. Johnny took the gin and tonic, sipping it as he watched her.

'Is this about Walsh?'

Anjli nodded. 'Kind of. I have some information for you on him, but I need some from you.'

Johnny thought this over. 'Depends on the ask,' he said.

'Danny Martin.'

'Ahh,' Johnny nodded slowly, finally realising why they were meeting. 'I saw the news last night. The body was Angela?'

'Yes.'

'Do you know who did it? News said there was a suspect.'

'There is, but he didn't do it.'

Johnny leaned in closer. 'So tell me who did,' he whispered.

Anjli considered her options. 'There's a lot going on here,' she said. 'I can't tell you, but in the questions I ask, you might get an idea on how things work here.'

'I think you're forgetting how things work,' Johnny snapped. 'How is your mum doing these days?'

'Better,' Anjli bit back another response. 'Thanks to you, Mister Lucas.'

'That's better.' Johnny settled back into the chair. 'Doesn't hurt to be a little respectful, does it? Ask me your questions, then.' He smiled as a thought occurred to him. 'But how will you explain to little Declan how you got the answers?'

Anjli ignored the jibe. 'Did Danny ever deal with other gangs? The Seven Sisters, perhaps?'

'Oh. So, it was Janelle?'

'No,' Anjli shook her head. 'But we've heard that Angela was spending time with Janelle's son Moses.'

'That surprises me,' Johnny mused. 'I thought Moses played for the other team. Lots of secret meetings with young blonds, if you know what I mean.'

Anjli mentally noted this. 'Did Danny deal with the sisters on your behalf at all?'

'Not that I recall,' Johnny mused. 'We had our run-ins with them, usually around Dalston and either side of the A10. Really hard to work out postal codes there, you know?'

'So you had a turf war?'

'More a turf disagreement,' Johnny admitted. 'Nothing serious, though. A few broken limbs, bust up faces. No deaths.'

'What about Derek Salmon?' Anjli asked. 'Did Danny ever deal with him?'

This was a question that Johnny Lucas wasn't expecting. 'DI Salmon? What's he got to do with this?'

'He's a person of interest.'

'Investigating plod now? Shame on you.' Johnny thought for a moment. 'That said, he's retired now, isn't he? Suppose he's fair game.'

He steepled his fingers together as he thought for a moment, taking in a possible new piece of information. Anjli decided not to give him the time to think too much on it.

'Was he on your books?'

'My books?' Johnny almost chuckled at this.

'Did he work for you? Like Ford did.'

'You mean like you do?'

Anjli bristled at this. 'I've already said, Mister Lucas, I help you because you helped my mum. I don't owe you and I sure as hell don't work for you like DCI Ford did.'

'Sure,' Johnny said mockingly. 'Whatever helps you sleep at night. Let's just say we had the occasional shared interest, but he never worked for me as such.'

Anjli didn't reply to this, writing in her notepad. Johnny's eyes twinkled in delight.

'So why would you think he worked for anyone?' he asked. 'Has DI Salmon been a naughty boy?'

Realising she'd given too much away, Anjli tried to change the subject. 'What do you know about Macca Byrne?'

'Birmingham thug,' Johnny hissed. 'Lowest scum out there. His dad used to be a total gent back in the day, though. Well, until he wasn't, that is. We sent out feelers to work with him, to do some joint campaigns, so to speak, and it was all going swimmingly, but then he poached a couple of my best men so I cut all ties.' His voice was darkening now, becoming more guttural, more angry. Anjli knew what this meant.

Jackie Lucas was coming.

'Best men?'

'Yeah. Bloody George Byrne made Chapman an offer he couldn't refuse. Bastard slipped out of Dalston with a couple of his hangers on that night, never to return.' There was a fire behind his eyes now, and Anjli knew that possibly the worst thing in the world that she could do right now was remind this psychotic gangster that someone had once betrayed him.

'Look, you're busy, and I've taken your time up,' she said, rising quickly. 'I'll leave you to things.'

'Wait.' Johnny's tone was sharp and commanding. 'I answered your questions. You owe me information on Walsh.'

Anjli nodded, feeling sick to her stomach. 'I asked about Derek, because Declan let slip earlier today that his father had a crime board. I'm assuming it was at his house. He said that Derek was on it and linked to you and a couple of other people.'

'Patrick Walsh put me on a crime board,' Johnny smiled. 'I'm touched.'

'But it means that Patrick Walsh, and now Declan is investigating you,' Anjli said. 'I don't know what the board is, or what it represents, but—'

'But you will,' Johnny interrupted, rising. He seemed more in control now. 'You will find out, and you will tell me everything. Private medical help can be so expensive, especially when it's *cancer*.'

'Come on, Johnny—'

'You mean Mister Lucas.'

'To be honest, I thought you already knew,' Anjli continued. 'I assume it was you who burgled his house today?'

'Why would I bother with such tawdry crime when I have you to do my bidding?' Johnny replied. 'I want to see the crime wall, DS Kapoor. Make it so.'

With a last smile, Johnny left the Angel & Crown, leaving Anjli alone, her legs shaking as the adrenaline hit.

She slumped back onto the sofa, moving to the red wine and downing the glass with shaking fingers. Johnny Lucas was right. While her mother was ill and needing treatment, he owned her. But for the moment she wouldn't give him the photos she'd taken while Declan was searching his filing cabinet, surreptitiously taken on her phone while pretending to read something on it. She wanted to examine them herself, to ensure that she wasn't putting anyone in Johnny or Jackie

Lucas' crosshairs when she eventually passed them to him. A line Johnny had spoken returned to haunt her memory.

'Sure. Whatever helps you sleep at night.'

And with that, alone in a gentrified pub, Anjli Kapoor began to quietly cry.

DECLAN SAT AT A TABLE ON THE UPPER FLOOR OF THE NELLIE Dean pub in Soho, a pint of Guinness in front of him, watching the Dean Street lunchtime trade through the window to his side. Although packed downstairs, many of the tourists didn't realise that there was a small rickety staircase leading to another floor upstairs, where trendy pie and mash dinners were served; this meant that even at lunchtime on a weekday you could usually find a table up there. And so, Declan sat at one, watching out of the window and waiting.

He didn't have to wait long. Only three sips into his pint, he heard movement on the stairs and Kendis Taylor walked into the upstairs bar, a white wine already in her hand. She walked over to Declan's table and sat down facing him with a smile.

'Cosy,' she said.

'They do great pies,' Declan replied.

'I've eaten already,' Kendis glanced at the menu anyway.

'I haven't, and I wasn't considering your opinions on it,' Declan smiled. Kendis smiled in return.

'You're looking better than when I last saw you,' she said. 'You've lost weight.'

'No, I've returned to my normal weight,' Declan looked down at himself. 'After the divorce, the suspension and Dad's death, I let myself go a little. Now I run when I can and I've even bought one of those exercise spin bike things.'

'Really? I am impressed,' Kendis leaned back, taking Declan in. 'And I didn't mention it last time, but I'm glad you dumped the beard, too.'

Declan looked at Kendis, the light from the window currently striking her smile, making it sparkle even more. He'd come to terms a long time ago that Kendis Taylor was the one he'd let get away. They'd both moved on: Declan with Lizzie, and Kendis with Peter. However, at times like this when he sat with her, every teenage thought and emotion returned like a truck slamming into him. He took a sip from his Guinness to hide his expression.

'So, business or personal?' he asked, waving around the pub, still ensuring that he didn't catch her eye. Kendis shrugged.

'Can't it be both?'

Declan laughed. 'Spoken like a typical journalist,' he joked. *'This is all off the record, but by the way can I chat to you on the record ...'*

Kendis nodded. 'Fair point,' she accepted. 'I wanted to talk about several things. I thought this could be a good time to do it.'

'No evening meetings at my house?' Declan was referring to the last time he'd seen Kendis when she had been waiting outside his then Tottenham apartment. She shook her head.

'Best to keep it to public places,' she said. 'Peter was a little ... well, he was jealous when he learned I'd seen you.'

Declan hid a triumphant smirk at this. He didn't know Peter, but there was a little shard of happiness in the heart of his soul when he heard of his discomfort.

'And we wouldn't want that, would we?' he said.

Kendis didn't answer, turning back to the menu once more.

Eventually she looked up.

'We're having issues right now,' she said. 'It's not really working.'

'Shit. I'm sorry,' Declan felt bad for his triumphant smirk now. 'I'm sure it'll work out.'

'I'm not sure I want it to work out,' Kendis admitted looking at Declan. 'It's been falling apart for a while now, and neither of us really knows how to fix it. And I think I want … *other* things.'

There was a long, awkward silence now, as if Kendis had expected or wanted Declan to reply to this. Instead, he stared at her in silence, his mind moving at a hundred miles an hour. He still loved Kendis, but neither of them were the teenagers they'd been before.

Could it work? Could he really put Kendis through the same legal problems that he'd had himself when he left Lizzie?

As if realising that she'd crossed a line, Kendis took a sip of her drink and carried on, changing the subject, suddenly all business.

'I'm doing a piece on Derek Salmon,' she said. 'We all know he's the prime suspect in the case.'

'And I'd like to know about your source in this,' Declan replied. 'More importantly, I'd like to know their connection to the Seven Sisters.'

Kendis shook her head. 'I can't, and you know that.'

She looked out of the window, staring down at the street below.

'All I can say is that my source knows it's coming from Mama Delcourt herself. That she had some kind of connection to Salmon in the past, and now she's calling in debts.'

Declan shook his head. 'Off the record? Quid pro quo?'

Kendis nodded, so Declan continued.

'Derek's dying. Months at best. He's made a deal with the Sisters to gain money for his family if he takes the fall. But he's trying to play them; if he's proven innocent saying nothing, the deal still stands. He'll make the money but go free.'

Kendis's expression changed slightly, as if she was about to smile, but thought better of it.

'But is he innocent?' she asked.

'You tell me,' Declan said, watching Kendis for any further reaction. 'You saw Dad's crime board. You saw Derek on it.'

If this had surprised her, Kendis Taylor didn't show it. Derek knew that Kendis had seen the crime board in his father's secret study because she'd already admitted to assisting Patrick Walsh with his memoirs and had been in the study to work on the book with him. Hell, she probably even wrote the book for him.

'He was dirty,' she sighed. 'Your father knew it, but he said that Derek was also a good copper, so he said nothing. And when he moved out of the Unit, Patrick ensured that Derek stayed where he was, at DI level. I think Patrick only saw him again when you started working with him.'

'So Derek worked for the Sisters ...' Declan thought back to his conversation in the car where Derek had expressed bitterness at having to go to someone he'd hated ... that he'd hunted. *Was all of this a lie?*

'Hold on. You twitched when I spoke about the family debt,' he said. 'Like you were going to smile, but then stopped.'

Kendis nodded. 'I thought you were joking. You weren't, were you?'

'No,' Declan leaned back in his chair. 'What am I missing?'

'Derek's family left him a decade ago because of his crime connections,' Kendis replied. 'Your dad told me this. Therefore, they would never take such money. Besides, his wife doesn't need it.'

'Why?'

'You should read the news more.' And with that she leaned back in her own chair, folding her arms and with a smug expression on her face. Declan knew she wouldn't tell him anything else.

'Dad could have told me about all this,' Declan muttered.

'Your father knew you could look after yourself,' Kendis explained. 'He was watching, though.'

'Derek played me for a fool,' Declan muttered. Kendis shrugged.

'If it makes you feel better, he played your father for years before he worked it out,' she replied. 'He started taking money from the Sisters. Little things, turning the head away type things. He also took some money from the Brothers Lucas, but that was more other people's game.'

'Monroe?'

Kendis shook her head. 'Anyway, we—'

'*Was it my dad?*'

Kendis stopped, looking directly at Declan. 'You don't want to open that door,' she said.

Declan nodded. 'I know,' he replied. 'But I have to.'

Kendis sighed. 'Lucas paid them all off, at one point or another. Salmon, Monroe, Wintergreen and Patrick.'

Declan frowned at the name Wintergreen. It was the name he'd seen with the USB drive the previous night. 'Who's Wintergreen?'

'She's not in the manuscript,' Kendis replied. 'You'll need to speak to Monroe for that.'

'Why can't you just tell me?'

'Because that's what your father told me. I just know the name.'

Declan considered this. So his father and Monroe both worked for Johnny and Jackie Lucas at some point. In a way, he'd expected this ever since Shaun Donnal had turned up at his father's house several weeks earlier.

'Thanks,' he said. 'I needed the truth.'

'That's a log line, not the truth,' Kendis explained. 'The truth is way more confusing.'

'Care to tell me about it?'

Kendis shook her head, looking at her watch. 'I'm on a deadline,' she replied. 'I can't stay long.'

'So, what was so important that you needed to meet with me?' Declan asked.

Kendis nodded, reaching into her pocket and pulling out her moleskin notebook. Opening it, she flicked through some pages until she found what she was looking for.

'When Angela went missing a year back, a guy on our crime desk did some research that eventually went nowhere,' she said, running a finger down the lines of shorthand. 'But he found some things, mainly to do with her birth.'

'Her birth?' Declan thought back to the conversation about the Nunnery. Kendis found the line she was looking for.

'Apparently she returned to the Mission when she was fifteen, demanding to know the address of the other family that were there the night she was born. She was claiming she'd done one of those ancestry DNA tests and it'd come out wrong. They called the police, she got violent. She was held overnight.'

'She'd realised that Danny Martin wasn't her father,' Declan mused. Kendis looked up from the page at this.

'You knew already?' she asked. Declan shrugged.

'Suspected, more like.'

'Ah, so you don't know everything,' Kendis said with a grin. 'You should check out the Mission House. There was a scandal there a while back.'

'What sort of scandal?'

'Something to do with a nun who died there, after an apparently bona fide *Virgin Birth*.'

'Which actually means she was too scared to say who the father was,' Declan smiled in return. Kendis shook her head.

'You'd think so, but no,' she replied. 'The nun in question, Sister Nadine stated that Saint Etheldreda's vicar, Father Barry Lawson was the, well, the *father*. Said he came to her one night and then disappeared by morning.'

'That doesn't really sound that Virgin-y.'

'Well yeah, but the problem here is the dates,' Kendis continued. 'The only time that Father Lawson could have conceived the child matched with a three-month stint of missionary work that he had in South Africa.'

'So Father Lawson appears as a vision, while he's thousands of miles away and impregnates the nun,' Declan nodded. 'Okay, I can see why they'd start screaming Holy Ghost at that. So what happened with the baby?'

'Died with the nun in childbirth, the same day as Danny Martin arrived,' Kendis said. 'Father Lawson himself was there to help. Which was another miracle, because apparently he was in Milton Keynes that same day at a Spring Festival food drive?'

She rose from the table, finishing her glass.

'I really have a deadline,' she said apologetically. 'But you should talk with Derek Salmon's wife before you speak with him again.'

And, with that she left, leaving Declan alone at the table, a new list of confusing clues laid out in front of him.

And what was worse; he'd lost his appetite.

13

REVELATIONS

Returning to Temple Inn, Declan found that Anjli and Billy were back at their desks, whereas Monroe's office was empty.

'Where's the Guv?' he asked. Billy looked up from his screen.

'Birmingham,' he replied. 'Went with our mental Doctor to go look at this new body.'

Declan sat at his desk, staring down at the little "British Bobby" Funko toy that Jessica had bought him a while back. It stared back lifelessly at him.

'You look like the problems of the world are on your shoulders,' Anjli said. Declan nodded.

'I was just wondering whether there are any coppers in London who aren't working for the bloody Lucas twins,' he muttered, his eyes still glued on the figure. If he'd looked up at that moment, he would have seen Anjli falter at the statement.

'Like who?' she asked. Declan now glanced up at her, but the moment had passed and Anjli had composed herself.

'Derek Salmon apparently worked at various times for both The Twins and also the Seven Sisters,' he said. 'My father knew but did nothing about it.'

'That was then,' Anjli returned to her desk, relieved. 'Things are different now.'

'DCI Ford would like to differ.'

'Ford was a degenerate gambler who couldn't stop betting on greyhounds,' Anjli snapped. 'I'm nothing like her.'

Declan stared in confusion at Anjli.

'I'm sorry,' he eventually said, 'I didn't mean to imply anything.'

'And I'm sorry. I didn't mean to snap,' Anjli replied, looking away. 'I'm still a little off after the chat with Danny.'

'Understandable,' Declan looked back to his desk. Growing up in the area made it far closer for Anjli. 'Did you find anything out? On your stroll through Mile End?'

Anjli nodded, sitting up. The worries on her face from a moment earlier were gone.

'We both have,' she said, pointing to Billy who now turned in his own chair to face Declan and Anjli.

'The body dug up in the Lickey Hills has a name now,' he said. 'Apparently the witness who showed them the body claimed it was a local girl named Gabrielle Chapman.' He turned his monitor to show Declan. On it was an image of a young girl, of around nine years old. 'This is her, an old school photo. It's the only record we have for her.'

'What do you mean?' Declan examined the photo. The image could have been a young photo of Angela Martin, but without a similar one to compare to, it could be anyone.

'Exactly what I said,' Billy replied. 'There are no official records of Gabrielle Chapman after Year Four. Her parents were in and out of trouble with the police, she was being bullied because of this, and so they took her out to home school her.'

'Rather than perhaps stopping whatever they did that brought them into trouble with the police?' Declan mused. 'Great parents.'

'Well, they didn't do it for long.' Billy brought up a newspaper clipping on his screen. On it was an image of a house fire, with the fire brigade on scene, the house a smouldering ruin behind them. The headline read:

SELLY OAK HOUSE FIRE KILLS TWO

'This was the only thing I could find on her parents,' Billy continued. 'Six years ago. Gabrielle would have been about twelve, maybe thirteen here. But after their deaths there's no note from Social Services, no adoption from family, nothing. It's as if she wasn't there. In fact, we see nothing else about Gabrielle until about two-and-a-half years ago, when she's arrested while with Macca Byrne at an illegal rave.'

'Eighteen months before her death.' Declan stared at the image of the fire. 'If they hadn't found a body, I'd have said that this was a fake identity scam.'

'Funny you should say that,' Anjli said, looking to Billy. 'Tell him what you also found.'

'I need Doctor Marcos to confirm this when she comes back from Birmingham, but I asked DC Davey to check Angela Martin's fingerprints to Gabrielle Chapman's ones,' Billy said. 'They're a hundred percent match.'

'Do twins have the same fingerprints?' Declan asked.

Billy shook his head.

'No,' he replied. 'They have the same DNA and appearance and all that, but fingerprints are unique.'

'Which means that the Angela Martin that was arrested in London has to be the same person as the Gabrielle Chapman who was arrested in Birmingham,' Anjli said.

Declan whistled at this. 'So we are talking identity theft.'

'It's the strangest bloody identity theft I've heard of.'

'Yeah,' Declan agreed. 'Angela Martin died at what age?'

Billy checked the notes. 'Seventeen years, four months.'

'And the Chapmans were the other family that gave birth that day?' Declan leaned back. 'I think there's more here than we're seeing right now.'

'Like what?' Anjli was leaning across the desk now, listening intently. Declan shrugged.

'Well, we know from Danny that Cheryl Martin only had one child,' Declan thought to himself. 'That's not something you can fake, especially with records existing from beforehand. All we need to do is check the hospital ultrasounds.'

'Likewise, Craig and Emma Chapman,' Billy brought up an image on his screen. 'They only had one child too.' He frowned. 'Came a month early, too. Looks like it was induced.'

'I think there's a third option here.' Declan rose, pacing as he worked it through in his head, speaking the process out loud. 'Apparently, when she was about fifteen years old, Angela Martin went back and confronted the Mission after doing one of those ancestral DNA tests, and having it come up wrong.'

'Wrong?' Billy looked confused.

'It would have shown her she wasn't a Martin,' Anjli said in reply. 'So if she wasn't Danny's kid, who was Daddy?'

'I would have said Craig Chapman, but they only had one child. Though I think there may have been another birth that day. A nun, claiming a Virgin birth, but who died during it.'

'You think it could have been twins?'

Declan stopped pacing around, stretching his arms, feeling his shoulders click tight from the hours of driving. 'I think it's the only plausible answer here,' he said.

'Then the twin girls go to different families, each unaware they're a cuckoo.' Billy walked over to the kitchen area, turning the kettle on, noting his colleagues' confused expressions to this. 'It's what they do. Cuckoos put their eggs in other birds' nests so that the other birds raise their chicks and they don't have to. Anyone want a coffee?'

'Cuckoos sound like dicks,' Anjli muttered. 'And I'll have a tea, no sugar.'

'Billy's right,' Declan continued. 'Not about the cuckoos, but about the twins. Coffee, white.'

'I'm right about cuckoos, too,' Billy grumbled as he poured coffee into two of the mugs.

'Fine, then as well as cuckoo birth practices, Billy is also possibly correct about the hypothetical twins,' Declan repeated. 'But if there were twins, and these became Gabrielle and Angela, then what happened to the other two babies?'

'If they both died, then it's a simple swap,' Anjli nodded. 'Nobody would be the wiser, unless one of the visitor's babies was visibly a distinct race. We need to find a nun who can confirm this. Going on the more believable thread that it wasn't God, who was the father?'

'That's the problem,' Declan said. 'We don't know. According to my source, the nun claimed it was the Vicar, but he was apparently doing missionary work on another continent.'

'Well, this explains how similar girls can be in two places, but it doesn't explain how they had the same breaks, the same tattoos, the same fingerprints and even the same apparent death,' Billy frowned, passing Declan and Anjli their drinks. 'That states more of a connection than just shared parentage.'

Declan sipped at his coffee, nodding approvingly at Billy. 'Hypothetically, let's say that Angela Martin learns that she has a possible twin sister at fifteen. Shortly after that, Gabrielle Chapman appears again in Birmingham. We know that there are two people as we have two bodies, but we also know it's one person as we've got the police reports and fingerprints that state Angela and Gabrielle were the same person. We're missing something and it's annoying.'

'Angela could have used her sister's identity,' Anjli suggested. 'And, as nobody had seen the real Gabrielle Chapman for years ...'

Billy considered this, but then shook his head. 'That doesn't explain the tattoos, or the broken arm.'

Anjli slumped. 'Oh, yeah.'

She then looked up with a smile.

'Christ, I'm an idiot,' she said, air-punching, rising and performing a victory jog around her desk before sitting back down in her chair and turning to the others. 'An utter idiot!'

'Let me guess, you have something,' Billy laughed.

'Oh yeah, I'd say so,' she said. 'Craig Chapman.'

'The Birmingham father?'

Anjli nodded. 'I was so busy thinking about twin girls, I'd forgotten about something I heard today. I spoke to ... well, to someone I know in Mile End earlier today. They mentioned to me that Johnny and Jackie Lucas had a guy who worked for them called Chapman, and that he was poached over to Birmingham by George Byrne. They never gave me his first name, and I didn't click until just now.'

Billy was already typing into the *HOLMES2* network, pulling up a file. 'Clifford Craig Chapman. Must have used his middle name. Did some time in the nineties. Not much, though. Shortly after, he moved to Selly Oak, in South Birmingham.'

'The house fire that killed two,' Declan leaned back. 'Anjli was right on the button.'

'So, Chapman left The Twins for Byrne. That's got to be something worth following,' Anjli said.

'More than that,' Billy looked up from his computer's screen. 'Says here that we arrested him for burglary at eighteen with a Daniel Martin.'

Declan almost shot out of his chair. 'Danny Martin knew Craig Chapman?'

'Enough to perform a criminal act with him.'

'Yet he didn't recognise him a few years later,' Anjli was unconsciously playing with her hair, twirling a strand around her finger as she spoke. 'I mean, they may not have even seen each other during the births, but what are the chances of the two of them turning up at the same place, at the same time?'

'I'll look into it,' Billy said. 'I can add it to the list.'

Declan picked up the Funko "Bobby" figure from his desk, staring down at it. There was a feeling in his gut, a hole in the pit of his stomach.

'Who was the arresting officer?' he asked. 'On the job that Danny and Craig were caught on?'

Billy tapped on the screen, pulling up the details – and then froze.

'Detective Constable Derek Salmon,' he breathed. Declan almost threw the Funko policeman across the room in anger but stopped himself.

'I need to speak to Derek,' he hissed. 'I think he's played us all.'

'But why?' Anjli asked. 'That makes no sense! He's dying!'

Declan went to reply to this, but suddenly remembered something insinuated by Kendis in the Nellie Dean. He turned to Billy. 'Amanda Salmon. Is there anything on her?'

'How do you mean?' Billy was already tapping at his laptop. 'Criminal record? Something else?'

'I genuinely don't know,' Declan replied apologetically. 'I just know that there was something off with his wife.'

Billy started searching through browsers as Anjli looked to Declan.

'You knew him,' she said. 'How well did you know his family?'

'I didn't, really,' Declan replied. 'They were falling apart when I first met him and divorced within a year or so. For most of the time I was with him, Derek was a very bitter divorcee.'

'Guys, I've got something.'

Declan and Anjli looked over to Billy as he pulled up a website on his screen. It was a local newspaper.

'Yeah, you definitely need to speak to Derek. He said he'd done this to gain money for his family, right?' Billy asked.

'Yes,' Declan warily said. Billy turned to face him.

'Amanda Salmon won the National Lottery two years ago,' he said. 'Not millions, but enough to pay off a mortgage and live comfortably.'

'So, all of this is bollocks,' Declan indicated the files on his desk. 'Derek didn't need the money, so why did he take the fall?'

'You need to ask him that,' Anjli said. 'He was your part-ner. Maybe he'll come clean.'

'And we still don't have a connection to Janelle Delcourt yet,' Declan muttered. 'I don't think this second body was in the Delcourt game plan.'

'We have one thing,' Anjli added. 'Moses was apparently dating Angela Martin. It was on the sly, but they knew it around Mile End. That could be enough for us to use as an excuse to visit the Delcourts. Also, I got the impression from my source that Moses was usually into the other sex.'

'Usually or always?' Billy asked.

'Does it matter?'

'There's a distinction. If he goes both ways, then she could date him while he dated men. If it's a singular direction, then she wasn't dating him. She was his beard.'

'Beard?'

'You know, his fake girlfriend to keep his appearance up.'

'Why do they call it a beard?' Anjli asked.

Billy shrugged.

'Because sixty years ago, having a homosexual relation-ship was still criminal in a lot of places. A fake partner needed a term that could be passed about and giving some kind of plausible deniability.' He thought for a moment. 'There's been a lot of unknowing beards out there. Girls that simply didn't know that the man they were dating liked men, but most of the time it was a business transaction, of a kind. The man needed to seem straight, and so did the woman. I did it myself when I was trying to stay in with my family.'

'So what, Angela Martin was gay too?' Anjli looked into the briefing room, where the image of Angela was still on the screen. 'Could this be why the Seven Sisters killed her? Or, maybe she wasn't, and then she learned about Moses?'

'We don't know that they killed her yet,' Declan corrected. 'All we know is that someone connected to the Seven Sisters knew where the body was. They could have been told in the same way that Derek was.'

The three officers sat quietly for a moment, each working out the next step in the investigation.

'Do we have anything on the iPad?' Declan asked.

Billy shook his head.

'We got into it using the fingerprint scanner, but it's been offline for so long, there's like a dozen OSXs that need to be updated before we can get into it,' he replied.

'While we wait, we need to find and speak to Father Lawson,' Anjli said.

Declan nodded.

'And we need to find out whether Angela Martin ever met Gabrielle Chapman, or just stole her identity,' he added. Billy was already tapping on the keyboard of his computer. Declan's computer *dinged*, and an image popped up onto the screen. Two photos linked; they were both police identification images of a seventeen-year-old girl. One half was Angela Martin, taken in Mile End. The other was apparently Gabrielle Chapman, taken in Moseley, South Birmingham. There was only half an image of both, however, the two photos stitched together to show both sides of one face.

The *same* face.

'Definitely identical, and with the fingerprints matching, we're most likely looking at the same person,' Declan said. 'Known associates for Gabrielle Chapman?'

Billy tapped on the keyboard again, and an image of Macca Byrne appeared on his monitor, as well as the blond boy that Declan had seen in the photo that had been in Angela's drawer. Seeing them, Declan glanced to Anjli, who nodded.

'We know that Angela Martin knew Macca and Harrison

Fennel from the photo in her bedroom,' she said. 'But it looks like she was with him under another identity.'

Declan leaned back in his chair.

'Gabrielle Chapman. Daughter of a man who worked for George Byrne.'

'And the daughter of a man who worked for The Twins, both of which weren't likely to be fans of George Byrne after they poached Craig Chapman,' Anjli muttered. 'Angels.'

Declan looked back to her. 'Sorry?'

'Gabrielle is the feminised version of Gabriel,' Anjli explained. 'Angela is the feminised version of Angel. It's been weighing on my mind. Seemed odd, coincidental.'

'Not if the nuns named them,' Billy suggested.

'Then we need to speak to these nuns as well,' Declan rose from his chair. 'But first, we need to find that priest.'

Anjli rose first. 'Perhaps I should do it?' she asked. 'You do, after all, have a very well-known past with the Catholic Church.'

Declan deflated a little. It was well known that one reason he'd been suspended in the first place was because he'd punched a dog-trafficking Catholic priest in the face on live television.

'Yeah, maybe you're right,' he said. 'Maybe it's time for someone to go chat with the Sisters, anyway. Let Monroe know what you found as well.' Declan was already walking to the door. 'He might be able to ask around while he's up in Birmingham. I have to go see my daughter first, so I'll go find the Delcourts later. Keep me updated.'

'Jessica?' Anjli asked. 'Is she okay?'

Declan frowned at the question. 'She's going on her first date.'

Anjli and Billy looked to each other and, knowing they

were thinking the same thing that Kendis had said earlier that day, that his innocent fifteen-year-old daughter might not be *that* innocent, Declan left the Crime Unit and walked to his car, his mind buzzing. There was no way that Angela's gravitating towards gang leaders in two distinct identities was a coincidence. Especially being the daughter of the right-hand man of the largest East End firm since the Krays. And if it *was* Angela taking on two identities, how did the *real* Gabrielle Chapman gain the same tattoos and injuries?

And why were they both killed?

The question that burned in Declan's mind the brightest though, was a simple one.

Why was the daughter of an East-End enforcer not only dating the heir apparent of the North London crew but also seemingly dating the son of the largest criminal power in Birmingham?

That was a question for another time, though. Declan had a bigger task ahead.

He had to be a *dad.*

14

DOUBLE TROUBLE

'I HATE THAT BLOODY WOMAN.' MONROE SAT ON A BENCH AND glared at Doctor Marcos. 'How dare she tell us to wait? I have seniority on her!'

'She's West Midlands police. You're City of London police. I don't think that works the same way up here,' Doctor Marcos leaned back on the bench, using the wall behind to rest against. 'But sure, Alexander. Argue with her again. I'm pretty convinced that will help us immensely.'

Monroe sighed loudly, a forced act for the Desk Sergeant watching them.

'Did you at least find out anything in the morgue?' he asked.

Doctor Marcos nodded.

'We need to requisition more things for ours,' she replied. 'This place has a ton of new toys that I'm just itching to get hold of.'

'I meant with the case.'

'Oh. In that case, no. They caught me before I could examine anything.'

Monroe looked to his phone, reading an email. 'The office has been busy,' he said. 'Seems we have a lot of additional information on this second body.'

'Like?'

'Like it shouldn't exist.'

Doctor Marcos grinned. 'Well, duh.'

The door opened, and Monroe glanced up at DCI Bullman as she emerged into the reception.

'Okay, your credentials match,' she said, passing two warrant cards back to Monroe and Doctor Marcos. 'But *she's* banned from crime scenes for another five months.'

'We're not at a crime scene,' Monroe rose now, facing Bullman. 'And *she's* here to see how you have an identical victim to ours.'

'That's easy,' Bullman opened the door, waving Monroe and Doctor Marcos through. '*You* got it wrong.'

Doctor Marcos went to reply, but Monroe placed a hand gently on her shoulder to pause her most likely expletive-ridden rant. 'How about we let the forensic experts look at that before coming to any conclusions?'

Bullman shrugged and pointed down a corridor. 'Third left. Touch nothing.'

Doctor Marcos nodded to Monroe and left the two DCIs in the hallway.

'Look, I think we got off on a poor footing,' Monroe said to Bullman, trying his hardest to give his best "charming" expression.

'You think?' Bullman folded her arms as she glared at Monroe. There wasn't more than a year or two between them. 'What gave it away? I think it was when you entered my police station demanding to see *the idiot that screwed up your case.*'

Monroe tried to smile. 'In fairness, we still don't know what's happened here.'

'That's not an apology.'

'No, it's not.' Giving up on the charm offensive, Monroe walked into the CID office, noting that the computers were definitely newer than the ones at Temple Inn. He understood now why Doctor Marcos had been like a child in a sweetshop. 'Is that the board?'

He pointed to a whiteboard leaning against a glass window, with a photo of the body of Gabrielle Chapman taped upon it.

'Wow. You're a super detective, I can tell,' Bullman was already walking towards it.

'We have a plasma screen,' Monroe replied, mentally scoring a point.

'Plasma screens are for people who don't know how to do proper police work,' Bullman mocked. Monroe twitched silently.

He really hated this woman.

Over the next half an hour, however, his impression of Bullman changed as she went through the status of her case; how a drugs bust had turned into a homicide investigation, and how a teenage informant had given them the lead.

'How was the kid involved?' he asked.

'He wasn't,' Bullman replied. 'Apparently his parents would fight a lot, so Alfie Mullville would hide out in woodlands for a few days. They were also serious heroin addicts, so the home life was probably not the best for him, anyway.'

'What would he do in the woods?'

'Live there,' Bullman said simply. 'The Lickey Hills cover over five hundred acres. A good square mile of woodland that a small boy can lose himself in. He says he did some kind of bushman survival course in school, so he knew how to make a little den, stay alive. And there's a forest centre nearby with a shop and café; he'd raid the bins at night.'

'A real Bear Grylls.'

Bullman actually smiled at this. 'I'm more a fan of Ed Stafford,' she said.

'So what, Alfie was in the woods and came across the burial?'

'It's possible,' Bullman pointed at a map of the Lickey Hills on the wall. 'As I said, it's only a square mile or so. We're not talking Sherwood Forest here. And Alfie would have been alone in the dark, with maybe a small fire. He'd have seen anyone drive in.'

'Did he say who the killer was?'

'Killers, plural. There were two, apparently. He said he didn't recognise them, but he was happy to look through mugshots. Found three suspects out of that.'

'Can I see them?' Monroe followed Bullman's finger once more to the side where three photos were pinned to the board. Three young men, all Indian, all dark-haired.

'And you think he was telling the truth?' Monroe asked.

'Christ no,' Bullman replied. 'He was making a deal to get his parents out of custody. I know he saw the killers, and probably even knew the killers. You could see it on his face. The fact that he picked these three men quickly while claiming he didn't get an unobstructed view means that we should look for the complete opposite. Blond Caucasians, most likely.'

Monroe moved across the crime board, examining it. 'Who does Alfie hang out with?'

'He's a loner, according to his teachers. That said, we have informants who claim he's part of Macca Byrne's group.'

She saw Monroe's expression.

'So you've heard of him?'

'In passing,' Monroe nodded at this. 'And it connects to our case.'

Quickly and without embellishment, Monroe explained to Bullman all that he knew about the Angela Martin case, leaving out the part where Derek Salmon claimed that the Seven Sisters had effectively hired him to take the blame. He talked about Moses Delcourt, and how there was a distinct chance that both bodies were sisters, but currently this was still in the realms of fantasy. And as he finished. Doctor Marcos and another forensics officer, a tall, slim Asian with a ponytail entered the room.

'This is DS Mistry,' Bullman introduced the forensics officer. 'Well?'

DS Mistry shrugged.

'Same person,' she said. 'But not. DNA is exact, the injuries and identifying marks are as close as dammit, but dental is slightly out and fingerprints are completely different. And, more importantly, don't match the ones we have on record for her.'

Bullman looked to the floor, avoiding Monroe's gaze, just knowing that it would be mocking.

'How did we not check the fingerprints before this?' she asked.

'Because we had the DNA match,' DS Mistry replied. 'DNA usually trumps fingerprints.'

'Usually,' Monroe couldn't help himself, and there was a slight touch of smugness in his tone. He could see Bullman biting back a reply, and that amused him greatly.

'They're twins,' Doctor Marcos said, breaking the atmosphere. 'Killed within the same timeframe as each other, give or take a couple of days. And with what looks like the same weapon. A garotte of some kind.'

Monroe looked to Bullman. 'What do you have on Gabrielle Chapman?' he asked.

Bullman shrugged.

'Recently? Tons of stuff. Before she was about fifteen? Nothing. She was a ghost. Dad worked for George Byrne, died in a house fire a few years back. Byrne always claimed it was an attack, that it was arson, but nobody claimed it. After that, Gabrielle disappeared into the system. It's more common than you'd expect, but it means that we have no records of where she lived or what she did until she's arrested with Byrne at sixteen.'

'Actually, you mean the body that *we* have did,' Doctor Marcos added.

'What?' Bullman now looked to Monroe, expecting some prank to have been played, but he seemed as confused as she was.

'As we said, Gabrielle Chapman's police custody finger-prints don't match her fingers,' Doctor Marcos explained. 'But they do match those of Angela Martin.'

Monroe stared at the board, making the same connec-tions that Anjli, Billy and Declan had, back in Temple Inn.

'If we ignore your body for a moment,' he muttered, 'I think this was simple identity theft. Angela came to Birm-ingham and needed to be someone else. Either to run away from something, or to run towards it.'

'Were they both devout Catholics? Her parents?' Bullman asked. Monroe looked to her.

'Cheryl Martin, Angela's mother was, and I can check if Danny was too, but it wouldn't surprise me if he was. Why?'

Bullman placed her hands together in a praying motion.

'Because Gabrielle Chapman was,' she said. 'From what the records state, she was constantly taking confession in a Catholic Church, Saint Wilfred's Church in Saltley before she died.'

Monroe looked back to the board. 'We should chat to someone there. Any chance of talking to the kiddie before we leave?'

Bullman shook her head.

'My men took him to school this morning,' she replied. 'You'll have to wait until after school finishes.'

Monroe grimaced. It looked like he'd be staying in Birmingham for a while longer than he wanted.

'That'd be great,' he said through clenched teeth.

STRIPE HADN'T GONE TO SCHOOL, EVEN THOUGH HE'D TOLD THE police he needed to. He claimed that his mock exams were coming, and the woman that they'd assigned to look after him dutifully took him back home, allowed him to get changed into his school uniform and then walked him to the gates of the school, informing him that if his parents weren't processed and released in time, she'd be there to wait for him.

But Stripe wouldn't be there for her to meet after school, for the moment she climbed back into her car and left, Stripe slipped out of the building through a side entrance and made his way back onto the street. School was a place that people could easily find him, and currently he needed a hiding place where Macca Byrne wouldn't.

He knew the moment that he'd made the deal, he'd done a stupid, terrible thing. You don't snitch on Macca Byrne's crew, and Harrison, no matter what he did, was definitely a part of the crew. All that Stripe could do right now was to lie low and pretend that this was nothing to do with him.

A mile north of Birmingham, and right beside the M6 motorway, was Star City, an entertainment complex that held restaurants, cinemas and bars. There were also places for kids to play, too: mini golf, bowling, lots of areas that a teenage boy could blend in with. If he could somehow break into the Vue Cinema, he could hide out in the back rows of the auditoriums for the entire day; the workers there were often students themselves and didn't care what was going on as long as it didn't bother the other people in the cinema. And so, Stripe sneaked in through the main entrance by asking to use the toilet, found a seat near the back and to the side of one of the larger screens, and settled in, hoping to hide out until it was dark.

The problem was that Stripe was a little noticeable. For a start, he was wearing a school uniform and was in a cinema during school time. Secondly, the visible white streak in his hair was very recognisable. He'd hoped that by coming here he'd avoid any problems, but he'd forgotten the fact that many of the junior staff who were employed here also bought drugs from Macca's people. He didn't know that since the night before, they had put the word out on the streets to find Stripe Mullville. And therefore it was only a matter of hours, in fact as the current film was ending and Stripe was about to sneak into another of the auditoriums, until one of Macca's boys, informed that Stripe was in the cinema somewhere, cornered him and politely suggested that Stripe follow him. Realising that there was nothing that he could do, and deciding to try somehow to bluff it out, Stripe agreed.

Macca was in the bowling alley next door, laughing with

his crew in the furthest lane from the entrance when Stripe arrived. He could see that Harrison and three others were playing with Macca, but they didn't seem to concentrate on it.

They were concentrating on him.

Seeing Stripe being brought over, Macca walked away from the others, waving for the young boy to join him at the American-style diner that backed onto the lanes. Sitting in a booth, he motioned for Stripe to sit opposite.

'You hungry?' he asked. Stripe had been, but now he found that his appetite had completely disappeared, replaced by a gnawing terror as to what would happen next.

Stripe shook his head.

'Milkshake then,' Macca nodded to one of his crew. 'Two milkshakes.' He turned his attention back to Stripe. 'You hiding from me?'

Stripe had been working out his excuse since the previous night; he knew that eventually he'd have to confront Macca, but he had hoped for more time.

'Me? No!' he exclaimed with a fake indignance. 'I'm hiding from the police.'

'You done something wrong?' Macca's voice was calm, collected.

'Nah man, I just don't wanna be seen with them while they arrest my parents, right?' Stripe continued to try to look tough, to bluff this out, but all that emerged was a whisper.

'I heard they were arrested,' Macca replied. 'Tough break. Do you know what their brief told them to do?'

'Don't matter. They'll keep quiet, so don't you worry about them, Mister Byrne,' Stripe said, looking over to the lane. He could see Harrison watching them intently. He forced his eyes to carry on past, as if simply looking about. 'The police got nothing, the stuff was gone, you know?'

'Clever,' Macca nodded. 'So they'll be out soon.'

'Yeah. I mean, I hope so,'

Macca took a milkshake passed to him, sipping at it. Stripe stared at the one in front of him, taking a sip for appearance's sake. It was vanilla.

'Problem is, I need to know if they spoke to anyone,' Macca continued. 'I heard that an hour after arresting your parents, the Fed in charge of the arrest dug up a body in the Lickeys.'

Stripe was ready for this. 'You think they told the police about a body?'

Macca shook his head. 'Nah, I don't think they ever met Gabby. *You* met Gabby though, right?'

'Once or twice,' Stripe whispered. 'I've not seen the news. Is she dead?'

'Yeah, she's dead.' Macca's tone darkened. 'And I want to know if your parents ...' he looked at Stripe now, observing him, '... if whoever told the police about the body being buried saw who did it. If they did, I'd want to know. You understand?'

Stripe nodded.

'Was it you?' Macca asked.

Stripe desperately wanted to say yes, to apologise for not saying earlier, but while in the cinema a thought had crossed his mind.

He knew that Harrison, Macca's right-hand man, had been one of the two people that buried the body that night, as he'd seen him. But that didn't prove that Harrison had been the one that killed her.

What if it had been Macca?

And, because of this one thought, Stripe kept his mouth shut.

If he realised this, Macca said nothing. 'Okay, cool,' he simply replied. 'So, why don't you stay with us until they release your parents, and then we can go ask them all together?'

'I need to get back to school, Macca. I need—'

'That wasn't a request,' Macca snapped, and suddenly the fearsome gang leader that Stripe had heard of so many times was sitting there. 'You're staying with us until I find out who showed the police Gabby's body. And then they're gonna tell me everything.'

Stripe felt his bowels collapse at that, and it took every urge in his body not to piss himself with abject terror.

'Sure,' he said, bluffing out his confidence once more. 'I can hang out with you guys. If you don't mind me kicking your ass at bowling.'

Macca laughed at that. 'You'll go far, little one,' he said, rising from the diner booth. Stripe however looked around.

'Is there a toilet nearby?' he asked. 'I'm lactose intolerant, and that milkshake's going right through me.'

Macca pointed at a door to the side of the diner and, leaving his schoolbag, Stripe rose quickly from the booth and ran through it. Macca picked up Stripe's bag and walked towards the others in his crew, now arguing about a strike.

But then he stopped.

'I've not seen the news. Is she dead?'

Macca hadn't said that Gabby had been on the news.

Something was off here.

Turning slowly, Macca started towards the toilet door. Behind him, Harrison had noted this change of direction and hurried to catch up with his master.

'You alright?' he asked. Macca didn't answer, opening the door and entering the men's toilets. There were five cubicles on the right and five urinals on the left. On the back wall were four sinks, with air-based hand washers secured to the wall by the side. Above the sinks were posters, but over one was a small window.

The top of the window had been opened, looking out into a rubbish area at the back of the cinema, which eventually opened out into Star City itself.

Apart from Macca and Harrison, the toilet was empty.

'He went through the window,' Macca hissed. 'Find him.'

Harrison turned and left the toilet at speed while Macca Byrne pulled out his phone and texted a simple message to one of his contacts. He only needed to send one. The contact would do everything else.

> Stripe Mullville to be found and brought to me ASAP. Ten grand to first to do it.

Pressing send, Macca looked out of the window.

Stripe saw who buried Gabby.

And Macca Byrne was going to have words with him.

15

TEENAGE KICKS

IT WAS SHORTLY BEFORE FOUR WHEN DECLAN ARRIVED AT THE house he had once lived happily in for many years. Walking up the drive, he felt slightly out of body, as if the last year simply hadn't happened, and he was now walking to the door of his house, to see his wife and daughter. He was so caught up in the thought that he almost tried to insert a key into the door, pulling himself out of the daydream in time to pause and ring the doorbell.

Lizzie answered it, her blonde hair long and loose around her neck, a chunky sweater over jeans completing the ensemble.

'You look like shit,' she said, pecking him on the cheek. 'Suppose you'd better come in.'

As Declan entered the hallway, pulling off his coat, Lizzie continued into the living room. Declan still loved her, and he knew that in a way she still loved him; they could have simply been cordial for Jessica's sake, but it had been the police force that pulled them apart, not an infidelity on either side, so there was an unspoken *life's a bit shit* attitude about the whole thing. And Declan had promised to always share the duties where his daughter was concerned.

'She'll be down in a minute,' Lizzie said as she sat on the sofa. There was a fresh mug of tea in front of her. Declan almost asked if she'd made one for him but bit his tongue. This wasn't his house, and she wasn't his wife anymore. Quietly, he sat beside her.

'So, have you met this Owen?' he asked. Lizzie nodded.

'In passing,' she said. 'When picking Jessie up, or when there's been a parent teacher thing.'

'There have been parent teacher things?'

Lizzie looked to Declan. 'Would you have gone if I'd told you?'

'Probably not.'

'Then shut up,' she looked to her watch. 'He should be here soon.'

'So what, they're going for a milkshake? That's a bit fifties, isn't it?'

'It's retro,' Lizzie replied. 'Seeing a film isn't cool anymore. And the shake place does gluten-free and vegan shakes.'

'Jessie's gluten-free and vegan?' Declan had a sudden fear that whenever his daughter had visited, she'd eaten meat feast pizzas under duress. Lizzie shrugged.

'Probably not, but who knows these days? Her hair's changed colour, by the way. It's now pillar-box red.'

Declan nodded. Jessica's hair had been bright blue the last time they'd seen each other. He'd learned after fifteen years that it was a coin toss to expect the same colour twice in a row.

Lizzie was fidgeting, as if unsure on whether to say something.

'Just say it,' Declan said. 'Whatever it is, just tell me.'

Lizzie nodded.

'Look, Declan,' she replied carefully, as if stepping on eggshells. 'We've been apart a while now, and I don't know if you've dated anyone yet or not ...'

'I haven't.'

'Oh. Well. Um.' Lizzie was floundering. Declan smiled.

'Are you asking my permission to go for a drink with Robbie Brookman?' he asked.

'For Christ's sake, Dec!' Lizzie rose now, fury in her expression. 'Are you stalking me? I told you—'

'Robbie called me last week,' Declan couldn't help it; he started to laugh. 'Asked if he could maybe take you out. It impressed me he called and I said to do it.'

Lizzie faltered for a moment. 'He called you first?'

Declan nodded. Lizzie sat back down on the sofa.

'Well now I don't know if I want to.'

'Don't be a grump, Lizzie,' Declan said, still chuckling. 'You're a beautiful, witty and intelligent woman who doesn't deserve a life of sitting at home waiting for her teenage daughter to come home at night. Make Jessie worry where you are for a change.'

'Thanks, Declan.' Lizzie smiled, and Declan could see that it was real. 'It means a lot you feel this way.' She looked at her watch again. 'I'd better check on Jess, make sure she's ready.' And with that Lizzie left the living room, leaving Declan on his own.

Finally alone, Declan released the pent-up breath he'd been holding. He wasn't fine with Robbie and Lizzie dating at all, but at the same time he knew that it was selfish of him to consider anything else for her. Earlier that same day, he'd wondered if he could make a future with Kendis; how was that any different to what Lizzie was thinking right now?

A knock on the door brought Declan back to the present. It was soft, nervous even. Declan looked to the stairs; nobody was coming down.

Looks like it's up to me to welcome our guest then, he thought to himself as he walked down the hall to the door and opened it.

Standing at the door was a sixteen-year-old boy. He was lanky and slim, his ginger hair spiked out in a trendy style. He wore a grey hoodie and denim combination jacket over black jeans, a striped T-shirt underneath. And to cap off the look, he wore Chuck Taylor Converse hi-tops, with what looked like Batman painted on the sides.

And he looked horrified to see Declan.

'Oh,' he said, looking around. 'I was looking for ...'

'Jessica? I know. She's getting ready,' Declan replied. 'I'm her dad.'

He moved back from the door, allowing Owen into the house, indicating that he should enter the living room.

'I didn't think you lived here,' Owen said, entering. 'I mean, she said—'

'That me and her mum were separated?' Declan nodded. 'We are. But when I heard that my dearest darling daughter, the light of my life and entire purpose of my existence was going on a date with a strange young man ...'

He sat facing Owen now, leaning in conspiratorially, Owen subconsciously leaning in to meet him.

'Well, let's just say that I moved everything to be here.'

'Well, it's a pleasure to meet you, Mister Walsh,' Owen held out his hand. It was trembling. Declan took it, shaking it.

'And you, Owen,' he said. 'Although it's DI Walsh. As in

Detective Inspector. As in *police.* As in if anything was to happen to my daughter to make her cry, I could ensure that you'd never be found again.'

Owen's mouth opened and shut twice as Declan leaned back.

'Only kidding,' he said. 'Although hurt my daughter and I'll ensure your life is a living hell.'

There was the sound of movement from the stairs, and Declan turned to see Jessica and Lizzie walking down them. Jessica was dressed in Doc Martens, a Fred Perry dress and a leather bomber jacket. With her bright red hair, she seemed to be half Mod, and half Punk.

'I didn't realise you were here already!' she exclaimed to Owen before hugging Declan. 'Or you!'

'I've been getting to know your date,' Declan said, looking to Owen and smiling darkly. Jessica nodded.

'I bet you have,' she said, turning to Owen. 'Did he do the Detective Inspector speech?'

'Yeah,' Owen said, reaching into his pocket and pulling out a five-pound note.

'And the "I could make your life hell if you hurt my daughter" one?'

'Yeah,' Owen repeated as he passed the note to Jessica. Declan looked at his daughter in hurt surprise.

'You bet on my reactions?' he asked. Jessica smiled.

'Come on, Dad, you're predictable as anything. Of course we made a bet on you.' She then passed the note to Lizzie. 'I bet Mum that you'd show your warrant card too, but she felt you were a little more restrained these days.'

'Et tu, Brute?' Declan was feeling severely got at here. Lizzie laughed.

'Go on, get out of here, the two of you,' she said, passing

the note back to her daughter. 'And have a shake on me, courtesy of your father.'

Jessica gave Declan a hug and then, with a shy look at Owen, a look that seemed to be shyly returned, the two teenagers left Lizzie and Declan alone.

'Were we ever like that?' Declan eventually said.

'Christ, I hope not,' Lizzie replied. 'Stay for some dinner?'

Declan shook his head. 'Work calls,' he replied. 'Thanks for letting me know about this, Liz. Even if it was so that I could be the butt of a joke.'

Lizzie embraced him, but for the first time in a long while it felt more like the embrace of a sister.

'Anytime,' she said.

'And call Robbie,' Declan reminded her as he left, realising that as he said it, it felt good.

Maybe it *was* time to move on.

STRIPE RAN DOWN THE STREETS OF SALTLEY IN AN uncontrolled panic. He knew that by escaping through the toilet window, he'd damned himself in the eyes of Macca Byrne, and the chances were that by now everyone in Birmingham would be hunting for him. Added to that, the police would have realised that he'd bunked off from school by now, and they too would scour the streets for him.

Crossing the road, Stripe saw an alleyway leading towards what looked like a church. But this wasn't any church, this was Saint Wilfred's Church in Saltley. Stripe had been here in the past and knew from his history books that if you ever needed to find sanctuary, or somewhere to hide, you ran to the church.

And, with the innocence and utter faith in this that only a child would have, Stripe turned and ran towards Saint Wilfred's.

'YOU'RE BLOODY KIDDING ME.'

The PCSO (or to state his full name, the Police Community Support Officer) that had accompanied Monroe and Doctor Marcos stared at his phone in a mixture of irritation and anger as he sat in the back seat of Doctor Marcos's Mercedes. Monroe, in the passenger seat, looked around to him, remembering for the first time in about fifteen minutes that there was even someone in the car with them.

'Problem?' he asked. The PCSO shrugged.

'Idiots,' he replied. 'The bloody Liaison Support Officers lost Alfie Mullville and now there's apparently a bounty out on him from Macca Byrne.'

'So, the bairn's on the run?' Monroe mused on this as Doctor Marcos turned off the A38 and onto a side road. 'That could make questioning awkward. What's your name again?'

'Holland,' the PCSO said. 'Like the country.'

PSCO Holland was in fact nothing like the country of Holland; he was a young, skinny brunette that wore a uniform that looked three sizes too big for him.

'Tell whoever texted you we need to be informed on any changes here,' Monroe ordered. 'We need to speak to this boy before we leave Birmingham.'

Doctor Marcos pulled the car to a stop beside a church, looking to Monroe.

'We're here. Want me in with you?' she asked.

Monroe shook his head.

'I'm just going to speak to the Vicar about Gabrielle Chapman,' he said. 'I'm not expecting much.' And with that he clambered out of the car, PCSO Holland reluctantly joining him.

The church was the same as many in the area, a literal Georgian block of religion amid a substantial garden, a square of grass and graves, an iron fence containing it while terraced houses from a far later time lined all four sides, a road going around it.

'Saint Wilfred's Church,' Monroe noted the sign as they walked up to the main door. 'What can you tell me about it?'

'Dunno,' PCSO Holland replied, still looking at his phone. Monroe sighed, starting to believe that Bullman had sent PSCO Holland along purely to annoy him.

Monroe wasn't a very religious man, and because of this, the interior of the church didn't really excite him that much. And so, with the reluctant Holland ambling along behind him, Monroe walked up to the altar.

'Hello? Anyone here?' he shouted out. 'DCI Monroe. I'm looking for a priest.'

There was a clatter from behind the altar, and Monroe walked over to it, leaning over it as he stared down at a small boy hiding half under the altar cloth, looking up at him in utter terror.

'Hello,' Monroe said, flashing his friendliest smile. 'You're not a priest.' The boy looked no older than twelve, thirteen even, although the white stripe in his fringe gave him an artificially older appearance. 'And who might you be?'

The boy rose to his feet, backing away from Monroe. 'They're after me,' he whispered. 'They'll be here any minute. You're a copper, right? You have to help me. It's the law.'

'Christ,' PCSO Holland muttered, staring at the boy. 'That's Alfie Mullville.'

Monroe looked up at a cross above the altar, an effigy of Jesus Christ nailed onto it.

If you're trying to make me a believer, he thought, *you're doing a bloody good job here.*

'Are you Alfie?' he asked.

The boy nodded.

'They call me Stripe,' he replied.

'Who's after you?' Monroe looked back to the entrance to the church as he heard faint footsteps approaching. It was likely just parishioners, but Alfie's terrified expression and tone had caused Monroe's adrenaline levels to spike, and he knew he was entering fight-or-flight mode. 'The police?'

'Macca Byrne.'

Monroe looked to PCSO Holland, ensuring that the officer had heard this. 'Macca Byrne is coming here?'

'People saw me,' Stripe explained. 'They'll tell Macca. He'll find me here. But churches are supposed to give sanctuary.'

'You might want to call for backup,' Monroe whispered to Holland, before turning back to Stripe. 'Why would Macca Byrne want you so badly?'

'Because I saw who killed Gabby. In the woods.' Stripe was panicking now, pacing as he spoke. 'I came here because Father Lawson was always nice to me. I thought he might be able to help.'

'Father Lawson? He's the priest here?' Father Barry Lawson was the name of the priest involved in the births of Gabrielle and Angela back in London. It couldn't be a coincidence that he was here, the priest that was taking Gabrielle's confessions. Monroe wondered whether the last email Billy had sent, the one he hadn't managed to read yet, had mentioned this. 'How can he help you?'

'I'd like to know that too.'

The voice had a hint of the Black Country accent, and Monroe turned to see a young man, dressed in black at the other end of the nave, five of his equally young crew behind him.

'I know who you are, Mister Byrne,' Monroe said, pulling out his warrant card. 'I'm DCI Monroe. This boy is under my protection. And we—' he looked to PCSO Holland and stopped.

Holland was already backing away from him, hands in the air, looking to Macca Byrne.

'He's not with me,' Holland said. 'I let you know about the boy. You leave me out of this.'

'You cowardly prick,' Monroe hissed. 'Turncoat bastard. You're not worthy of the uniform you wear.'

Holland said nothing, looking to the floor as, at the back of the church, Macca Byrne chuckled.

'Oh, dude,' he said to PCSO Holland. 'Did you just screw up. We'd already been told the kid was in here. You just shit away your career for nothing, you prick.'

And with that, Macca Byrne and his men started down the nave towards Monroe and Stripe, pulling wicked looking knives out of their pockets as they did so. Monroe looked around. Even without the weapons, a six on one fight wouldn't be pretty. Now, it was looking to be pretty damned brutal.

'You don't want to do this,' Monroe said, as calm and as official as he could.

Macca smiled.

'Actually, Mister Fed man, I pretty much do.'

And with that, Macca Byrne and his crew moved in.

———————

16

MOTHERS AND FATHERS

D ECLAN SAT IN HIS A UDI AS HE READ THROUGH HIS NOTEBOOK. He'd thought that the last case that the Last Chance Saloon had investigated was complicated, but this was getting crazy. The day was almost over, and he still needed to speak to Janelle Delcourt and then return to Tottenham to have it out with Derek Salmon, while Anjli and Billy were trying to lock down the elusive Father Lawson.

Looking down at his phone, Declan read the email report that was currently displaying on it for a third time. DC Davey had picked up a crime report from the previous night and passed it on to Declan, unsure if it was relevant in any way; a Birmingham man partying in Islington had been found, passed out on the floor with the word CHITS cut into his chest and covered in an extensive amount of his own blood. He didn't want to press charges and claimed that he didn't know the men that attacked him, but there were two things unsaid that had screamed out when Billy found it.

The first was that the man, Ricky Johnston, was a known associate of George and Macca Byrne. The second was that the estate they found him in was an area known to be controlled by the Seven Sisters, and more importantly Moses Delcourt himself.

Declan wondered if he'd be able to use this somehow. He still didn't know how he was going to speak to Janelle; the Sisters were known not to speak to police. And he currently didn't have any backup.

Deciding that if he didn't go now he never would, Declan eventually climbed out of the Audi, locking it behind him as he stared across the road at the row of shops that faced him: an international supermarket, a cab company and a Brazilian café stood shoulder to shoulder, facing the housing estate the other side of the road that was currently behind Declan. A minute or two's walk south was Seven Sisters overground station, and a hundred yards north was the Seven Sisters Underground stop. If you were a crime family called "Seven Sisters", you couldn't find a place that was better suited for your branding.

If crime families had branding, that was.

Above the shops were houses, and beside those was a Jehovah's Witnesses church. If passing though, you'd think that it looked no different to any other London high road.

But Declan knew better. Seven Sisters was part of his old patch, and although he'd never locked horns with Moses or his mother in the years he had worked here, he was still very much aware of the ins and outs of the gang, including where their base was.

Walking into the Brazilian café, Declan walked past the tables and chairs, moving through the evening trade, feeling their eyes locking on to him as he walked up to the counter at the back, the smell of what seemed to be some kind of black bean stew hanging heavy in the room. A Brazilian man, wearing a simple white shirt and black trousers, looked up at him.

'Good evening to you, mon! Table for one?' he asked, his accent seeming to bounce from Brazilian to Jamaican in the process. Declan pulled out his warrant card, showing it briefly before placing it away.

'Sure. But out the back,' he nodded to a door at the back of the café. 'A little more private.'

'That's just the apartments upstairs,' the man replied genially. 'We don't have tables back there.'

'You sure?'

'I'm sure.'

Declan leaned in.

'Then instead, why don't you tell Janelle Delcourt that Detective Inspector Declan Walsh is here, and has some questions about Derek Salmon,' he whispered. 'And, tell her that if she doesn't speak with me in the next five minutes, I'll be arresting her son for murder.'

The man at the counter paused before speaking softly in return, his accent disappearing completely.

'You sure that's the message you want passed?'

'Not really, but I don't really have a choice right now,' Declan forced a smile. 'I'm alone and I'm looking for new friends.'

'That ain't the way to make friends.'

'I'm a trendsetter.'

The man considered this, and then, motioning for Declan to stay right where he was, he walked through the back door to the café, into the area that he had claimed had nothing of importance. Declan knew that the correct thing to do was to wait until a reply came down, to see if Mama Delcourt would speak with him, but he was in a hurry. And to be honest, he always found that things moved quicker when the interviewee was on the back foot. Moving quickly, he grabbed the door before it closed and, giving the man a second to continue up the stairs, unaware of the unlocked door below, Declan quietly made his way through it.

It was a well-known "secret" amongst the people of Tottenham and Seven Sisters that the houses above these shops had been smashed through, refurbished and turned into one enormous house: a stately home in the middle of Tottenham, and accessible by several entrances. Two storeys high and seven shops wide, there was enough space here for several families' living space and multiple offices, but although the Seven Sisters were seven individuals, only one family lived here.

The Delcourts.

The man in the white shirt had knocked on a door above Declan; the sound was metallic, and Declan knew from the tone that the door was likely an armoured one, which made sense. If a drug dealer could armour their door, the Crown Prince of North London and his mum would do the same. Waiting out of sight, he listened.

'What?' a muffled voice spoke from the other side.

'There's a police officer in the café,' the man's voice now. 'Says he wants to speak to Mama Delcourt, or he's arresting Moses.'

Laughter from the other side of the door paused the conversation. Then the voice spoke again.

'Is he new around here?'

'Dunno, man. I never seen him before. Says his name is Detective Inspector Walsh. Wants to talk about Salmon.'

'Probably wants a kickback, then.'

There was a click of a lock and the *shunk* of a bolt, and

Declan knew that this was likely the doorman opening the armoured entrance in order to come down and check things out. There was probably CCTV in the café that could be examined, but that would be grainy, and he probably wanted a proper look at the "mad copper" before they decided on what to do. Knowing that timing was of the essence now Declan started up the stairs quickly, moving swiftly past the surprised man in the white shirt, bringing up his foot and kicking hard at the door as it opened, slamming the door back, and sending the doorman tumbling.

All of this had happened in the space of a second, and by the time the man in the white shirt was shouting for help, Declan was already through the door and slamming it shut. The doorman was on the floor, dazed, his forehead bleeding from where the metal door had slammed into his face. Declan moved quickly, passing the concussed man, but the doorman was less concussed than Declan had hoped and rose, pulling out a Beretta pistol and aiming it at Declan, pulling the trigger.

He never finished the action. Declan, seeing this, had allowed his muscle memory to take over. As a member of the Military Police before joining the police, this wasn't a new experience for him, and he moved almost on autopilot, moving in, grabbing the gun and spinning it around in one swift motion, tearing it from his opponent's hand and shifting the Beretta's angle so it was now aimed at the doorman.

Weighing it in his hand, Declan nodded. At least half a clip full.

'You clean your gun a lot?' he asked. The doorman, shocked at the speed of what had just happened to him, shook his head.

'Not my gun,' he said. 'You're gonna die for this.'

'Probably, if your gun misfires,' Declan replied, grabbing the doorman and moving in behind him, leading him along. 'Now, which room is Janelle Delcourt in?'

'Who wants to know?'

The voice was calm, assured and young. Declan turned to one door on the left as Moses Delcourt emerged into the hall.

'Detective Inspector Declan Walsh, City of London Police,' Declan said. 'I'd show you my warrant card, but I'm a little busy.'

'I can see,' Moses was almost amused. 'I heard of you, Walsh. You worked this patch, yeah?'

'Among others.'

'Why the aggro then?' Moses pointed at the gun. Declan shrugged.

'Your mum's been ignoring our calls and I'm a little impatient,' he said. 'And as for this? The nice man here was saying it's not his after aiming it in my face, so I removed it from him and was going to return it to its rightful owner. You don't know who that might be, do you Mister Delcourt?'

'Nah man,' Moses replied, probably knowing that whoever claimed that gun also claimed the crimes connected with it. 'Let Kayas go though, yeah? He's done nothing.'

'Give me free passage and I will.'

There was a long moment of silence.

'Mum's busy right now,' Moses said.

'So I'll wait.' Declan heard a noise from behind him, so backed Kayas the doorman towards a window where he could see all sides of the hall.

'Talk to me instead,' Moses suggested. Declan nodded.

'You sure you want me to do that?' he asked. 'I'm investigating the murder of Angela Martin, and currently, all the signs are leading to you being the killer.'

This was not the statement that Moses Delcourt had been expecting.

'You think I did it?' he asked, his eyes widening in genuine surprise.

'No, but as I said, the signs lead to you.' Declan replied. 'Someone wants the police to take you down. Even to where the person who confessed to it is saying that you and your mum made him do so.'

Taking a risk, Declan pushed Kayas to the side. Spinning the gun so that the hilt was now facing Moses, Declan offered it to him.

'I needed to gain your attention,' he said. 'And, at the moment, I have a case that's way beyond just you and Angela and is currently about to kick a gang war off.'

Moses looked at Declan for a long second before taking the gun from him.

'I've got my own theories on who killed her,' he said.

'Which one?' Declan replied.

'Which what?'

'Which body,' Declan continued. 'You see, we have two identical bodies and one woman, with two identities that connect to both you and Macca Byrne.'

The door to the side crashed open and two burley young men in hoodies ran in. Moses however waved them back.

'I don't talk to police,' he said. Declan nodded.

'Then talk to me as someone who just wants to get this solved,' he said. 'Because currently I'm seeing too many pieces on this chessboard.'

Moses thought for a moment. The room was silent, with the men in hoodies glaring at Declan.

After a few long seconds of this Declan went to speak again, but the slightest hint of movement from behind alerted him and he spun around to face Kayas, swinging a baseball bat at his head, connecting hard.

As he fell to the floor, losing consciousness, Declan realised that this had been a terrible idea ...

As Anjli and Billy arrived outside of Our Lady of the Sea, it started to rain. Pulling up her coat collar, Anjli hammered on the door to the church.

'The sign said it's open until ten,' Billy, ignoring the rain, said as he showed a noticeboard beside the corpse gate.

'Well, they obviously forgot about that today,' Anjli replied, looking at her phone. 'Bloody place doesn't have a phone number online, either.'

Billy glanced at the web page on Anjli's phone, seeing a photo of Father Lawson.

'I can see why the nuns all liked him,' he whistled. 'He's a looker.'

Anjli turned to Billy in mild disgust. 'Put it back in your pants.'

'Hey, I'm just saying that if he was twenty years younger I'd be confessing—' he stopped as the door unlocked and opened to reveal a man in the doorway. Moving into the light, Anjli and Billy saw that it was Father Lawson.

'Can I help?' he asked. 'It's quite late, but you sounded insistent.'

Anjli showed her warrant card.

'I'm DS Kapoor, this is DC Fitzwarren,' she started. 'We need to speak to you about a birth.'

'Christenings can be discussed—' Father Lawson started but stopped himself. 'This isn't a normal call, is it?'

'No, sir.'

'You'd better come on in, then.'

Entering the nave, Anjli and Billy followed Father Lawson back to the altar. He sat on a pew at the front, indicating for the two detectives to join him. 'So what can I do for you?'

'Angela Martin,' Anjli pulled out her notebook, opening it. 'You may have seen on the news that we found her this week.'

'Yes, terrible thing,' Father Lawson nodded. 'Although I don't see why I'm talking to you about that.'

'She was born at Saint Etheldreda's Mission House,' Billy chimed in. 'At the time that you were running it.'

'I wouldn't really say I ran it,' Father Lawson said. 'The nuns did that. I was connected in an advisory manner.'

'What kind of advisory manner?' Anjli looked up.

'In the manner given to a priest when the Catholic Church wanted a man involved.' Father Lawson raised his hand apologetically. 'I don't make the rules. Poor child. How terrible.'

'We believe that on the night she was born, there were quite a few babies in the Mission,' Billy added. 'We were hoping you could explain this a little more to us.'

'I don't understand what you're saying,' Father Lawson's expression had hardened slightly. This was definitely a conversation that he didn't seem to want to have.

'We're saying that on the night that Angela Martin was born to Daniel and Cheryl Martin, we believe that there were three other babies born the same time. One was to Craig and Emma Chapman, down that day from Birmingham, but the other two, twins we believe, were to a nun.' Anjli looked at Father Lawson as she spoke, watching his expression. 'A nun who apparently claimed that you were the father.'

'Ah, yes,' Father Lawson nodded slowly, his expression unchanged by this revelation. 'Now I understand. Sister Nadine. She had ... well, to be brutally honest, she had an infatuation with me. Claimed that I came to her in the night and seduced her when I was in Africa on missionary work. No way I could have done the deed, so to speak.'

'What did the nuns say about this?' Anjli carried on, watching Father Lawson's expression intently. The man was a hell of a poker player; he gave nothing away as he spoke.

'Well, most of the nuns assumed that Sister Nadine had simply been a naughty girl and was trying to find a way out. But some nuns, the more, well, passionate believers among us, were quite excited about this. Claimed a virgin birth.'

'And you didn't? Claim this as such? I mean, surely to have an *Angel of the Lord* come down looking just like you would give you some kudos back in Rome.'

Father Lawson brought his hands together, as if praying. 'Let's just say that I'm not as cloistered as the nuns,' he said. 'I understand lust, as I've seen it. Sister Nadine had lust. And whoever the poor man was that she seduced, she convinced herself that it was, well, me.'

'So she fantasised about you?' Anjli stared at Father Lawson's hands in prayer as if trying to gain some meaning from them. Father Lawson shrugged.

'I was away for close to four months around the time,' he said. 'Back and forth from Africa and attending my other parishes. Who else could it have been?'

'And were you there at the birth?' Anjli asked. Father Lawson shook his head.

'No, again I was on secondment to a church in Beachampton, which is near Milton Keynes,' he said. 'I was performing a sermon the same moment if I recall correctly. I know this because this isn't the first time that I've had someone say I was in two places at the same time. I have, that is, I had a twin brother.'

Billy looked down at his notes. 'We found records that stated you were in Seminary school with a brother, but it didn't state you were that closely related,' he said. 'Were you identical?'

Father Lawson nodded. 'Oh, very much,' he replied. 'We utilised it terribly as children growing up, constantly getting each other into terrible trouble. And then we both saw the light in our teenage years. We both wanted to be priests, but Stephen, poor Stephen, had his own inner demons. At the end, we went our separate ways. But I know that he pretended to be a priest, pretended to be *me* frequently. I suppose that often it was harmless, and Stephen was trying to use the lessons they had taught him in Seminary School, and I felt sorry for him. I told no one, nor mentioned this to the Bishop.'

He smiled.

'To be honest, he was always the better priest out of the two of us.'

'So could he have been the one who fathered Sister Nadine's children?' Anjli suggested. Father Lawson's expression changed, as if he was about to say something but then decided to alter tack.

'I've heard that suggested by people,' he replied. 'That or God really visited Sister Nadine that night, but I'm afraid that although I'm a believer, I'm not that much of a believer.'

'A DNA test would answer it,' Billy said to Anjli.

'That would be difficult,' Father Lawson sighed. 'My brother disappeared after being released after a lengthy spell in prison, and we found his clothing and a goodbye note on a beach in Kent. A body was never found, and we never heard from him after that.'

'I'm sorry to hear that,' Anjli replied, noting this down in her notebook. 'When was this?'

'Around six months ago,' Father Lawson replied. 'We never spoke much after his arrest, but if you do find anything more about what happened to him, please let me know.' Father Lawson scratched at his neck, under his dog collar.

'I'd so like to reconnect with him again.'

'We understand that you also have a church in Birmingham,' Billy stated from his notes.

'Yes,' Father Lawson affirmed. 'The joys of more faithful than followers require priests to perform double duty these days, I'm afraid.'

'Did you ever see either Gabrielle or Angela after the birth?' Billy turned to a new page in his notebook.

'Both, actually. They came to find me specifically,' Father Lawson rose now, walking to the side of the pews and picking up a glass of water. He took a mouthful of water, swallowed, and then finished the glass before placing it down and walking back. It was a simple motion, but Anjli couldn't help but wonder if he did this to gain himself some valuable thinking time.

'Angela learned somehow that her parents weren't her real ones, and came to speak with the nuns in Poplar,' he continued. 'She was looking for closure, and the nuns realised that she had to be one of Sister Nadine's daughters. And no,' he raised his hands, 'I was not there that day and have no idea what possessed the nuns to pass off the babies as other people's children. All I can think is that they genuinely believed that these girls were brought to them by Angels.'

'So the nuns passed her to you?' Anjli was walking now, pacing around the front pews as she tried to work the logistics out.

'Yes,' Father Lawson replied. 'They said that they couldn't help anymore. Angela Martin came to visit me here in Deptford, and then a week later, out of nowhere, Gabrielle Chapman started attending confession in my Birmingham Diocese.'

'And you didn't find that strange?' Billy asked. Father Lawson leaned in.

'To be honest, I thought nothing of it at the time,' he explained. 'You see, I was utterly convinced that it was Angela, playing some kind of game with me. I don't think I ever met the real Gabrielle.'

Anjli walked back to the two of them, motioning for Billy to rise.

'Thank you for your time,' she said, shaking Father Lawson's hand and then, strangely, bending over to kiss it. Father Lawson pulled it away.

'No, that's only for Cardinals,' he explained. 'I'm happy with a handshake or a fist bump.'

'Sorry,' Anjli replied with an embarrassed smile. 'Dunno what came over me there.'

'You're not the first one to do it, so don't worry,' Father Lawson smiled in return.

'I like your tattoos,' Anjli pointed at the two sets of dots on Father Lawson's hand. 'What do they mean?'

Father Lawson pulled his hand back automatically, before pausing and bringing it back into view. 'Sorry,' he said. 'I've had them so long I forget they're there.' He showed the five dots.

'I was given these by a tribe in Africa,' he said. 'They used dots to tell stories, and they invited me to create my own, as a way of bonding with the tribal leaders. This set, the ones that look like the five on some dice? It's based around the Gospels: Matthew, Mark, Luke and John stand around the figure of Christ in the middle.'

'And the other one?'

'The Holy Trinity,' Father Lawson looked down at the tattoo, a faint smile on his face. 'The Father, Son and Holy Ghost.'

Anjli nodded, putting her notebook away. 'That's a lovely story to have on your hands,' she said. Confused why the interview was ending so quickly, Billy shook hands with Father Lawson before being almost frogmarched out by Anjli; he looked to her in confusion when they emerged outside.

'What the hell?' he asked. 'I still had questions!'

Anjli kept him walking.

'That's not Father Barry Lawson,' she said. 'When he put his hands together in prayer, I saw something. When I kissed his hand? I was checking his fingers and needed a closer look.'

'Never took you for a hand fetish kinda girl.'

Anjli punched Billy on the arm as they continued out of the gate and onto the street. 'Idiot. The tattoos.'

Billy shrugged. 'I thought that was a lovely story, of how he integrated with the indigenous tribes.'

'They're prison tattoos, Billy,' Anjli explained as they arrived back at Billy's car. 'Five dots in that pattern are known as the *quincunx*; the four dots are the walls or the gatehouses, the dot in the middle is the prisoner. It's found on people doing long stretches. And the three dots is a common prison tattoo that means *my crazy life*.'

'What, that prison is crazy?' Billy looked back to the church, as if expecting Barry Lawson to be following them.

'No, it's given to show that the inmate is crazy.' Anjli climbed into the car. 'Come on, we need to get back to the lab before I wipe any fingerprints off the glass I just stole. I want to know exactly who that was we spoke to, as it sure as hell wasn't the priest we were supposed to meet.'

'He said that Stephen Lawson was dead,' Billy looked back to the church.

'Yeah, I don't think that Stephen's the dead one in that relationship,' Anjli replied as she started the car and pulled out into the Deptford traffic.

17

THE CALVARY COMETH

MACCA BYRNE SMILED AS HE REACHED MONROE, STANDING tall, barring the way to Stripe, still cowering beside the altar. PCSO Holland was now sitting on a pew across the church, as if by staring at the floor he wouldn't be a part of this, and Monroe wished more than anything that he could give the coward a punch in the teeth before Macca and his men started.

But they never started, as a gunshot, echoing through the church, stopped them.

It was as if everything paused for a second; nobody moved and then, slowly, *oh so* slowly, Macca and his men started turning back towards the door of the church, as if awaiting a second, more fatal gunshot to strike.

At the rear of the church, beside the door to the nave, stood Doctor Marcos, a vicious-looking gun in her hand, aimed at the ceiling where she'd most likely fired. Monroe fought back an irrational urge to shout at her for possibly creating an incredibly expensive hole in the church roof and instead quietly thanked whichever Guardian Angel was looking over him at that moment.

'Bringing knives to a gunfight? That's not the Birmingham way,' she said, walking towards the small congregation, keeping the gun aimed at Macca as she did so. 'Also, the numbers seem a little out of whack here. How about I kneecap a couple of you to make it fair for the old man?'

'You with him?' Macca asked with the assuredness of a man who had faced people with guns before. Doctor Marcos grinned.

'I'm not *with* him, if you get what I mean, but I do work for him, so yeah.' She cocked the gun, the click echoing ominously in the empty church. 'Now then children, I suggest you get the hell away from my Detective Chief Inspector before I forget I'm police and I blow your goddamned balls off.'

His wicked looking butterfly knife hidden away once more, Macca raised his hands, slowly backing away from Monroe, allowing Doctor Marcos to pass by.

'Understood,' he said. 'We were just leaving, anyway. This was a misunderstanding. We'd heard that a paedo was touching a teenage boy in here.'

'Well, then I admire your civic mindedness,' Monroe replied, his racing heart finally slowing down. 'And now we're all friends here. If you wouldn't mind sending your boys away, Mister Byrne, I'd really like to have a chat with you.'

'Yeah? About what?' Macca turned angrily at Monroe with the face of a man who didn't expect to be questioned. 'You gonna ask me the same questions that all the other Feds ask? You got nothing on me.'

Monroe shrugged.

'I'd be surprised if they asked you these questions,' he

said casually. 'I was intending to talk to you about Moses Delcourt and Gabrielle Chapman. Or is it Angela Martin?'

Macca stopped, as if the statement had thrown him off track for a moment.

As Macca Byrne looked to his men, Monroe could see there was the slightest chance that the young gangster might have actually considered this, but, as Macca went to reply, in the distance they could hear the faint sound of police car sirens.

'Sorry, I called in the cavalry,' Doctor Marcos smiled. 'Didn't think that PC Useless there would do much police work.'

Macca spat on the stone floor of the church, glaring now at Doctor Marcos as she walked over to Monroe, gun still aimed at her opponents. 'You want to talk, while she wants to arrest me.'

'Actually, I really want to shoot you.' Doctor Marcos waved the gun again. 'It's amazing what they let you get away with in the police force.'

'A minute ago, you wanted to cut me,' Monroe interjected to Macca. 'Amazing how fast change occurs, isn't it?'

Macca moved forward, but Doctor Marcos stopped waving the gun around, now aiming the weapon directly at Macca's head.

'Please, try it,' she said. 'I have kill trophies. I 3D print them up myself. I could always do with another. And who do you think an inquest would believe? Little old me, scared for my life or you, the knife wielding thug and son of a crime lord?'

For the first time, Monroe saw the gun close up, and almost stepped back in surprise. It took everything he could to bluff it out, turning back to Macca.

'I can't let you have the kid,' he said. 'But know that I will find the murderer.'

But Macca Byrne wasn't listening, already pushing his crew out of the nave door and into the early evening before the police could catch them. He looked back to the altar before leaving, staring directly at Stripe now, who'd emerged from behind the altar to watch Macca leave.

'You'd better hope they keep your parents in the nick,' he hissed. 'Because when Mummy and Daddy get out, I'm gonna make sure you never see them again.'

And with that Macca Byrne joined his crew, running off into the Birmingham evening.

Now alone in the church, Monroe looked to Holland, who currently wore the expression of a man who was about to be violently sick, as he sat on the pew at the front of the nave.

'You puke in here, laddie, and I'll wipe it up with your goddamned face,' Monroe snapped, his face red with anger. 'Sit on that pew and cuff yourself. Abetting a criminal. Christ almighty. And you!' Now he turned back to Doctor Marcos. 'Does SCO19 know you stole one of their Glocks?'

'Yes!' Doctor Marcos snapped back irritably. 'Well, probably. I mean, I'd discussed with them about examining the comparisons between ammunition and simunition markings in barrels. Andrews seemed interested in seeing the results, so I took that as permission to borrow one of them.'

'And filling it with blanks?' Monroe replied. 'At least I hope to god they were blanks!'

Doctor Marcos answered this by pulling the magazine and passing it to Monroe. In it he could see the simunition rounds, the plastic heads of the bullets filled with blue paint.

'I'm a chemist,' Doctor Marcos explained. 'I knew what

was likely to happen the moment I saw Peter Pan and his band of merry reprobates enter the churchyard on a mission, and I had a forensics kit in my car. I mixed some things together, threw it to the floor, so it smashed in the test tube and made an enormous bang that covered the sound of the glass.'

She smiled.

'By the time they turned, all they saw was a woman with a gun. Bang.'

'And a bloody paintball gun at that,' Monroe groaned. 'What would you have done if they called your bluff?'

'I would have shot them in the face,' Doctor Marcos shrugged. 'Didn't you ever see *Byker Grove* on TV? They spent a year with that subplot.'

Monroe held out his hand.

'What else did you steal?' he asked. Reluctantly, Doctor Marcos pulled out a simunition grenade. Monroe snatched it from her hand, pocketing it.

'You're a nightmare,' he muttered. 'When we get back, I want that Glock passed on to whoever runs the SCO19 teams up here.'

Deciding instead to ignore this, Monroe turned to face Stripe standing beside the altar.

'You've been a hard boy to find,' he said. 'And there seem to be many people looking for you.'

Stripe nodded.

'You gotta keep my mum and dad safe,' he said. 'Macca's mental. He'll hurt them.'

Monroe looked to Doctor Marcos briefly. 'At the moment, laddie, I'm more worried about keeping you safe,' he said. 'Now, tell me more about Father Lawson?'

At that point the door to the church crashed open, and

three police officers moved into the nave, looking around in confusion.

'You're late, boys,' Monroe said. 'Macca Byrne and his men were here, but it was all a massive confusion.'

The police officers moved to the side as DCI Bullman stormed into the church, striding purposely down the middle of the nave towards the altar.

'I left you for ten minutes,' she snapped. 'That's all it took for you to create an incident that's taken up half my team.'

'No offence DCI Bullman, but I think your team has people on it that are creating their own incidents,' Doctor Marcos said, pointing with the gun at PCSO Holland. 'That little shit there was the one who alerted Macca's gang to our whereabouts. Or, rather, the small child that they were hunting.'

'This one?' Bullman walked over to Holland, staring down at him. 'You sent Macca Byrne a message?'

PCSO Holland said nothing, a slight nod of the head his only answer. Bullman nodded to herself, as if accepting this.

And then she brought her arm back and swung at PCSO Holland, punching him hard in the face, sending him tumbling off the pew and onto the cold hard floor of the church.

'Take this little bastard to the cells,' she said to the police officers who had entered with her. 'And have him take the uniform off. I won't have him shame us anymore.'

As the police officers escorted Holland out of the church, Bullman walked back over to Monroe.

'Sorry,' she said. 'I didn't know.'

Monroe shrugged. 'It happens to all of us,' he replied. 'Literally. A few weeks ago we learned that one of our own was passing on information and actively hindering a case.

Grassing to a wannabe gangster is non-league compared to what we've seen.'

He looked to Stripe.

'That said, you can understand why I feel untrusting towards your team right now,' he said. Bullman went to reply, to contest this, but stopped, nodding. There wasn't a thing that she could say right now to build trust in her team, when one of them had literally thrown police into harm's way.

'I can see why you'd think that,' she replied. 'And from now on Alfie Mullville—'

'Will be in my care,' Monroe interrupted, holding a hand up to stop Bullman's angry response. 'You can be as pissed off as you want right now, but I just had six men threaten my life with knives, brought here by the man you sent to liaise with us. I trust you, but currently my faith in your Command Unit is a little tarnished right now.'

'So what, you're stealing my case?' Bullman squared up to Monroe, who shook his head.

'Not at all,' he replied. 'We have our own case that seems to link with your case. And anything we learn we'll immediately share with you. But the boy stays with us. And I'd suggest you put his parents somewhere safe and witness-protection like for the moment too.'

He looked around.

'And who the hell looks after this place?'

There was a polite cough and Monroe turned to see a small, overweight man in a clerical collar standing by the church entrance.

'And where were you when we needed you?' Monroe asked.

The man stepped forward, holding out his hand.

'Father Dulaney,' he said softly. 'I was out back when I

saw Macca and his boys enter. I thought nothing of it until the police arrived.'

'A gang of six thugs enter here looking for a square go at me and you thought nothing of it?' Monroe was astounded. 'Am I missing something here?'

Father Dulaney shrugged apologetically. 'Mister Byrne is a regular here,' he explained. 'I assumed that he was here to pray.'

'Macca Byrne is a devout Catholic?'

Father Dulaney paused before answering, as if trying to find the most tactful explanation here.

'Let's just say he was a fan of confession,' he said.

'Did he confess to you or Father Lawson?' Bullman asked, realising what the priest was insinuating.

'Oh, Mister Byrne and many of his friends preferred Father Lawson,' Father Dulaney said. 'That's why I found it strange that Mister Byrne was here today, but not unnatural. You see, Father Lawson is at his other church right now.'

'Other church?' Now it was Bullman who looked confused. 'He has more than one?'

'Oh yes,' Father Dulaney looked nervous now, as if giving away some kind of terrible secret. 'The numbers of new, ordained priests have fallen over recent years, down eighty percent in some areas of the UK. Because of that, we have more churches than priests right now, and many of our new priests come from Africa. We find ourselves spread thin, so to speak. Many of us will have "linked" churches; that is, churches that are not a priest's particular parish, but will have a connection to the priest, ensuring that they will spend some of their time there, over their own parish.'

'Basically, you're saying that you time-share priests?' Monroe asked. Father Dulaney smiled.

'That's pretty much exactly what I'm saying,' he replied. 'Father Lawson has his own church in London, but for years now has also been coming up here to take confession and perform some of our services.'

'And both Gabrielle Chapman and Macca Byrne came here to see Father Lawson,' Monroe spoke it as a statement rather than a question, turning to Bullman.

'Well, bodies aside, now I know we're working on the same case,' he said. 'The Father Lawson he's talking about is the same one we've been looking for. And there's an entire circle of people we're seeing here that not only seem to know everyone else but are all connected to both Gabrielle Chapman and Angela Martin. Who, according to the finger-prints in police records seems to be the same person, even though we have two bodies with different ones.'

Monroe looked to Stripe, still standing by the altar.

Poor little bugger hasn't got a clue what he's got himself into, he thought to himself.

But that wouldn't stop Monroe from using the boy to find out the truth.

18

AGAINST THE WALL

OPENING HIS EYES PAINFULLY, WINCING AT THE LIGHT THAT HIT them, Declan half expected to find himself in the boot of a car that was being driven somewhere far away and quiet, or more likely tied to a rickety wooden chair in a North London basement, naked, with electrodes attached to rather sensitive areas. What he'd done was stupid with a capital S. You simply didn't walk into the Seven Sisters' castle, attack their men and then expect to walk out. And, considering that the last thing that Declan remembered was a rather pissed off and embarrassed doorman smacking a baseball bat into the back of his skull, he almost hadn't expected to wake up at all.

Instead, he lay on a plush sofa in an ornate, red wallpapered lounge. The sofa was leather, very expensive, and Declan was currently sprawled face first on it. Moving his head and instantly regretting it as a wave of pain shot through his skull, Declan spied a mug of tea on a table in front of the sofa, while across from him sat Moses Delcourt, patiently waiting for his guest to waken.

'You're alive,' Moses said, matter-of-factly. 'And you're not bleeding. Although you'll have a wicked bump there tomorrow. You've got a tough skull, fed. You should be lucky.'

'Where am I?' Declan clambered ungracefully into a sitting position, looking at the mug warily. 'Is that for me?'

'Milk and lots of sugar,' Moses nodded. 'Good for shock. And as for where you are? You're in the throne room of Janelle Delcourt. It's where you wanted to be, right?'

Declan took a sip of the tea, feeling the hot, sweet liquid slip down his throat. It was good.

'I expected you to be a little more aggressive towards me right now,' he said.

Moses shrugged.

'Gotta admire a guy who comes in like you did,' he admitted. 'Although Kayas acted in self-defence, before you consider dragging him in. You held a gun to his head. He was defending me.'

Declan nodded. 'You won't hear me say anything against him,' he said. 'He got the drop on me. I'm good with that if he is. Although he aimed the gun at me first.'

Moses looked around the room, and Declan followed the gaze. The wallpaper was expensive, gold patterns on a deep-red background. The carpet was burgundy; it was thick and obviously equally expensive. The lamps in the room were brass with misted glass shades, but they were more of a brushed gold rather than a hard, shiny surface, making them warmer and more subtle. The furniture was antique mahogany or leather, and on the wall was an oil painting of Janelle and Moses Delcourt, created a few years earlier when Moses was in his mid-teens, in an ornate golden frame.

Moses saw Declan's gaze.

'Yeah, it's a bit Buckingham Palace, ain't it?' he said with a grin. 'Mum's idea. She's the Queen of North London, so why not live like a real one?'

'I must get her interior designer's details,' Declan replied. 'And arrest them.'

Moses laughed at this. 'You're genuinely not scared, are you?' he asked. Declan shook his head carefully, still unsure if it would fall off if he moved it more vigorously.

'I've been in worse scrapes,' he admitted. 'And besides, if you wanted to hurt me, you would have done it already.'

'Let's just say you piqued my curiosity with the "other body" bollocks you were spouting,' Moses sat back in his chair. 'And if someone is setting me and Mum up, I'd like to know about it.'

Declan placed the mug onto the table, looking back to Moses.

'You'll let me free when we're done?' he asked. 'I'm not going to be rolled up in a rug and dumped somewhere, or left in the street with words etched into my chest?'

Moses smiled at the last line, but the humour never reached the eyes.

'Let's just say that currently you're walking out the front door.'

Declan nodded at this. 'I can deal with that,' he said. 'You mother joining us at all?'

'My mum don't hang out with feds and tradespeople,' Moses replied. 'You're both. So you speak to me.'

Declan shifted position on the sofa.

'Okay then, I can deal with that. As I'm speaking to you, Mister Delcourt, I'll start with some simple questions. Where did you meet Angela Martin?'

Moses stiffened at the name.

'I didn't kill her.'

'I never said you did.' Declan motioned to his jacket pocket. Moses nodded, so Declan reached in and pulled out his notebook. Flipping it open, he pulled out a pen and started to write. 'I know that you're being framed for it though. Whether or not you killed her, someone has it out for you and I'd like to work out who.'

'Who said it was us?'

The question was innocent, but Declan could feel the weighted implication. Answering this was pretty much giving someone a death sentence, as it would place them at the top of the Delcourt, and therefore the Seven Sisters', hit list.

'Derek Salmon,' he replied. 'Came to us saying that he had to confess to the crime because of a deal he'd made with you and your mum. Said that if he did this, you'd look after his wife and daughter. He's terminally ill, you see.'

'We haven't spoken to Salmon in ages,' Moses muttered. 'Since he quit the feds, in fact. And we sure as hell didn't pay him to find a body.'

'I know that now,' Declan replied, putting the notebook down, allowing Moses to see that he was effectively taking the conversation off the record. 'His wife won the lottery and wants nothing from him. My problem – well, actually my problems – are these.' He counted off on his fingers. 'First, why was Derek aiming us at you? Or, rather, why was he aiming *me* at you in the first place, when he must have known we'd work out it wasn't you? Which gives me a subsequent second question of why me? Why would he throw me to the wolves on a case that was obviously being made up as he went along?'

'You'd have to ask him that,' Moses replied.

Declan nodded.

'I intend to,' he said. 'Right after I finish here with you. But there's more.'

'This the other body bit?' Moses leaned forwards. 'About time.'

'So Angela Martin was seen in Birmingham with Macca Byrne,' Declan said. 'In fact, we arrested her with him. But you know this already.'

'Go on.'

'But it wasn't Angela that was arrested,' Declan continued. 'It was Gabrielle Chapman, who we're still trying to gain information on. She's the other body we found, killed in the same manner and here's where it gets interesting, she had the same historical injuries and tattoos as Angela. And we have witnesses that say that this woman, this "Gabby Chapman" was the one seeing Macca Byrne. Not Angela.'

Moses stared at Declan silently for a moment.

'But you knew that already, didn't you?' Declan spoke it as a statement. Moses shrugged.

'I have sources, and I'd heard rumours.'

'Like what?'

Moses grinned. 'I don't deal in tittle-tattle,' he replied. 'So he was with this other girl. Why should this matter to me?'

'Well, there we have another problem,' Declan sipped at the tea as he continued. 'When we checked her record, Gabrielle Chapman's fingerprints matched Angela Martin's ones. So even if Gabrielle was seeing Macca, it was Angela arrested with him.'

Moses nodded, still calm. 'Sounds like you got a girl, my girl, playing at being two girls. But then there's another girl, who seems to be the same as my girl.'

Declan watched Moses, looking for anything that could give away what the younger man was thinking. There was nothing. It was almost as if Moses had prepared for this conversation; that he expected the questions that Declan was asking.

Moses knew all this already.

'It's definitely not your usual crime scene,' Declan replied. 'I have to work out who killed both girls, seemingly around the same time and why they were identical. I mean, that's twins, right? But then that brings up a question about parentage. And all I have is an ex-police officer, a corrupt one who is trying his best to say that you did it, without actually saying that. So I need you to stop pissing about, stop playing whatever game you're starting here and tell me what the hell is going on.'

Moses went to reply, to argue, but then stopped. Silently he took a sip of his own mug before looking back to Declan.

'I didn't know who her dad was at the start,' he said. 'I swear. We met at a friend's house party. She must have been about fifteen back then. I was sixteen, almost seventeen. She was different to the other girls. Later, I realised it was because of how she grew up, you know? We got on with each other ...' he paused, as if trying to work out how to phrase the next line. 'And after a while we started seeing each other.'

'And her dad?'

'He was well pissed off that she was seeing me,' Moses actually chuckled at this. 'His bosses and Mum didn't exactly get on.'

'He knew it was you?' Declan asked. 'She told him?'

'Oh yes,' Moses nodded, pulling up his hoodie to show a small scar on his stomach. 'Sent some prick around to cut me, warn me off. Didn't work.'

Declan thought back to his conversation with Danny Martin.

'She was seeing some lad. Black kid; didn't know the name. From North London.'

Danny Martin had lied. *What else had he lied about?*

'Her father also said she was on drugs at the end,' Declan continued, moving the subject on. Moses nodded.

'I don't take the stuff, but Angie became addicted. And when she did, that's when things fell apart. They're all druggies up there, even the kids. I tried to get her to stop, but she was a thunderstorm, you know? You couldn't stop her doing anything she didn't want to do.'

'Did she ever mention a sister? Or a connection in Birmingham apart from Macca?'

'No, man. Not that I knew. And when she met Macca, she introduced us.'

Declan looked up from the notebook. 'I bet that didn't go down well with the Sisters.'

Moses leaned in, lowering his voice now. 'Mum never found out. We had a plan. We were gonna create mad trade routes down the Grand Union, just like they did in *Peaky Blinders.* He was gonna source the gear, and then I'd sell it down here. Feds have that cool numberplate tech on the roads, but they don't follow barges.'

Declan nodded at this. 'You sure you should give away such trade secrets?' he asked with a smile. Moses shrugged.

'Don't matter. Never gonna happen now.' He looked out of the window, up at the sky. 'There was something that was weird though,' he continued. 'She weren't religious at all. Her dad was super Catholic, all into the guilt and everything, but she couldn't give a shit. Tossed all the crosses he kept giving her away. And then out of nowhere she has this rosary, you know? The beads and cross and stuff?'

'I know a rosary.'

'Well, she had this wicked one made of Paracord and I think metal balls. Vicious bloody thing. She'd hold it in her hand and when she was in a scrap, she'd flick it at whoever she had a problem with, and the cross at the end was like a whip.'

'It didn't break?' Declan remembered the broken rosaries that he'd seen in Angela's bedroom. None of those seemed to be as sturdy as the one Moses spoke about.

'Nah, man. This thing was hardcore,' Moses was grinning now as in his mind he relived the moment. 'She was a real bitch sometimes. But you didn't mess with her. That's how I know that it was someone who she knew, who she trusted, that set her up to be killed. She wouldn't have expected it, you know? That way you could stab her in the back.'

Declan nodded. 'Did she ever mention a Father Lawson?' he asked.

Moses started laughing.

'Yeah, but it was a joke, you know?'

'How so?' Declan didn't see the humour. Moses shrugged.

'She kept calling ol' Lawson her father, because he was her Father, you get it? Father Lawson being called Dad?'

Declan got it. And he believed that he understood the joke far better than Moses Delcourt did. Touching the back of his head and happy to see that it wasn't bleeding still, he rose from the sofa.

'I'll find who really killed Angela,' he said. 'Don't take this into your own hands.'

Moses rose to meet him. 'I'll do what I damn well want,' he said. 'You might have all your clues and your Sherlock Holmes shit to do, but I know that someone killed Angie to stop what we were doing, and I'm gonna make them pay.' He grinned; a dark, humourless, violent smile. And for the first time, Declan saw the man that terrorised North London.

'You're more than welcome to come at me again if I do,' he said. 'But I'll leave you in a far worse state than unconscious on my mum's sofa, you get me?'

Declan did. And, nodding a farewell, he left the Seven Sisters' stately home, walking out of the Brazilian café and over to his car. Only once he sat in the driver's seat, the door locked, did he finally let out the breath that he'd been holding. The recklessness of the situation hit him like a freight train.

They could have killed him.

Staring up at the car roof, Declan took a deep breath to calm himself. There was something still nagging at him, something that Moses had said at the end.

'Someone killed Angie to stop what we were doing, and I'm gonna make them pay.'

Moses had spoken in the plural, not the singular tense. Which meant that he believed her death affected more than one person. Who were the others?

Declan tabled that thought for another time as he indicated and pulled out into the road. He had another stop to make, and it was nearby.

He was going to get the truth out of Derek Salmon.

19

SISTERS AND MOTHERS

Billy and Anjli sat in Billy's car outside Ursuline Convent, a 1970's red-brick monstrosity of a building that bore more similarity to a council estate than a Catholic Nunnery.

'I never thought about where nuns went to die,' Billy muttered. 'I thought it was more like birds, you know? You just never see the bodies.'

'You thought they just disappeared, like Jedis?' Anjli asked, amused. Billy shrugged.

'They have magic powers,' he replied. 'I've never felt comfortable around them.'

The reason for their visit was Sister Margaret, a nun in her eighties who, at one time, was Mother Superior at Saint Etheldreda's Mission House, but in recent years had moved to Ursuline, to finish her years in quiet contemplation.

Billy's phone buzzed, and he answered it on speakerphone.

'Yeah?' he said. The voice of DC Davey came through the speaker.

'It's Davey,' she said. 'I've got your print results.'

'Blimey, that was fast,' he replied, looking to Anjli. 'We only dropped them off an hour back.'

'Yeah, but glass is easy to gain them from, and it helps that he was in the system,' DC Davey explained. 'And, with you already saying who you thought it was, it was easier to narrow down.'

'Was it Stephen Lawson?' Anjli asked.

'Yeah,' DC Davey replied.

'Were you able to get DNA from the glass?'

'That's a longer and more complicated task,' DC Davey's voice was cagier as she answered. 'But if we manage it, we'll let you know. It helps that he was drinking water, and not some kind of carbonated drink, but if you find better DNA, it'd be good to know. I've already contacted Belmarsh Prison, where Stephen was jailed to see if he was ever swabbed while there. If so, I can compare that to Angela's DNA and see if something comes of it. Davey out.'

The phone call disconnected. Anjli considered this.

'He killed his brother,' she said. 'It has to be.'

'Let's arrest him,' Billy went to start the car. Anjli placed a hand on his arm.

'We'll send uniforms in,' she smiled. 'We, however, are going to speak to some nuns.'

Billy's shoulders slumped as he nodded.

'Fine,' he grumbled. 'But if they talk about the *damnation of homosexuals*, I'm going to have a debate.'

Getting out of the car, Billy looked around at the terraced Victorian houses on the other side of the road.

'That said, I do like the area,' he said. 'I wonder how much the houses are around here?'

'Way more than I can afford,' Anjli replied as she started

across the street towards the Convent. 'You probably have enough stuffed into your sofa though.'

Billy chuckled.

'There was a time, Kapoor, where you wouldn't have been far wrong,' he said before locking the car and following her to the Convent door.

———

THE CONVENT ITSELF WAS SMALL AND QUIET, EFFECTIVELY A retirement home for nuns. Sister Margaret had a small room on the first floor, a shared bathroom beside it; inside the room the walls were painted cream and the functional furniture was pine. The paintings on the wall were simplistic and religious in attire, comprising Mary, Jesus, Mary and Jesus together and a crucifix, and there was a narrow Murphy bed that folded up into a pine bookshelf cabinet. By the window was a long desk that also doubled as a sideboard, and a kettle rested beside the lamp, an empty mug beside it.

On the other side of the room was an armchair, and here Sister Margaret sat, currently knitting as Anjli and Billy entered.

'Sister Margaret? I'm—' Anjli started, but Sister Margaret held up a knitting needle, cutting her off.

'I lost count,' she eventually complained. 'I'll have to do the row again.' She looked up to her two visitors with a smile.

'Please, sit,' she indicated the bed. 'I have little furniture. It's not really required by us.'

Sister Margaret was Irish, although Anjli believed she was more Republic of Ireland because of her softer accent. She was short, only five feet in height, and wore the "old lady" frame of a woman who had once been overweight but was now far slimmer because of advancing age. She wore a long black dress with a white collar and contrary to popular culture she didn't have a full black and white wimple on, instead wearing a more casual looking grey one that covered her hair. The only other item of clothing she seemed to wear were thin rimmed glasses, which she now placed on to stare at Anjli and Billy.

'They said you wanted to talk about Father Lawson?' she asked. Anjli nodded.

'How long were you at Saint Etheldreda's for?' she asked.

Sister Margaret shrugged.

'Ooh, now I don't know that rightly,' she said, thinking. 'I'm eighty-six now and I joined when I was nineteen, so a good long time, I'd say.'

'And you were there when Father Lawson was there?'

'I was there when he was just a child!' Sister Margaret laughed. Billy looked to Anjli before speaking.

'What do you mean by that?'

Sister Margaret leaned closer, placing the knitting to her side. 'Those two were the bane of the East End as kiddies.'

'Barry and Stephen?' Anjli watched Sister Margaret as she spoke. 'You knew them?'

Sister Margaret nodded.

'Aye, they were always getting into trouble. Eventually their parents, good Catholics the Lawsons were, they put them into Sunday School, and at the time I was running it.'

'So you put them on the path then?' Billy asked.

'Aye, for the good or bad of it,' Sister Margaret nodded. 'Eventually they both went to Seminary College, but Stephen didn't have the temperament for it. He was too wild, too much of a free spirit for the church. He had lustful intentions.'

'A ladies' man?' Billy smiled, but Sister Margaret looked horrified at this.

'God no!' she exclaimed. 'He didn't like the ladies, if you get my drift.'

Billy looked to Anjli now. 'At all?'

'Now why would you think that?' Sister Margaret asked. 'Where are these questions going?'

'Angela Martin and Gabrielle Chapman,' Anjli said. And at these two names, Sister Margaret crossed herself.

'Poor wee kiddies,' she said. 'I heard what happened.'

'We heard that they were the daughters of a nun.'

There was a moment of silence, as if Sister Margaret didn't understand the question, before a spark of recognition returned and she carried on as if the pause hadn't happened.

'Aye, Sister Nadine. A mistake, bringing her into the order.'

'She claimed that Father Lawson was the, well, the father of the child.'

Sister Margaret sighed. 'So she did. It was very much an embarrassment for many of us.'

'So you don't believe it was a vision from God?'

'Oh Christ no!' Sister Margaret paused, looked to the ceiling and crossed herself again. 'No, that was definitely the work of man.'

'But Father Lawson was in Africa.'

Sister Margaret looked confused at this. 'What do you mean?'

'I mean that Barry Lawson was out of the country,' Anjli replied. 'I'm assuming if Nadine saw Father Lawson, she was actually seeing his twin brother?'

'Are you dim in the head, lass? I already told you that

Stephen Lawson didn't like girls!' Sister Margaret calmed a little as she continued.

'And Barry didn't like tropical climates.'

Anjli realised what the nun was saying. 'You're saying that it was Stephen who went to Africa?'

'Oh, to be sure, we knew that the two of them were playing the same part, but priests are in such short supply these days and Barry always kept Stephen on a short leash. But Barry had his weaknesses, too. And when the Bishop learned of, well, let's say Barry's indiscretion, that stopped.'

'The church knew of this?' Billy shook his head. 'Of course they did. They're the church.'

'They knew some.' Sister Margaret sat back in the chair, getting comfy. 'And Stephen wasn't going to let his rather lucrative sideline go.'

'Sideline?'

'Oh yes.' For a woman in her later years, Sister Margaret's memory seemed remarkably bright here. Anjli assumed that it was because criminal activities amongst the priesthood was a little more interesting than the usual day-to-day activities of a nun. 'Stephen was bringing in certain illegal substances from Africa every time he went over there,' Sister Margaret explained. 'Sold them straight on to Daniel Martin.'

'You knew Danny Martin?'

'Of course I knew him!' Sister Margaret looked to Billy. 'Are you sure she isn't touched in the head, boy? The Martins were some of the most devout Catholics you'd see around here!'

'So Danny Martin and Stephen Lawson worked together,' Anjli was writing this down now. 'Was Barry a part of this?'

'No, never,' Sister Margaret vigorously shook her head at this. 'That is, I don't think so. No, I'm right. He was never a part. But once Nadine was pregnant, we knew that Barry had been foolish. Stephen and Daniel, they used this for leverage. Stephen started playing "Barry" more now while the poor lad went to his other church in Beachampton.'

'Was it Barry or Stephen then that was here the day of the birth?' Anjli asked.

'Stephen,' Sister Margaret replied. 'That was a weird day to be sure.'

'Why?' Now Billy was asking the questions.

Sister Margaret shrugged.

'Well, we didn't really have births back then. We stopped in the seventies. But Daniel Martin was an old school Catholic family and Cliffie Chapman was a local too, although he'd moved. They both came in through Father Lawson, but it was Stephen who was there on the day.'

'Did they talk to each other?' Anjli was realising what happened that day.

'Why would you think that?' Sister Margaret asked. Anjli shrugged.

'Well, we know that Daniel Martin and Craig – sorry, Cliff – Chapman worked together, and you've already said that Stephen worked with him too. I'm guessing that it wasn't a coincidence.'

There was a long silence. Sister Margaret sat, looking nervous.

'I didn't know,' she whispered. 'I mean, we knew that there were drugs, but it was Africa, you know? They couldn't be that bad.'

'Go on.' Anjli leaned forward.

'They met,' Sister Margaret admitted. 'They talked a while. I can't remember how long for, but it wasn't more than half an hour. I only passed by once, but they were talking about trade routes.'

'Then what happened?'

Sister Margaret started to cry.

'Then it all went wrong,' she said. 'Sister Nadine, she went into labour. And so were the women, the wives. One was a breach, the other way too early. Things were going bad. We called Father Lawson – Stephen Lawson – out, begged him to help us. The babies, they were dead.'

'Which babies?' Billy asked. 'Nadine's?'

'The others,' Sister Margaret wiped away her tears. 'Father Lawson said this couldn't happen, that this would be a terrible thing, and we, well, we believed him. He went to speak to Sister Nadine; she'd given birth but was poorly. I don't know what happened, but he returned and told us that the babies were alive. But Sister Nadine didn't seem to be. We checked, and he was right. She had passed.'

'He killed her?' Anjli was astonished at this. Sister Margaret shook her head.

'No, no, he wouldn't have ...' she said, but her tone gave away an uncertainty to this. 'He wouldn't have ...'

'So then what happened?'

Sister Margaret took a deep breath. 'We swapped the babies,' she admitted. 'We gave one each to the families, but it was a crazy time as an ambulance had arrived for the Martin lady. She was losing blood after her birth. The families left, and we buried Sister Nadine and her ... *their* babies.'

This was the moment that Sister Margaret broke down, sobbing uncontrollably. 'Oh Jesus, forgive me!' she wailed.

Anjli looked to Billy; her face devoid of all expression.

'What happened after that?' she asked coldly. Sister Margaret looked up, gathering her composure once more.

'We never talked of it,' she said. 'When Father Barry returned, he was furious. Told Daniel and Stephen that they were barred from his church, that he would never help them again. Neither Stephen nor Barry told Daniel that his newborn child was our Angela, our *Angel* ... I think they were scared of some kind of retaliation.'

There was a long moment of silence before Sister Margaret spoke again, and this time Billy and Anjli allowed her this time to compose herself some more before continuing.

'Anyway, about a year later Stephen killed two men in a café and was put away. After that, Father Barry and Daniel seemed to reunite, to rekindle their old friendship. But by then I'd moved up to Alum Rock with many other nuns.'

Billy wrote this in his notebook. 'And when Angela came back?' he asked.

'That was years later,' Sister Margaret replied. 'She found out the truth, you see. We told her to speak to Father Barry. We hoped this would be his time to tell her the truth, but I don't think he did.'

'When was the last time you saw Father Barry Lawson?' Anjli asked, rising from the bed. Sister Margaret shrugged.

'I avoided him after his brother's incarceration,' she said. 'It turned him, it did. Made him a different person.'

'Thanks for that,' Billy said, rising to join Anjli. 'And God be with you.'

Anjli looked at Billy with a what the hell expression, and he shrugged. Shaking her head, Anjli turned to also say farewell to Sister Margaret.

But she was already knitting once more, already forgetting the two police officers in front of her.

She'd probably forgotten Father Barry Lawson, too.

20

INTERVIEW TWO

DECLAN WAS IN THE INTERVIEW ROOM WHEN DEREK SALMON was brought in.

'About bloody time one of you turned up,' he said, sitting down on the chair facing Declan across the table. 'I've been in here over twenty-four hours since you left me. They'll start charging me rent.'

He was wearing the same trousers as he had the previous day; Declan could still see the mud flecks on them from the trip to Epping Forest but instead of the suit jacket and the shirt he'd been wearing when he was arrested, Derek Salmon now wore a white tee shirt under a light grey hoodie. Declan wondered whether they'd allowed someone to pick up some clothes for him, some kind of professional courtesy to someone who once worked in the building or whether they'd just found some items in the lost and found box and tossed them to him.

Arriving at Tottenham North, Declan had realised very quickly that Salmon was becoming a bit of a celebrity right now, with the Last Chance Saloon being cast in this story as the unit helping him "clear his name". Police loved a good underdog story, especially when it involved one of their own, and a tale of a copper that was proving their innocence was pretty much catnip to the plod. After all, the alternative was that one of their own had been dirty for years.

Which, in this case seemed to be more accurate.

'Sorry,' Declan muttered, holding his anger in check until the police constable who'd brought Derek in left the room.

'Do you need anything else, Derek?' the constable asked before leaving.

'Nah, Mike. Just my medicines. I'll take them with dessert,' Derek smiled at the constable as he left through the main door, closing it behind him. 'Good man, that. Helps people out.'

'You seem to be doing okay,' Declan said, forcing a smile. 'It's almost like people here believe you're innocent.'

'I have you and your sterling work to thank for that,' Derek replied. 'Also, what did I hear about another body being found?'

Declan rose from the chair, pacing around the room. 'It's a confusing one, I'll admit, Derek,' he admitted. 'There are so many twists and turns in this case—'

By this point he had walked up from the side and, with one quick movement, and before Derek could respond, Declan grabbed the front of his hoodie, dragging him to his feet and slamming his back against the wall.

'What are you doing?' Derek exclaimed as Declan leaned in close.

'You might have everyone here fooled, but I'm wise to you now, you crooked bastard,' he hissed. 'I can't believe that I believed you. I actually fell for your act like that bloody idiot who just walked out of here.'

Derek stared at Declan silently.

And then he smiled.

'Press the button, you cocky little shit,' he breathed. 'Stop pissing about and start this interview. I got things to do.' And with that he brought up his left hand and, with a sharpened pinkie fingernail, he scratched at Declan's cheek.

It didn't draw blood, but it hurt like hell and Declan stepped back, letting go of Derek's hoodie.

'What the hell?' he snapped. Derek shrugged.

'You just rammed me against a wall,' he replied. 'You think I wouldn't take a shot back at you?'

'You used me,' Declan said. 'You were my mentor, and you used me.'

'And you were the son of the man who killed my career,' Derek sat at the table once more, straightening himself out as he did so. 'How do you think it felt, watching you climb the ranks because of *him*? To be forced to wipe your arse every day because of *him*?'

'My father?'

'*Of course I mean your father!* Bastard was as corrupt as I was! Oh, don't tell me you didn't know. We all lined our pockets, even your darling DCI Monroe. But no, suddenly Patrick gains a conscience and I'm damned for all eternity! Stuck at DI rank while shits like you overtake me!'

Derek was reddening in the face now, but his anger wasn't abating.

'You know how many times a day I wished him dead? And then God answered my prayers! No longer did he have anything on me. Granted, it was weeks before I would die myself but screw it, a win's a win! Now I could do what I wanted. And what I wanted was to bring you both down. You and Monroe.'

'Join the list,' Declan snapped back as he sat in the chair facing Derek. 'How is all of this bringing us down?'

'Because you've started a gang war,' Derek said with a smile. 'You've kicked a hornet's nest and people are going to die because of it. And the people upstairs will go *the media are pissed at us! Why did that idiot DI ask questions when someone confessed to the murder and even showed us the body? Why did his DCI agree to this?*'

Declan stared at Derek Salmon now with the look of a man who was seeing someone for the first time. Derek was right. The higher ups would have a field day on this. Monroe's team had been handed an open goal here; it was Declan's faith in his onetime mentor that was going to bring them all down.

'Personally though, I wanted to see you fall, you cocky little prick,' Derek was enjoying the role of an angered victim a little too much. 'All those years wiping your arse and fixing your cock ups, you aged me more than cancer ever did. And I've not even started yet. I'll be haunting you way beyond my death.'

There was silence in the room as Declan glared at his old mentor.

'Press the sodding button,' Derek hissed.

'So you hold all the cards then,' Declan eventually spoke. 'Care to explain some things to me?'

Derek looked at the recorder. 'You're not being professional here.'

'I'm learning from the best,' Declan replied. Derek

thought about this and then nodded, as if taking the compliment.

'So what do you want to know?' he asked. 'You better hurry, I'm watching *Bake Off* in ten minutes. They put a TV in my cell and everything.'

Declan leaned back, considering this. 'Did you kill her?'

'Isn't that the whole reason you're on the case? To prove otherwise?'

'We know you worked for The Twins and also the Seven Sisters. Did you work for George Byrne?'

'Ooh, now that's an interesting line of questioning,' Derek clapped his hands in a slow applause. 'I wonder though if you're missing the point of this though.'

'Probably. Are you really dying?'

'Yeah. So you can imagine my delight when your bastard of a father did it first.'

Declan bit back a reply. He knew that Derek was just trying to get a reaction.

'Did you work with Danny Martin?'

'Several times.'

'You knew Angela well?'

'Well enough.'

Declan nodded to himself. 'You knew she wasn't his daughter?'

Derek laughed. 'Everyone knew that, boy. She looked nothing like him or his wife. It had to be Lawson's.' Derek paused, as if realising he'd spoken out of turn.

'Nice,' he said. 'That won't happen again.'

'Why do you want a gang war?' Declan asked. Derek shrugged.

'I don't,' he said. 'But the kids do.'

'Moses and Macca?'

'Among others.'

'There aren't any others.'

'You sure about that?' Derek chuckled. 'Shame. I actually thought you'd made some headway here.'

'You're just playing with me now,' Declan stood up, the interview over.

'I wouldn't have done any of this, you know,' Derek admitted. 'If you'd just rolled over and died after punching that priest. But no, you had to do one last thing, solve one last case, didn't you? And in the process kill the career of DCI Ford.' He laughed. 'The Twins might not have given a damn about her, but Danny Martin used her for everything he did. And losing her blindsided him.'

'You're talking about the Bernard Lau case?'

'Damn right I'm talking about that,' Derek leaned back, crossing his arms. 'They suspended you. You were out. There was no way that you'd get out of that. And then DCI Ford decides that she wants you as her own patsy, but royally screws it up. And then you get a nice new job, all thanks to Alexander Goddamned Monroe.'

'And that's when you did all this,' Declan shook his head. 'I never realised how much you hated me.'

'You haven't even begun to realise how much I hate you,' Derek said. 'I made deals, boy. Deals that were worth it.'

'With Danny Martin?'

'Screw Danny Martin,' Derek sneered. 'He's a jobsworth. I mean the bigger names. The Byrnes. The Delcourts.'

'Yeah, about the Delcourts,' Declan replied. 'I forgot to mention something.'

'What's that?'

'I told the Delcourts how it was you that showed us the body. It quite surprised them, considering that you never spoke to them after you retired. Moses himself had a few thoughts on what he wanted to do with you.'

'Lucky I'm in here then,' Derek smiled. 'Safest place to be.'

Declan nodded slowly, as if agreeing.

'Shame it's not for you, though,' he replied. 'Derek Salmon, you're free to go.'

'What are you saying?' Derek rose from the chair now, confused. Declan shrugged.

'We have enough evidence to show that you were coerced by as yet unknown people to confess to the crime,' he explained, walking to the door and banging on it. 'Knowing this, we can happily allow you to return home, free of all guilt.'

'But you told the *Sisters* about me!' Derek was no longer smiling. 'They'll be waiting!'

'Not my problem,' Declan said. 'I did my part of the bargain. I set you free without stating on the record that you'd told me you'd been pressured by them.'

'But you did tell them!'

'Not my problem.'

'But you can't do this! I haven't seen ...' Derek's face was ashen. 'I haven't confessed to Father Lawson.'

'Yeah, you know him, don't you?' Declan smiled now. 'And it makes sense, what with him knowing Danny Martin. Shame it's not him now.'

'What do you mean?' Derek was wheezing now, visibly scared. Declan shrugged.

'My team, the ones you wanted to destroy? They seem to believe that Father Barry Lawson is actually Stephen Lawson in a dog collar.'

'Stephen Lawson's in prison.' Derek was now visibly sweating.

'Stephen Lawson got out six months back. And, we believe, is currently pretending to be his brother. We have police out looking for him right now, according to the last text I received.'

Declan grinned as the door started unlocking.

'But don't worry,' he explained, tapping the side of his nose. 'You'll still get absolution, I'm sure.'

'There is no absolution from him, you dopey bastard!' Derek exclaimed, now grabbing at Declan. 'You can't send me out there! He'll kill me! I need police protection!'

'You want protection? Give me something I can use,' Declan replied. 'Tell me who gave you the burial site. Tell me who murdered Angela Martin and Gabrielle Chapman.'

Before Derek could reply, the door opened and the police constable who'd brought him in leaned into the room.

'Everything alright?' he asked.

Declan looked to Derek, who nodded slowly.

'Fine,' he said. 'I'll tell you. But not until tomorrow.'

Declan looked to the constable. 'Take Mister Salmon back to his cell and keep him there,' he said. 'I don't want him missing *Bake Off*.'

As Derek passed him, however, he grabbed his one-time student by the arm.

'You were never going to let me free, were you?' he asked. 'You played me as much as I played you.'

'As I said, I learned from the best,' Declan stepped back as the constable took Derek by the arm, leading him out of the Interview Room. 'But I didn't mean you, Derek. I meant my father and Alex Monroe.'

The hurt look that crossed Derek's face as he was led

away was enough for Declan. Now alone in the Interview Room, he thought back to what Derek had said. There was one thing that was going to weigh on Declan's mind for the rest of the night.

He still didn't know who killed Angela Martin and Gabrielle Chapman.

21

DUALITY

ALEXANDER MONROE HADN'T INTENDED TO STAY THE NIGHT IN Birmingham, but here he was, kipping in the Ready Room, half wrapped in a knackered old pink blanket that was fraying at the edges and smelt weirdly of Battenberg cake, while Stripe Mullville slept on the sofa across the room. Doctor Marcos had claimed a custody cell, stating that she always slept well when nicked, and Bullman, the only local involved here, had disappeared for the night, returning to her home and a proper bed.

It was about one in the morning when DI White entered the room, walking quietly over to Monroe and tapping him on the shoulder.

'Sir,' he whispered. 'You've got a visitor.'

Monroe rubbed the sleep out of his eyes and stared blearily at White. 'You're Bullman's man, aren't you?'

White nodded. 'We met briefly when you arrived. I was with the boy when his parents were arrested.'

Monroe looked over to Stripe, now awake and watching the two of them.

'You know this man?' Monroe asked. Stripe nodded.

'He was nice to me,' he said. Monroe nodded back at this, looking back to White.

'So who's visiting me at—' he looked at his watch, '—this bloody stupid time in the morning?'

'One of George Byrne's men,' DI White sat on one of the other chairs now, not bothering to whisper now that everyone was awake. 'We picked him up during a nightclub fight and he asked immediately to speak to you. Arresting officer brought him directly here.'

'Do George Byrne's men often get what they ask for from the police?' Monroe asked, half joking. It was Stripe that answered, his voice devoid of all humour.

'Yeah.'

Monroe looked back to the boy, considering this for a long moment.

'I don't want to leave him alone,' he said to White. 'If Bullman trusts you, and if Alfie here says it's okay, will you wait with him while I speak to this lad? Or can you go wake up Doctor Marcos and bring her here?'

White nodded. 'I can wait,' he said. Monroe shook himself out of the tattered blanket, offering it to the DI.

'Want this? No? Good choice.' He tossed it back on the chair.

Stretching his arms to remove the kinks in his shoulders caused by his cramped sleeping position, Monroe left DI White and Stripe together, walking out into the corridor. A young female constable stood there, patiently waiting for him.

'You another one on Byrne's payroll?' he asked sardonically. The constable stared at him silently for a moment, and Monroe felt the daggers strike from her gaze.

'You ever done something to keep the peace that's a little against the rules?' she asked. Monroe thought for a moment and then nodded.

'I worked in East London, so yeah, I did that.'

'Then get off your high London horse, Guv,' the constable snapped back. 'We're on a knife edge here. Byrne owns half the coppers in Saltley and Aston, and when he dies his son'll likely burn half the city down in triumph. You work with the Devil, doesn't mean that you're *owned* by the Devil.'

She showed Monroe to an Interview Room down the corridor.

'In there. CCTV is turned off, you'll be alone.'

Monroe nodded, walking past the constable. He stopped though, looking to her.

'It starts like that, you know,' he said. 'You think that by working with the cancer you'll beat the cancer, but soon the working with becomes working for. And that's when you can't get out.'

'Did you get out?' the constable asked. 'Because you're sounding like this is a bit familiar to you. *Sir.*'

Monroe thought for a moment. 'I thought I did, but now I'm not so sure,' he said. 'Stay safe out there.'

With a last nod of thanks, he entered the Interview Room.

There was a young man sitting in the room. A familiar young man. Tall with blond hair, he wore a black polo shirt with charcoal jeans over expensive looking tan Chelsea boots.

'I recognise you,' Monroe said, sitting opposite him. 'Come to finish what you couldn't start in the church?'

'Just here to talk,' the man said with an ease that made Monroe feel for a second that *he* was the one being interviewed here. 'I had myself arrested so I could speak quickly to you. My brief will be here soon, and he'll have me out in minutes, so let's get on with it. I'm Harrison Fennel.'

'You say the name as if you expect me to know it,' Monroe replied. Harrison shrugged.

'Wasn't sure,' he said. 'We work for the same boss, after all.'

'Unless you mean Her Majesty the Queen, laddie, then you've mistaken me for someone else.'

Harrison smiled at this, pulling out his phone, something that should have been taken from him when he was processed, and tapping on the screen. A website flashed up; he read from it.

'Employee. Noun. A person who is paid to work for someone else.' He looked back to Monroe.

'The question is, of course, who's been paying you over the years?'

'I don't work for The Twins,' Monroe snapped. 'I don't know what you've been told, but we ended our relationship a long time back.'

Harrison shrugged. 'I ended mine too,' he replied. 'Don't mean that they don't still think I work for them.'

Monroe leaned back in his chair, staring at the man in front of him. 'You work for Macca Byrne. You're close to him.'

'I'm his right-hand man,' Harrison said with a hint of pride. 'Have been since we met in senior school. I was a year above him.'

'But you work for The Twins.'

'It's complicated.'

'So uncomplicate it for me,' Monroe finished. 'Explain to me why you're mixed up in all this, and why the hell I'm talking to you right now.'

Harrison sat silently for a moment, and Monroe couldn't

work out whether the man was sulking, refusing to answer or simply trying to put together what he needed to say.

Eventually he started talking.

'My dad, right? He worked for The Twins, mainly gopher stuff. You know, *gopher* this, *gopher* that …' he chuckled at his own joke. 'But he left with Craig Chapman when Chapman moved up here to work with George Byrne. I'd only just been born around then. Don't remember much of London.'

'Okay,' Monroe leaned forward, painfully aware of the fact that it was early in the morning, and that he'd only had a couple of hours of broken sleep. 'So how does that lead to you working for The Twins?'

'Because my dad never stopped working for them,' Harrison explained. 'While Craig cut all ties, my dad went up with him on Jackie Lucas's orders. To monitor them, to see what they'd do.'

'Spy on them.'

Harrison cocked his head sideways.

'My dad the spy,' he said, his expression brightening. 'Yeah, I can see that. Anyway, unlike James Bond, it turns out the whole move was nothing. Still, my dad still kept tabs on the Byrne gang for the Lucas brothers, doing what they'd paid him to do. And then, when I was old enough, I started in the family business too.'

'You knew Angela Martin?' Monroe asked. Harrison nodded.

'I knew Angela,' he said. 'I loved her.'

'Did she reciprocate that love, though?' Monroe mentally filed away this attachment. Declan had mentioned a photo found in Angela Martin's room of her, Macca and Harrison Fennel.

'Her dad was our liaison,' the boy continued, ignoring the

question. 'We'd drive down to London and meet with him. And sometimes she'd turn up.'

'Did you see The Twins?'

'Never The Twins,' Harrison admitted.

'So, what went wrong?' Monroe asked. 'Because we've got bodies that show that something happened.'

'Angie went off the rails,' Harrison looked down at the table, remembering. 'She was out on the town with Moses Delcourt, as her dad had set that up through some copper he knew. The plan was to unite the London gangs, but we soon learned that no matter what Moses thought, he wasn't gonna rule North London.'

'Why?'

Harrison chuckled. 'Because he had a cock, bruv. The clue's in the word *Sisters*. Christ, he has a sister, Molly, yeah? Twelve years old and into ponies. Wants to be a vet when she grows up, doesn't care about the world her family's in. Even she's more likely to replace her mum than him.'

'So how were you getting around that?'

'Angie. She was gonna get in tight with Mama Delcourt, maybe even become one of the other six Sisters. That way she was in the room with her when things were decided. Having her courted by Moses also gave a legitimacy to him. And, down the line, she could take over and unite that way, with the traditionalists seeing her as the new Matriarch, while the progressives get to follow the son.' He chuckled. 'If they married, she'd be *Mama Delcourt* too. They wouldn't even have to change the nametags.'

'But something stopped this.'

'Yeah. Moses had ambition beyond his mum and London,' Harrison shook his head. 'Started talking to Macca Byrne about their parents. Both were living under shadows, you get? Anyway, Macca gets really into this. I see it all, as I'm in school with him. His dad's a genuine piece of shit and doesn't see what his son brings to the table. So Macca decides that maybe he should go sit at another table and plans to do this with Moses. Within two years they'd convinced themselves that a plot from a TV show was the way forward. Drugs from Birmingham into London via the canals. Meanwhile, I get a call from Danny Martin, saying he wants me to cut the air supply between Angie and the Byrnes. Ensure she's not a part of their world.'

'So how did you get around that?'

Harrison smiled. 'Angie had a backup plan already. Turned up in town calling herself Gabby Chapman. Technically, Angie Martin never turned up. Even when she was arrested, she was under this new identity.'

'So you never met the real Gabrielle Chapman then?'

Harrison shook his head. 'Mate, until the end I didn't even know there *was* a real Gabrielle Chapman,' he explained. 'I mean, my dad knew her dad and all that, but I didn't mingle. And by the time I joined, they were all dead in a fire. Or so I thought. Anyway, I thought Angie had found someone to do her a new identity. And it was golden, too. She had photos, a provisional licence, a passport, everything.'

Monroe nodded. This was a part of the story he understood. At this point Angela Martin would have found out the truth about her parentage.

'I'm guessing she wasn't talking to her father at this point either?' Monroe offered.

'Nah, they'd had a falling out,' Harrison nodded. 'She was effectively AWOL, working with Moses. She was still talking to the priest though, so we assumed that she was keeping people updated.'

'The priest?'

'Lawson. She'd go to confession, but she was really just passing the news and getting orders from London. He was part of the firm too. Even though she wasn't talking to her dad, she was still moving towards a common goal.'

'Which was?'

'War,' Harrison said the word as if it was nothing more than a thought, ignoring the huge implication such a term could give. 'We realised early on that Macca and Moses wouldn't work well. Macca was a pipe smoking crackhead and got Angie into smoking it, doing a little meth, screwing her up. I knew I could get her off it if I got her out of Birmingham, but Moses found out, started kicking off.'

'How did he find out?' Monroe asked.

Harrison laughed.

'You know, I think the crazy bitch actually told him herself,' he said. 'One of those *he's a better shag than you* moments. Right threw him off his game. And that's when the problems started. That's also when I saw Danny Martin's actual plan.'

'Which was?'

'To take over everything.' Harrison rested his arms on the back of the chair as he relaxed. 'He didn't want Angie anywhere near him by then, but he was happy to use her to set Macca and Moses against each other and then, once they killed themselves and their turfs were decimated, to walk in, take it over and somehow throw the whole shit show on Mama Delcourt, get her removed and get Angie to take over the Seven Sisters before he took it from her. Three turfs become one.'

'But it didn't happen,' Monroe nodded. 'Because Angela was on drugs?'

'I dunno,' Harrison admitted. 'It was around then I stopped getting messages from London. Even the priest wasn't in the loop anymore.'

Monroe rubbed at his eyes, the tiredness returning.

'God save me from complicated stories,' he whispered. 'And bloody Father Lawson.'

Harrison actually laughed at this. A banging on the door interrupted them, and Monroe saw the constable enter once more.

'Hurry it up,' she said. 'His brief's arrived.'

The door shutting again, Harrison leaned across the desk.

'Look,' he started. 'I wanted to speak to you because we got shared history. And if you accuse me of anything, I can ensure your career is dead instantly, yeah?'

'Go on,' Monroe replied, resisting the urge to strangle the little scroat.

Harrison nodded.

'Angie got her orders from Lawson during confession in his Birmingham church, but at some point her dad had gone into business for himself. She was way out of control too, a liability. She could have given any of us up at any point. It was stressful.'

'And then?'

'And then she disappears. Danny Martin drives up, I thought it was to find her, but he picks me up in the middle of the night and drives me to a Mission House in Alum Rock, where like, nuns lived, yeah? In there was a body. It was Angie, but like a fake one. She was dead. An overdose, I think.'

'Danny Martin took you to see his daughter?'

'I know, it sounds crazy,' Harrison replied. 'But that's how it was. Danny explained that this was Gabby Chapman, and he needed her buried, forgotten about. Didn't say what happened. Said that if I didn't, he'd tell both of the Byrnes about everything I'd done. I had no choice. We took it to the Lickeys.'

'So you and Danny Martin were who the witness saw in the woods?'

'Yeah,' Harrison nodded. 'I thought I saw someone, but then nothing was said for another year. I thought I'd got away with it.'

He looked to the floor, as if remembering the moment.

'There was something that struck me as weird that night though,' Harrison whispered, as if scared that even mentioning this would incriminate him, 'When I went to take the body away I saw these bruises on the neck. Like someone had strangled her with a cord. But Danny was convinced it was a drug overdose, even showing me the needle marks.'

The door opened and a suited man, round rimmed glasses framing his narrow face, stood there.

'You can stop your questioning,' he said. 'My client is free to go.'

Harrison rose, his mannerisms morphing immediately into those of an arrogant, mocking man.

'Toldja you had nothing,' he said to Monroe, nodding to the solicitor in the doorway. 'Toldja I'd be out.'

And punctuating his interview with a back kick that knocked the chair over, Harrison Fennel left the Interview Room, leaving DCI Monroe very much awake ...

... and incredibly confused.

IN TOTTENHAM NORTH, THE DESK SERGEANT LOOKED UP AT the monitor screen as the doorbell buzzed. On it, a man dressed in a long black overcoat waved at the camera. Reluctantly, the Desk Sergeant buzzed the outsider in, checking the time. Two in the morning. Nobody good ever arrived at a police station at two in the morning.

Shaking the rain off his coat, the man walked up to the counter with a smile, and the Desk Sergeant noted for the first time that the man was a priest, the coat's lapel now exposing his dog collar.

'Bit late for house calls?' he said, sitting up. The priest smiled.

'Never too late for God, my son,' he said cheerfully. 'Although I'm here on serious business. You have a man in custody. Derek Salmon?'

'What about him?'

The priest pulled a Bible out of his coat. 'He's very ill,' he explained. 'They called me because his family is worried he'll go to Hell without being shriven.'

'Sorry, Father, I'm an atheist. What does that mean exactly?'

'Confession, my son. To be absolved of all sins in God's eyes.'

'And you need to do this at two in the morning?'

'I do this when I'm asked,' the priest explained. 'He called his family tonight and begged them to organise it. It's a simple act, but one that he obviously requires. And when you're as ill as he is, the Last Rites don't seem so very far away.'

The Desk Sergeant considered this for a moment and then nodded.

'Okay, I'll let you in and get someone to take you to his

cell,' he said, already buzzing the door to the inner area open. 'Just wait in the corridor.'

The priest made the sign of the cross.

'Thank you. And I hope you find God yourself one day.'

'Yeah, good luck with that one, Father.'

And with that, Father Lawson smiled at the Desk Sergeant, gave a small, respectful nod and then entered Tottenham North Station, mentally and physically ready to give Derek Salmon his Last Rites.

Because you always needed them right before you died.

22

REVELATIONS 2

I<small>T WAS EARLY IN THE MORNING BY THE TIME THE POLICE</small> reached Our Lady of the Sea Church in Deptford. Even though the order to arrest Father Lawson had been given hours earlier, it was deemed a minor arrest, more of a pick-up than a manhunt. And as such the graveyard shift, finding the church locked up for the night had simply waited until the next shift arrived before passing it to them.

Father Lawson still hadn't returned, and the consensus was that he'd somehow learned that he was being looked for when he had been at Tottenham North. But then Tottenham North was having their own issues that morning, and everything was a little muddled. There was another priest who worked at Our Lady of the Sea, but nobody had found a way to contact him until six am, and it was a tired and cranky Father Callie who opened the door for the police to enter.

'I told you, we don't live in the bloody place,' he snapped as the police; two police constables, a Detective Sergeant Anderson and three CSI officers entered. 'You need to try his lodgings.'

'We've already done that,' DS Anderson explained. 'We're hoping that there's something here that could help us find him. Or maybe he's hiding in here?'

The police made their way through the church, checking underneath the pews and examining the sacristy – the small room to the side of the altar where the priests kept their vestments – but there was nothing to be found. In fact, it was only after a good hour of searching that PC Masters, fresh out of Hendon and looking for a way to get herself noticed found herself once more wandering into the crypt under the church. They had looked it over earlier, but only a cursory glance with a torch; there were no hiding areas under there. But one part of the crypt had nagged at her, made her walk back down to examine it, her torch moving across the stone memorials towards the back of the crypt, and the Marlowe mausoleum.

There were air fresheners hanging off it, as if in tribute, or as little decorations.

'Sarge?' she cried out. 'Sarge!'

After a couple of moments, Anderson appeared.

'We've looked down here,' he said.

'I know,' PC Masters replied, pointing to where her torch shone. 'But there's something off about this.' She was walking along the crypt now, with Anderson reluctantly following her.

'Is it the man we're looking for?' he asked mockingly. 'No, unless he's hiding behind it.'

'Well, what do you think it is?' Masters almost snapped, before adding, 'Sarge?'

Anderson walked up to the stone, sniffing. The air was filled with a fresh mint smell, the four air fresheners doing their job well, but there was something else.

Something sickly.

'Get a crowbar,' he ordered suddenly. 'We need to open this.'

Masters left quickly and a few minutes later returned with a crowbar and the other officers, all curious to see what the DS had found. Using the crowbar, digging it into the side of the stone, Anderson and one of the forensic officers levered the stone away, allowing it to crash to the floor. Behind it was an old, mahogany coffin, and the sweet, sickly smell was even stronger, like roast meat that had been forgotten about for months at the back of a fridge.

Anderson looked at the forensics officer, who nodded.

'There's a body in there,' he said. 'And not one that's been embalmed. You can smell it.'

'How do we get it out?' Anderson reached for one of the coffin handles with one hand, holding his tie over his nose with the other, but the forensics officer stopped him.

'No way, man,' he shook his head. 'Let the big guys come in and sort it. This is above ground, yeah? If this has been in the coffin for months, then it'll be like a pressure cooker. You pop the lid, and it'll explode.'

Anderson looked down at his suit. He liked this suit.

'Clear the crypt,' he commanded. 'And get someone in who can sort this.' He turned to Masters, who looked like she was trying not to throw up.

'You okay?' he asked.

She nodded, but her face showed that this was a lie.

Anderson couldn't help himself. He took a long, deep breath, smiling as he looked at her.

'Mmm, just like chicken nuggets,' he said, laughing as PC Masters, grabbing a hand to her mouth ran from the crypt.

The forensic officer stared at him, shaking his head.

'You're such a prick, Ken,' he said.

IT WAS SEVEN AM BEFORE THE FULL CSI TEAM ARRIVED, AND they covered the crypt with tarpaulin before they carefully removed the coffin. By this point they had removed DS Anderson and the others out into the nave of the church, the forensic officers helping the CSI team while the PCs stopped the curious public entering.

Anderson had apologised to Masters by this point; he wasn't a bad man, just a stupid, thoughtless one he'd explained. Masters had politely thanked him, but he knew that this was something that wouldn't be forgotten, and he'd probably get shit for it down the line.

One of the forensic officers emerged from the crypt, pulling off their hood and mask. Rising from the pew he was currently sitting on, Anderson walked over.

'Well?' he asked. The officer nodded.

'There's a second body in there,' he said. 'Dumped in on top. We'll have to check, but it looks like it's been in there about six months or so. It's a middle-aged man and he's in what looks like clerical clothes.'

'Looks like?'

The forensic officer nodded. 'The clothes get exposed to all the chemicals that the corpse produces, and they decompose too. Luckily the stiff white collar they all wear is a little more recognisable.'

'Do we know who he is?' Anderson was already pulling out his phone. The forensics officer nodded.

'Yeah, he had a wallet in his pocket,' he said. 'Father Barry Lawson.'

'Can you give me anything else?' Anderson asked. The officer thought for a minute.

'We're doing an on-site examination and it's not great conditions,' he replied. 'But there is one thing. It looks like the body was circumcised.'

'Do Catholics get circumcised?'

'Not usually, no,' the officer looked back to the crypt as Anderson lowered the phone.

'That's got to be a mistake,' he said.

'Possible, maybe, I don't know what to say,' the officer shrugged. 'We'll have more later, when we give it a full examination.'

As the forensics officer walked back to the crypt, pulling the hood of his PPE suit back on, Anderson stared at the phone.

How the hell was he going to explain this?

MONROE SLEPT LITTLE AFTER HIS MIDNIGHT VISITATION, AND BY eight the following morning he was already pacing as Doctor Marcos entered the Ready Room where he'd made his base.

'I need to get out there,' he complained. 'There are too many things pissing me off right now.'

'Like what?' Doctor Marcos sat on a chair, resting her feet on the coffee table. 'I heard you had a visitor.'

'One of Macca's boys,' Monroe nodded. 'Told me he worked for Danny Martin. But even though he explained a few things, I can't help but feel that he left me with more questions than answers.' He started counting off on his fingers.

'First, he confirmed what Anjli and Billy found out last

night: that Stephen and Barry Lawson were sharing the same identity themselves, although he didn't seem to know as much as Sister Margaret did. And there's a niggling, a worry in the back of my mind that says we're missing something big, that there's still a part of the puzzle involving Father Lawson that we haven't considered.'

'I might have something on that,' Doctor Marcos replied.

'You haven't let me get to two,' Monroe muttered.

'This is more important than two.' Noting that Stripe was still sleeping, Doctor Marcos led Monroe out into the corridor.

'Had one of my friends contact me ten minutes ago,' she said. 'Seems they found Barry Lawson.'

'They arrested him?'

'No,' Doctor Marcos shook her head. 'They found his body. Six months old, they reckon, wedged into a coffin under the Deptford Church that he was the priest for.'

'That matches with what we have,' Monroe thought to himself. 'We know from the fingerprints that Anjli and Billy spoke to Stephen Lawson.'

'Yeah, but they're got some discrepancies with the body, so I'm waiting for an update.'

'Like what?'

'Well, the body was apparently circumcised. Catholics rarely go in for that sort of thing.'

'Maybe it was done in Africa?'

'If it was, then we have a new problem,' Doctor Marcos lowered her voice. 'The mad old nun that Anjli spoke to yesterday said that Stephen was the one sorting the drugs in Africa for Danny Martin.'

'You think that if it is circumcised, it's Stephen's body?'

'It's a possibility. I mean, come on Alex, none of this

bloody case has been by the book.' Doctor Marcos folded her arms. 'She said that Barry told Stephen and Danny that he was done with them, that there would be no more African drugs. Yet a year later, he's back on track with Danny.'

'Because we arrest Stephen for murder,' Monroe nodded. 'The fingerprints matched him to the scene.'

'I'm forensics,' Doctor Marcos shrugged. 'I know I can fake fingerprints. All you need is—'

'An inside man,' Monroe spat in sudden fury. 'Bloody Derek Salmon. He was the arresting officer. Stephen makes a very public show, and then Barry gets arrested for it. Derek swaps the prints on the gun for Barry's, and "Stephen" takes the fall, claiming he's been set up.'

'We already know that Barry and Stephen shared the role,' Doctor Marcos added. 'Stephen just carried on.'

'And then six months ago Barry Lawson, the real Barry Lawson, is released early.' Monroe was scratching at his beard now as the lines of enquiry in his head started picking up speed. 'He fakes a suicide, kills his brother and regains his identity.'

'So, then what?' Doctor Marcos asked. 'If it was you? If you gained your life back, only to see that your children, taken from you, had been murdered a couple of months before you got out?'

Monroe nodded. 'I'd want to gain vengeance on anyone who hurt them,' he said. 'And I'd use whoever loved them to help me.' He looked back to Doctor Marcos.

'Macca Byrne was meeting with Lawson after this,' he said. 'The priest told us that last night. What were they talking about? I think there's more going on here than we thought. We need to call Declan and the others—'

'No,' Doctor Marcos continued. 'That might not be a good idea right now.'

'Why?' Monroe asked, suddenly concerned at this change of attitude.

'Because Lawson's body wasn't the only thing I was told about today,' Doctor Marcos said. 'Derek Salmon died last night, and before he passed, he raised an official complaint about Declan.'

'Salmon's dead?' This genuinely surprised Monroe. 'They can't pin that on Declan! The man was dying!'

'They can when they found traces of Declan's DNA under Derek's fingernail,' Doctor Marcos finished. 'And Declan never recorded their conversation.'

'Christ!' Monroe slammed his fist against the wall in frustration. 'Bloody fool! We need to call him.'

He paused.

'No,' he said. 'Then they'll say we're colluding with him.'

'Don't worry,' Doctor Marcos smiled. 'I've got it in hand. Anyway, I have some autopsy news, too.'

'Cause of death?' Monroe remembered Harrison's testimony the previous night. 'Was it strangulation?'

'No, although there were marks on the neck. Surprisingly, it was a drug overdose,' she confirmed.

'Why surprisingly?' Monroe nodded a *hello* to DI White as he walked past, the Birmingham detective looking suspiciously at the two officers whispering in a corridor.

'Because the autopsy showed that Gabrielle Chapman had a sizeable brain injury,' Doctor Marcos said. 'Old wound. Maybe from when her adopted parents died. She wouldn't have been responsive. She sure as hell wouldn't have been partying around.'

'Well, that explains why we never heard of her between

the fire and Angela's arrival,' Monroe considered. 'But if she couldn't take care of herself, who looked after her?'

Turning back to the Ready Room, he stopped completely still.

'He picks me up in the middle of the night and drives me to a Mission House in Alum Rock, where like, nuns lived, yeah? In there was a body. It was Angie, but like a fake one. She was dead. An overdose, I think.'

'The bloody nuns,' he whispered, remembering Harrison's words once more. 'We need to go to Alum Rock.'

'What about the boy?' Doctor Marcos asked. 'I'm in the morgue. You can't leave him in there.'

'I'll take him with us.' Monroe looked up to see DI White returning from wherever he'd been to. 'You busy, lad?'

'Lad?' DI White paused with a smile. 'Not been called that for a while. What do you need, sir?'

Monroe smiled.

'I need a chauffeur to a nunnery,' he said.

23

MEETINGS

Billy rarely started his day with breakfast meetings, but the text he'd received on the way to work that morning had intrigued him enough to consider it.

8C 8.30am returning a favour RH

Billy knew very well what the cryptic message meant, and he knew who was returning the favour here, but it was sent so cryptically, as if deliberately ensuring that the sender couldn't be recognised concerned him. However, it wasn't far from Temple Inn, so he diverted his morning commute and headed instead towards Bank.

Turning into Change Alley, opposite the historic Royal Exchange, he stopped at a black door, one of many doors along the alley, pressing the buzzer. The door clicked open, unlocked from someone deep inside the building, and Billy quickly entered.

The Eight Club was an exclusive members' club in the

city's heart and was situated under the building that Billy had entered, walking down the five wrought-iron staircases to the reception. He wasn't a member of the club, but he'd been to enough events here to know where he was going. Arriving at the reception desk at the bottom of the staircase he gave his name to the receptionist and was waved through into an underground bar area, where sofas and tables shared the space with expensive looking pool tables.

Rufus Harrington was playing pool at the end table. He wore jeans, and a short-sleeved black shirt, his tan brogues expensive. He still wore his brown hair shaved at the sides and slicked back, the amount of gel in it making it look like a Lego hair piece, and he had a large cygnet ring on his left middle finger, one with a masonic emblem that he was currently resting the pool cue on as he took his shot.

'William!' he exclaimed after he took it, walking over and slapping Billy on the arm. 'Glad you could make it. Drink?'

'It's eight in the morning.'

'So a spirit rather than a pint, then?'

Billy took a lemonade instead and walked with Rufus over to his table, against a far wall of the underground room.

'I wanted to thank you properly,' Rufus said as he sat at the table. 'Your little titbit about Devington Industries tanking saved me a small fortune. I sold high, bought back in low and almost doubled my portfolio. I really owe you there.'

Billy didn't reply; he sat silently, sipping at his drink. The last time he'd seen Rufus, he'd given him the insider knowledge that Devington Industries was about to have a bad news day following the rooftop drama and subsequent suicide of Susan Devington, right before she was going to be charged with multiple murders. He had passed this on with the implicit suggestion that Rufus would reconnect Billy with his family, but since then he had heard nothing from the City banker.

'Is this to do with my family?' he asked. Rufus shook his head.

'Sorry dude, still working on that. But I wanted to return the favour. You told me to sell my shares, to get out before the shit storm started, remember?'

'I don't think I used those words exactly,' Billy muttered. Rufus shrugged.

'Either way, I'm telling you the same. But it's not shares, it's your job. The people you work with. Get out, as there's a shit storm coming for you.'

'What do you mean?' Billy leaned forward, placing his glass down.

'I mean that there's someone seriously gunning for you all right now, in particular some bloke named Walsh. And they won't stop until all of you are mashed up under their boot.'

Billy nodded slowly at this. 'Do you have a name?'

'Yeah, but it's not one I want to repeat, so you get this once.' Rufus looked around the club, checking they were alone. 'Charlie Baker.'

Billy almost laughed. 'Christ, Rufus. I thought you were telling me about a credible threat,' he said. 'Charles Baker is toothless since he dropped out of the Leadership contest.'

'Don't be so sure,' Rufus replied, stone cold serious. 'His wife died a week or two back. Hanged herself, probably because of the shame of his earlier infidelities coming out. He might have shit the bed politically, but now he's a widower, and he's got the sympathy vote. Everything he lost, he regains in a public and transparent revaluation of his life, during a post-grieving period of course.'

He lowered his voice even more.

'Charles Baker will be the next Prime Minister. They even delayed the Leadership battle for a month or two just to fix his PR. He's part of some high up Star Chamber thing, so I'm told, by the people who know.' He tapped his cygnet ring. 'Babies out-of-wedlock mean nothing these days, especially when it was while he played for the other team. And he was effectively a victim in the Victoria Davies case, not a suspect. But your team made him look bad, made a fool of him. He'll want to close this chapter of his book before he moves on, and that includes exterminating anything that can cause him a problem.'

Rufus rose from the sofa, looking down at Billy.

'Get out, while you can. This isn't your fight. And if you try, you'll lose. Try their breakfast menu. On me.'

With that, Rufus left Billy alone at the table. Billy leaned back, considering the news. Charles Baker had been a suspect in the Devington case, and Declan had eventually saved his life on the top of Devington House in a tense confrontation that ended with the death of Susan Devington. But in the process, rumours of infidelity, insider trading and of Baker being connected to parties involved with several murders had leaked out. His political career had been cut short; Billy had believed.

But what if it hadn't? Baker had stepped down as Secretary of State for the Home Department, but he still consulted with his replacement. Technically, he had the Security Service and the National Security Council under his spell, not to mention whatever this Star Chamber was that Rufus had been so secretive about.

Finishing the drink Billy looked across to the pool tables, nodded a thanks to Rufus Harrington and left the Eight Club.

Things were about to get terribly bad.

———

THE GRAVELLY HILL INTERCHANGE IN BIRMINGHAM HAD BEEN known under a different name for fifty years; to many locals it was Spaghetti Junction, a five-level interchange where the M6 motorway met the A38 Aston Expressway and the A5127, while spanning two railway lines, three canals and two rivers. It was an incredibly busy location, but the surrounding areas were less so. While cars sped above them, people could happily, and more importantly, quietly stroll down the Birmingham and Warwick Junction Canal, meeting the River Rea before following the canal north, past Star City and eventually joining with the River Tame, following the route of the M6 above it, as you walked eastwards, meeting up with the Rea once more just north of the A47, Brompton and Washwood Heath.

It was a good place for quiet conversations; the cars above could cause problems with recorders, while the multiple routes out of the area gave you the opportunity to escape if things went wrong, or if the police had gained wind of your activities. And it was here, at the junctions of the rivers Tame and Rea, that Macca Byrne met with Harrison Fennel.

Macca was as ever in his black clothes, blowing into his gloved hands while Harrison wore a pale-blue tracksuit with blue trainers. He was nervous as he arrived; the text from Macca had been brief and commanding.

'Problems?' he asked as he approached from the Rea side of the junction, looking around, checking to see if they were being watched. It had been a long time since Macca had been alone with Harrison. It was refreshing yet a little concerning to see him alone now.

'I heard they arrested you,' Macca said, a little louder than Harrison had expected, as if playing to a crowd. Looking around but seeing no one, Harrison shrugged.

'Deliberately,' he replied. 'I thought I might get into the station and get word to Stripe, get him to turn for us.'

Macca nodded. 'Good plan. Did it work?'

'Nah, man. That old fed we saw in the church had him tight.'

'I heard that you were tight with that old fed too,' Macca watched Harrison. 'Something you want to tell me?'

'Sure,' Harrison said, forcing himself to stay calm. 'The old bastard recognised me from the church, took me into an interview room. Wanted to know about Gabby's death, talked about Angela Martin.' He watched Macca's face as he said the name, but nothing was given away. 'Anyway, I said nothing. The questions he asked were weird, so I just waited for my brief to arrive.'

'You did the right thing,' Macca smiled for the first time. 'Man, it's so hard right now, you see? I have to be careful that Moses don't get no hold in Birmingham.'

'I got you,' Harrison said, and was surprised to realise that he actually meant it. 'I've known you since we were kids, bro. I'd take a bullet for you.'

'There's no need to go that far,' Macca replied, reaching into his pocket. 'But I do need you to do something for me.'

Harrison tensed, but relaxed when Macca pulled out a small envelope.

'When the time's right, I need you to pass this message,' he said.

'What is it?'

Macca smiled. 'It's a call to war,' he smiled. 'Put it some-where safe and read it later, yeah?'

Harrison unzipped his tracksuit top, sliding it into an inside pocket. Macca looked out across the water.

'I mean, you'll need to read it when you copy it out and send it to Danny Martin, won't you?'

Harrison froze, his expression visibly the stark realisation that Macca Byrne knew. The riverside was silent for a moment, with neither man talking, but then there was a movement from the side, and Harrison turned to see Wesley O'Brien emerge from the bushes at the back of the bank, fury on his face. He wore the same camel jacket and black jeans over trainers he'd worn the last time that Harrison had seen him, at the Jam House, but, as he walked up to Macca, Harrison realised that this time Wesley wasn't there for George Byrne's son.

He was here for *Harrison*.

'Looks like you were right, kid,' Wesley said. 'Look at him. He's already shitting himself.'

'You told your father?' Harrison looked to Macca. 'You didn't even speak to me about this?'

Macca shrugged, looking to Wesley standing beside him. 'I told Wesley, not Dad,' he said. 'I wanted a witness to the message who my dad would believe.'

Harrison pulled out the envelope.

'This message?' he asked. Wesley nodded.

'Turncoat bastard,' he hissed. 'Always knew there was something off with you.'

Harrison shook his head, backing away, but stopped as he realised that he was now at the edge of the bank. 'I don't work for Danny Martin no more,' he said.

'Yeah, but you did, right?' Wesley continued while Macca stood silently. 'Like your dad did?'

Harrison shook his head. 'He made me do it. And it was only small things, bruv. I swear.'

'Like burying Gabby?' Macca nodded slowly. 'Yeah, I know it was you, H. That's why you got yourself arrested, to tell Stripe to keep his mouth shut. I should have guessed, really. Every time he saw you around, he damn near shit his pants.'

Harrison looked across the river now, as if realising why they were at such a secluded place. This wasn't a meeting; this was an execution.

'It's not what you think,' he said. 'That wasn't your Gabby. Danny got me to do it.'

'We know,' Wesley spat at the floor in front of Harrison. 'I asked about. I know you were with him that night.'

Harrison went to reply, to deny everything, but then a sudden calmness came over him. An acceptance of what was about to happen. The cars seemed to stop. The birds stopped chirping.

'This message you want me to pass,' he said, his voice relaxed and assured. 'I'm it, aren't I?'

'Yeah.' Macca turned to face Harrison, and for the first time in the meeting Harrison saw the knife in Macca's hand. A hunting knife.

The same knife that they'd made Dave Ewan hold a few days earlier before they'd beaten the living shit out of him.

A knife with Dave Ewan's fingerprints on.

'The message,' Harrison said. 'The one in my pocket. When they find it, they'll see it's from the Delcourts to your dad, isn't it?'

Macca smiled sadly. 'Yeah,' he said. Wesley was fidgeting now.

'Give me the blade, son,' he said. 'I've wanted to gut this little—' Wesley didn't finish as Macca Byrne spun to the side, ramming the hunting knife deep into Wesley's chest.

'Didn't see this coming, did you?' he hissed as he twisted the blade. 'My dad ain't around to bail you out this time, you piece of shit.'

But Wesley couldn't reply; his eyes were already glassy and dead as he slumped against Macca, who gently helped the body to the bank of the river. Looking around to confirm that there were no witnesses, Macca quickly removed the blade from Wesley's chest and placed it into the hunting sheath that it came with, tossing it into the undergrowth that Wesley had emerged from earlier, the path he'd made both entering and exiting it plainly visible for all to see.

Harrison meanwhile had removed the envelope carefully, wiping down the edges to remove any fingerprints he may have placed on it, stuffing it into the inside pocket of Wesley O'Brien's camel coat.

'Man, you scared the shit out of me,' he said. 'I genuinely thought you were grassing me out.'

'I had to think fast,' Macca explained as, with a vicious kick to the side of the body, he flipped Wesley O'Brien's body over the edge of the bank and into the river. The body would float away and be found, while the blood on the bank would give the forensics a field day. And then they'd find the knife with Dave Ewan's fingerprints still on the sheath, and the note inside Wesley's tracksuit. 'He wasn't lying when he said people had told him about your chat with the fed. I was just lucky he came to me first. Turned up literally a minute or two before you did, I had to work with what I had.'

'So, what now?' Harrison asked, but Macca was already on his phone, waiting for it to connect.

'The grown-ups are taking an interest now, so it's time we move everything ahead,' he said, turning the phone onto speaker mode as it connected. 'It's me, bruv. We need to bring it forward. We've just left a message in a river, when you hear about it, you know what to do.'

'Do we have a location yet?' the voice of Moses Delcourt echoed out of the speaker.

'Lawson's sorting that out now,' Harrison leaned in to speak. 'I'll get Danny, and what we just did will bring Macca's dad.'

'You think George Byrne will do this?' Moses seemed amused at the idea. Macca glanced across the river, watching the dead body floating down it.

'We just sent him a message he can't ignore,' he said. 'He'll be there.'

'Then I'll get Mum to turn up,' Moses agreed. 'Man, it'll be good to end this.'

Harrison nodded, even though Moses couldn't see him.

'All I care about is finding out who really killed Angie,' he said. 'And then killing them.'

With that, Macca ended the call, looking to Harrison.

'You ready for today?' he asked. Harrison nodded.

'Yeah,' he said. 'Today all debts get paid.'

Macca looked back to the body, now floating down the river. 'Thanks for your service, bro,' he said as he joined Harrison in walking westwards down the Rea, heading back towards Star City and Saltley.

The body would be found soon, and the note would leak back to George Byrne.

That note would start a war that only one man could stop. But before that, they had to ensure that nobody could stop this, and that meant silencing Stripe Mullville and the fed he was hanging around with until the job was done.

It was going to be a busy day.

———

24

JIGSAW PIECES

DECLAN DIDN'T HEAR ABOUT DEREK SALMON'S PASSING UNTIL he arrived at the office that following morning, and it was DCI Farrow, standing nervously beside the entrance to the building that informed him.

'You're a bloody lucky man,' he said as they walked up to the upper level. 'You're useless with administration, so your records haven't updated your change of address.'

'Why's that lucky?' Declan asked.

'Because the police raided your apartment in Tottenham this morning,' Farrow explained. 'They want you in the Interview Room right now, talking about last night.'

'What about last night?' Declan was already having a sinking feeling about this conversation. 'Is this the Delcourts?'

'This isn't the bloody Delcourts,' Farrow snapped. 'Derek died, Declan. He made a complaint, saying you attacked him, claimed he scratched you in defence. They found skin under his fingernails. Will it be yours?'

Declan nodded, still confused. 'He scratched me. It was
...'

He sighed.

'It was when I rammed him against a wall.'

'Jesus, Declan. You're better than that.'

'He was fine when I left him!' Declan exclaimed, looking
back to the office entrance as footsteps could be heard up the
stairs. Instead of a police unit hunting him, though, it was
Billy and Anjli. 'He was going to speak to me again today!'

'What's happened?' Anjli asked, seeing Farrow.

'Look,' Farrow checked his watch. 'I'm here as a favour,
but you need to disappear. Go hide yourself somewhere far
away, and I'll throw some red tape around to delay your next
inevitable suspension or arrest. But you need to sort this,
Declan. You need to prove you didn't speed up the death of a
dying man before his Last Rites.'

'Last Rites?'

Farrow nodded. 'Last person to talk with him was a priest
who came on his family's request.'

'What priest?'

'What's this got to do with anything?'

Declan shook his head 'Guv, there's nobody in his family
who would have done that,' he said. 'If a priest turned up, it
was on his own volition. Did they get the name?'

Farrow tried to remember. 'Actually yes,' he said. 'Father
Barry Lawson.'

Anjli stepped between Declan and Farrow, diverting both
gazes. 'Keep the body there, sir,' she commanded. 'You hear
me? Don't let anyone touch it.'

Farrow looked to Declan in surprise at being spoken to
this way. 'Do all of you act like—'

'She's right, sir,' Declan replied. 'Barry Lawson isn't Barry

Lawson.' He thought back to the conversation he'd had with Derek the night before.

'There is no absolution from him, you dopey bastard! You can't send me out there! He'll kill me! I need police protection!'

'Derek knew this,' he said. 'H as good as told me that if Lawson got hold of him, he was dead.'

'Actually, we think he might be Barry Lawson,' Anjli continued. 'That is, he *was* Barry, but was arrested and sentenced as Stephen. Doctor Marcos was sent some forensics on a body found that led her to believe this.'

'What sort of forensics?' Farrow asked. Anjli smiled.

'*Willy* forensics, sir. Stephen Lawson was circumcised. As was the six-month-old body they found.'

Farrow shook his head. 'I don't want to know,' he said. 'I shouldn't even be here.'

Billy was at his desk now, reading more from his monitor screen.

'According to the arrest report, Stephen Lawson walked into a café, and *Godfather*'ed some drug dealer in Stoke Newington. Shot him twice in the head. Looked around the café, shouted *nobody effs with Stephen Lawson*, then dropped the gun and ran.'

'So basically everything someone does if they want to be caught,' Anjli shook her head. 'I'm guessing it didn't take long to find him?'

'Less than a day,' Billy carried on reading. 'They picked him up in Poplar. Fingerprints matched the gun. He didn't have an alibi, claimed he'd been sparked out all day, and that his drink must have been spiked ...' Billy looked up, surprised.

'This matches what Doctor Marcos sent us today, that Barry may have been framed. Stephen Lawson claimed all the way through the trial that he wasn't Stephen but was *Barry* Lawson. And that Stephen had set him up with the arresting officer.'

Declan sighed. 'Let me guess. Derek Salmon.'

'Give the lady a prize,' Billy said. 'I mean, I know you're not a lady, but it's how the saying goes.'

'It would explain why he killed Derek Salmon, hypothetically,' Declan added. 'He'd blame him for setting him up, giving him a life in prison. Likewise, his brother.'

'And that means he'll be looking for Danny Martin next,' Anjli nodded. 'I'll go find him, see if he's not dead yet too.'

Declan looked to DCI Farrow. 'Guv, we'll need any CCTV you have of Father Lawson coming and going last night. And we'll need someone to examine Derek's body while Doctor Marcos is in Birmingham.'

'I know a solid SOCO,' Anjli said. 'Rajesh Khanna. Did some work at Mile End.'

Declan nodded. 'I met him on the Bernard Lau case,' he said. 'Knew his stuff, I thought.'

'Make a call, bring him in,' Farrow ordered. 'And Declan, get out of here. Don't use the pool car, as they have trackers.'

'Thank you, sir,' Declan said, genuinely grateful. Farrow shook his head.

'I just didn't want to be the guy who suspended you twice,' he said. Billy and Angela moved now, but Declan spoke, stopping them.

'I'm sorry,' he said. 'All of this, it's on me. Derek did it because he had an issue with my dad. And he wanted to make me look bad, to destroy my career. And in turn, he's affecting all of you. So I just wanted to apologise. I know we can fix this.'

'It's not on you,' Anjli replied. 'This was going to happen

no matter what. We just need to work out what the powder keg is going to be that kicks everything off.'

'Let's hope we do that before all the shit falls on us then,' Billy said. 'Need a lift to Euston?'

But Declan was already out of the door.

'Well,' Farrow said. 'Who else wishes they hadn't got up today?'

MONROE HADN'T HEARD ABOUT DECLAN'S INEVITABLE suspension; instead, he'd made his way, with Stripe reluctantly following along for the ride to the Alum Rock Nunnery, hoping to find that last clue about Gabrielle Chapman. DI White had agreed to act as chauffeur; partly because he knew where the Nunnery was, but more because of the embarrassment that the unit had after the PCSO Holland incident.

'Here,' he said, passing Monroe a coffee as the DCI climbed into the passenger seat. 'I got you a coffee. The stuff we have in there is shite.'

Monroe gratefully accepted the hot drink, sipping at it as they made their way through Birmingham. 'How long you worked with Bullman?' he asked. White shrugged.

'Few months,' he replied. 'She's a maternity cover, believe it or not. Came in while DCI Cao had her daughter. You got kids?'

'No,' Monroe said, looking out of the window, letting the coffee warm him. 'Never seemed to find the time for it.'

White glanced at Stripe in the back seat through the rear-view mirror. 'Well, you seem to have a way with them,' he said. Stripe however was looking through the window too, a concerned look on his face.

'This ain't the way to Alum Rock!' he exclaimed. 'We're too far north.'

'I'm avoiding Saltley,' White explained. 'You're too famous in that area right now. We're heading south through Washwood Heath.'

Monroe heard the fear in Stripe's tone and looked at White from the corner of his eye. There was something wrong; DI White was nervous as he drove.

'You want to tell me what's the matter, lad?' he asked.

White ignored him.

Monroe went to pull his phone out but stopped. His hand wasn't working. Slowly, he turned his head to White.

'What ... did you ... do ...' he whispered.

'I'm sorry,' White said, still avoiding Monroe's gaze. 'I had no choice.'

Unable to move now, Monroe looked at the coffee cup in his hand as his grip relaxed, and the now-empty cup fell to the floor. 'You son of a ...'

Alexander Monroe slumped in his seat, the seat belt the only thing keeping him upright.

'What are you doing!' Stripe moved forwards, moving between the seats to examine Monroe. 'Are you okay—'

He didn't finish the line, because DI White brought his left arm back hard, elbowing Stripe in the face, sending him flying back into the back seat, blood streaming from his nose.

'Sit down and shut up,' White said as he turned off the A4040, moving into a small industrial area. Driving for another hundred yards, he pulled to the side, turning off the engine. Quickly, and without speaking, he pulled out his handcuffs, cuffing the unconscious Monroe's hands behind his back[SP1] . He looked to Stripe, now staring terrified out of the window.

'You stay quiet, and nothing bad'll happen, yeah?' White said. But Stripe knew that this was a lie as he could see the two figures of Harrison Fennel and Macca Byrne walking towards the car.

Opening the door, DI White left the vehicle and walked over to the two men.

'We just found the body,' he said. 'George Byrne is on his way to identify it right now. What are you playing at?'

'It's not a game,' Macca Byrne said, pulling out an automatic pistol. 'It's war.'

And with that, Macca Byrne shot DI White point-blank in the face.

As the dead detective fell to the floor, Macca stared into the car, smiling when he saw Stripe.

'Hey, little buddy!' he said, putting the gun away. 'Are we gonna have fun together!'

Macca Byrne leaned into the car, pulling out Monroe's unconscious, handcuffed body while Harrison opened the back door, pulling the terrified Stripe out by his arm.

'That looks painful,' he commented as he saw Stripe's broken nose. 'Enjoy the pain while you can, kid. It's gonna get a lot worse.'

Positioning[SP2] Monroe's body into the boot of a nearby and waiting car, Macca climbed into the driver's side as Harrison, pushing Stripe in front of him into the back seat, climbed in.

Leaving the body of DI White on the street beside his police pool car Macca Byrne drove off into the morning sun.

25

AN INVITATION TO MEET

Moses Delcourt stormed through the Seven Sisters building, shouting his mother's name. Anyone who saw him knew to remove themselves from the situation; his face was one of fury, with murder on his mind.

'Mum! Where are you?'

Eventually a door opened and Anita Taborsky, one of the Seven Sisters; a haggard, harridan of a woman, easily in her seventies with long white hair pulled into a bun, her physical appearance contrasting with the vibrant, expensive dress she was wearing, stared out at him.

'Your mother is in counsel,' she said. 'You must wait—'

She didn't continue as Moses stormed past her, entering a dining room containing an enormous table with chairs all around it. On these chairs sat five more women of varying ages, with Janelle Delcourt sitting at the head of the table.

All were now glaring at Moses.

'We're in session,' Janelle started. Moses just laughed.

'Don't give me that, Mum,' he replied. 'Everyone knows these are just set dressing. You're the one that gives the orders.' He leaned across the table now, almost spitting in anger.

'Like the one to kill Wesley O'Brien.'

Janelle Delcourt had an incredible poker face, but even she couldn't keep an element of surprise off it. 'Who?'

'George Byrne's right-hand man was found in a Birmingham river an hour ago,' Moses explained, his voice rising in anger as he progressed. 'They found the knife nearby; it has Dave Ewan's fingerprints on it. And in the jacket was a message, a little wet but readable. It said *Macca is next, love the 7S.*'

Janelle looked to the other women in the room. 'Well, it certainly sounds like us,' she smiled. Moses slammed his hand on the tabletop, the loud impact echoing around the room.

'Dammit, Mum!' he cried out. 'Macca and his dad were my problem to sort! Not for you to send your paedo mate over to do my business!'

Janelle stared at Moses for a long moment.

'Everyone out,' she commanded. The other women in the room rose silently from their chairs, leaving Moses and his mother alone.

'The next word from your mouth better be "sorry", young man,' she said, her tone ice cold and dripping with venom. 'I have sent no one to Birmingham. And I sure as Hell have sent no messages to that little druggie shit or his prick of a father.'

Moses went to speak, to reply to this, but paused.

'Sorry,' he replied meekly. 'I'll sort this.'

'Birmingham was your idea, your plan,' Janelle rose from her chair, now standing across the table from Moses. 'I let you play gangster because that's what you wanted. You think I didn't know that you planned to work that druggie bitch girlfriend of yours into this room? You were never getting this. Never!' She punctuated this by grabbing the small tumbler in front of her and hurling it at the fireplace, where it shattered in a minor explosion of glass shards.

She stopped, letting the silence hang ominously over the room for a moment.

'I already knew that this has gone too far, regardless of who the bodies they found are,' she said. 'I knew before you did. And I already have a plan. I'll be leaving shortly to hold peace talks with the Byrnes. Peace talks that we now need to ensure happen because you couldn't keep your cock in your pants!'

Moses stared sullenly at his mother. 'Where?'

'A house in Beachampton, near Milton Keynes,' Janelle said. 'It's been organised by a third party.'

'Who's gonna be there?' Moses raised his chin defiantly, as if daring his mother to ignore him.

'George Byrne for Birmingham and Danny Martin, speaking for The Twins,' she replied. 'It's being organised by a priest we all know. He's playing Switzerland in this war.'

'I'm coming with you,' Moses said. It was a statement, not a question, but Janelle didn't even argue this.

'Oh, I know you are,' she snapped. 'This is your bloody cock up, so they have specifically requested you. So grab your things as we leave in an hour.'

Moses turned and silently walked from the room, passing the other Sisters in the hallway without a second glance.

He couldn't look at them.

If he had, they would have seen his smile.

George Byrne sat in his office overlooking St Chad's
Queensway, otherwise known as the A4400 and one of the
main ring roads around central Birmingham, watching the
traffic passing by. He wasn't seeing the cars, or the dual
carriageway though; in his mind he was looking at a time,
long ago, when he played in the streets with his best friend
Wesley.

For over thirty years George Byrne had held his offices
north of the A4400, and south of the Birmingham and
Fazeley Canal; people called it *St Chads* now, or "just south of
Newtown", an area of decrepit buildings, cheap warehouses
and forgotten pubs. But George stayed there not because of
the price, but because of the history. This was the Gun
Quarter of Birmingham. All along Price Street were remnants
of the history of the Quarter; gun shops that still eked out a
trade in this day and age, many now transformed into
sporting goods or shotgun stores, some now converting their
trade into air pistols and toys. Next door to him was Horton
Guns, and across the street was The Bull Pub where he took
most of his meetings and his lunch. Again, he didn't go there
for the closeness of the location, but for the history; since 1729
there had been a hostelry selling beer there, and in the mid-
nineteenth century gun workers were paid their salaries
there.

George liked to pay his men there too.

The Gun Quarter had first filled orders for the
Napoleonic Wars and supplying the soldiers of the East India
Company. They armed the Crimean War, sent arms across to
the USA, mainly for Confederate soldiers during their Civil
War, soldiers including General Custer, who was known to
use a Birmingham *Galand & Somerville .44* pistol. Even in
World Wars One and Two the Gun Quarter stepped up, with

local firm Webley & Scott creating the official British sidearm for the Army.

George had found one hidden away in the wall when he'd first taken over this office. He'd taken it as a good omen.

George had loved guns. He'd loved the power that holding one gave him. And, with Wesley beside him, he'd used guns to build the empire that he now held.

But Wesley was gone now.

The call had come through ten minutes earlier; Wesley's body had been found in a river, and the police were searching for a weapon nearby. There'd been a note with the body, the contents of which had been passed on.

MACCA IS NEXT, LOVE THE 7S

George had already tried to contact his son, but he wasn't answering his phone and nobody knew where he was. This worried George, as even though he hated the little shit half the time, he was still his blood. And that trumped everything.

More than anything, though, he was angry. He knew that Moses and Macca were spoiling for a fight, ever since that junkie bitch came onto the scene. He'd thought that when they removed her, things would have changed, but a couple of months later things had simply got worse. It didn't help that Macca had visited that bloody priest more, although George couldn't fault a man for finding God.

His phone rang; for a second George stared at it, surprised. Nobody called his land line anymore. He'd even considered removing it, as most of his conversations were done on his smartphone these days. Picking it up, he listened.

'George?' The voice was familiar, and southern.

'Danny,' George replied. 'What d'ya want?'

'Just heard about Wesley,' the voice down the phone continued. 'I wanted to say how sorry I was.'

'Not as sorry as she's gonna be,' George hissed.

'Come on, George. Do you seriously think this was on her?'

'She left a note.'

'No, her son left a note. I've seen the photo too. It's more of this Moses verses Macca bullshit that's been building up recently. They cut up a guy in Islington, for Christ's sake.'

'They cut up my guy in Islington.'

'Because your son beat up one of her lieutenants,' Danny continued. 'It's a circle.'

'Yeah?' George rose now as he shouted down the phone. 'If it is, it's one that your bloody daughter drew.'

There was a long pause down the line.

'My daughter, my real one died at birth, and I've paid my penance for what happened to that junkie replacement,' Danny replied coldly. 'You were there.'

George rubbed at his temple with his free hand.

'Yeah, of course,' he said. 'It's just—'

'I know,' Danny interrupted down the line. 'I get it. But this needs to stop.'

'And how you gonna manage that?' George asked, staring out of the window again, watching the cars pass by.

'Father Lawson's setting up a peace talk today, neutral ground, halfway between both of you. I'll be there and so will Mama Delcourt. Alone, no crew.'

'Her boy?'

'I can't say, but she'll most likely bring him, especially as he's a part of this. You'll bring Macca?'

George nodded to himself.

'If I can find the little bastard,' he said. 'Send me the details. But if that priest gets out of line—'

'Come on, George. He's worked hard for us all over the years,' Danny replied. 'We can give him this one moment. And, let's face it, this is all on us, anyway.'

George didn't say goodbye, he simply disconnected the call, staring at the phone.

So Mama Delcourt and her son want to talk peace.

Pulling out a drawer in his desk, he reached to the back of it and removed a cloth package. Unwrapping it, he stared down at the 1887 Webley Mark I revolver that he'd discovered in a wall a long time ago.

It had been Wesley's pride and joy. He'd spent hours working on it, and because of this the revolver was cleaned, oiled and ready to use.

And today it would execute Janelle Delcourt and her son.

IN A GLOBE TOWN BOXING CLUB, JACKIE LUCAS STARED AT Father Barry Lawson with cold fury.

'I don't like you,' he said. 'I don't like priests in general.'

'I understand that,' Father Lawson replied. 'And I'm here purely as a messenger. Daniel has decided that we should play peacemaker in this war between North and South.'

'Danny Martin should have asked me first.' Jackie picked up a small free weight in his hand, staring at it for a moment before hurling it at the wall. *'He should have asked me first!'*

'Mister Lucas,' Father Lawson stayed calm in front of the unhinged maniac in front of him. 'I've worked with your organisation for a very long time now. I've made you and Daniel an extensive amount of money.'

'And lined your own pockets,' Jackie snapped. 'And treated your brother like shit!'

'I did,' Father Lawson nodded, but Jackie noticed a hint of a smile on the priest's face. 'And I will face God very soon about that. But I've agreed to allow this meeting, and I will host it today. George Byrne, Janelle Delcourt and Danny Martin will be attending. I was greatly hoping you would have joined us for these peaceful negotiations.'

'I don't play well with others,' Jackie snarled. 'Now get out of my club before I drag you into the ring and beat the living crap out of you.'

Father Lawson stared coldly at Jackie Lucas for a long moment before finally nodding.

'I'll give Daniel your regards,' he said. Jackie spat onto the mat he stood on.

'You tell Danny that we're done if he does this,' he said. 'I've let his actions over the last year fly because of all the shit with Angie. And you too, for that matter. But, once this is done, he moves on. You both do. Tell him that.'

Father Lawson nodded and turned from Jackie, leaving the club.

'I'll pray for you both,' he said as he walked out of the door and onto the street outside.

Father Lawson had never met Declan Walsh before. Even though Derek Salmon had spoken of him many times, and even begged Father Lawson to frame Walsh while ending his pain, he'd never shown a photo of the man to the priest. And that was why, as Father Lawson emerged out of the Globe Town Boxing Club, turning westwards towards Bethnal Green, he didn't recognise the man standing on the corner of Bullards Place and Warley Street, watching the entrance to the building.

And as for Declan, he stood calmly, watching the priest leave, allowing him to turn north down Morpeth Street, moving out of sight before following.

Because Declan recognised Father Lawson.

And Declan Walsh wanted *closure*.

———

26

MISSING PERSONS

THE MOMENT THE NEIGHBOURS HAD HEARD THE GUNSHOT, THE police had been called. And the moment that the tracker on the car had shown it to be DI White's car, DCI Bullman and Doctor Marcos had raced to the scene.

By the time they arrived, the scene had been locked down by the Washwood Heath police, a young police sergeant currently in discussion with several worried-looking PCSOs, pointing out areas to cover as the forensics team finished setting up a tent over the body.

Exiting the car first, Bullman strode over to the sergeant.

'DCI Bullman,' she said, flashing her ID. 'You the Duty Officer here?'

'For my sins,' the sergeant replied. He was tall with short-cut balding hair, giving him a Jason Statham-esque vibe. 'Sergeant Parker, ma'am.'

'Who's the Divisional Surgeon?' Doctor Marcos asked, already pulling blue latex gloves out of her coat pocket. The sergeant shrugged.

'Nobody here yet, ma'am,' he said.

Doctor Marcos nodded.

'Then I'll take it on until someone does,' she said. Bullman however grabbed her by the arm before she could continue on.

'Five months,' she whispered. 'No crime scene duties—'

'Dammit Bullman, Monroe was in the car,' Doctor Marcos snapped. 'You can damn well arrest me if you want, but I'm attending the scene and I'm the best qualified here.'

Bullman looked around the street, at the police constables, the forensics officers. They all seemed so young.

'Go,' she said, loosening her grip. 'Find out who killed my man.'

Pulling a mask on, Doctor Marcos walked off towards the car where three forensic officers were already working. Bullman turned to see a PCSO walking an old lady towards her.

'This is Mrs Baldwin,' the PCSO, a young Indian woman explained. 'She saw everything.'

'What did you see?' Bullman asked. Mrs Baldwin pointed to the car.

'The man there stopped the car and two other, younger men came out of one parked there. The man, the dead one that is, he got out and faced them. They shot him, grabbed an old man out of the front and a small kiddie out the back.'

'Was the old man fighting them?'

'He looked like they'd knocked him out,' Mrs Baldwin said. 'Sorry, but by that point I'd moved away from the window as I was calling you.'

'Did you see the two men?'

'It was a way away, and I didn't have my glasses on. But one of them, the one that fired the gun, was black.'

Bullman frowned at this. 'You mean a person of colour?'

'No, I mean black. Black jacket, black trousers. Looked like a funeral director.'

Bullman nodded at this. There was only one person who fitted that sort of description.

Macca Byrne.

She shook Mrs Baldwin's hand. 'Understood. Thank you. The constable here will take you somewhere comfortable for your statement.'

Leaving the witness to the PCSO, Bullman walked over to the white incident tent, pulling on her own gloves and mask as she did so. Peering in, she looked to the floor, where in a puddle of dried blood she could see the dead body of DI White.

They had shot him in the face, his features mangled by the impact. His greying hair had a tinge of pink to it, and his hands were empty, open.

He was talking. He was negotiating. And they killed him.

Leaving the tent, Bullman walked over to the car now. Doctor Marcos was at the passenger side door now, sniffing a coffee cup that had spilled onto the floor. Beside it was Monroe's discarded phone.

'They ensured I couldn't track him,' Doctor Marcos showed the phone angrily.

'Looks like White was stopped by Macca Byrne and a henchman,' Bullman said. 'He stopped the car and got out to speak to them, maybe try to reason with them. Strange they were here though, I thought with the Delcourts killing Wesley O'Brien, they'd all be returning to the nest and hunkering down.'

Doctor Marcos rose from her kneeling position by the door, motioning silently for Bullman to follow her.

'We need to talk,' she said, looking around, ensuring that

as they passed the crime scene perimeter that no other officers followed them. 'Somewhere private.'

There was a minibus next to them; Doctor Marcos slipped behind it, out of sight of the police. Confused, Bullman went to follow but found herself facing a furious Doctor Marcos who'd brought a wicked-looking scalpel up to Bullman's throat.

'Don't move,' Doctor Marcos hissed. 'You even twitch and I will nick your carotid artery. You'll spray everywhere, but I'm not afraid of blood. And you won't be too, as you'll be dead in ten seconds or so.'

'What the hell?' Bullman replied, staying completely still.

'The coffee cup,' Doctor Marcos explained. 'It was on the passenger side. If White was driving, then Monroe would have sat there. And he would have drunk it.'

'So?'

'It looked like coffee, but there was an oily slick on the sides. Examining it, there was a hint of salt and soap to the touch and smell.'

'GHB?'

'Oh, you know your date rape drugs then? Good. Yes, *Gamma Hydroxy butyric Acid*, better known as Liquid Ecstasy. Now I've not done a full test on the cup yet, but I'll bet you whatever you want that there was a shit ton of GHB in Monroe's coffee, enough to knock him out. And if that's the case, then the only way it would have happened was if he was given the coffee by someone who put it in. And as White was the only other person in the car ...'

'You think White did this?' Bullman was appalled.

Doctor Marcos shrugged.

'So far, since we got to Birmingham, we've met a constable and a PCSO who both worked for the Byrnes.

What's a Detective Inspector to add to the list? And as he worked for you …'

Tired of this, Bullman knocked the scalpel away.

'I'm not working for the Byrnes,' she hissed. 'God, I only moved here a few months ago to cover maternity duty! And there may be rotten apples, but that's not the entire unit!'

She looked to the sky, sighing.

'This isn't right. It doesn't scan correctly. Macca Byrne shot White, but if he was helping them, why would they do that?'

'Maybe White worked for the father? Not the son?' Doctor Marcos added. 'Also, why did they take Monroe rather than shooting him too?'

Bullman thought for a moment. 'They need him for something.'

Doctor Marcos nodded. 'That's what worries me.'

Bullman held her hands up. 'We friends now?'

Doctor Marcos nodded, placing the scalpel away. 'I just want my DCI back.'

Bullman placed her hands on Doctor Marcos's shoulders.

'Never hold a knife on me again,' she said, bringing her knee up hard, connecting with Doctor Marcos's midsection, sending her gasping, winded to the floor. 'Unless you intend to use it.' Bullman moved out from behind the minibus, returning to the crime scene. Doctor Marcos smiled to herself as she regained her breath.

'Ooh, I like her,' she muttered to herself before pulling out her phone and pressing speed dial.

'It's Rosanna,' she said into it when the call answered. 'Gather the babies. Code red.'

DECLAN HAD FOLLOWED FATHER LAWSON ONTO THE CENTRAL Line at Bethnal Green and had changed trains at Tottenham Court Road for the Northern Line. He'd kept his distance, always ensuring that although he was still in view of Father Lawson, he was never too close, too obvious. And, staying at a distance, he followed the priest off the train at Euston, and up the escalators into Euston Station itself.

Not realising that he was being followed, Father Lawson bought a ticket from the machine on the concourse, with Declan a couple of people behind in the queue paying close attention to the destination. He wasn't sure whether he'd read the screen right, but when it was his turn to reach the machine, he noted that there was a receipt on the floor, forgotten by Father Lawson when he left that stated that he had bought a single to Milton Keynes, which matched what Declan had seen. Buying similar, Declan turned and walked across the concourse towards the giant screen above the train platforms, looking for the next train there. It was a train to Birmingham New Street, although the platform wasn't announced yet.

Noting that there was a good twelve minutes before the train left, Declan used this time to work out his next steps. He'd deliberately left his phone in the office and needed another to contact the others, to let them know that something was occurring. He briefly considered stealing one from a commuter, but instead wandered over to a phone stand in the middle of the concourse, one aimed purely at international travellers who needed a burner while in the country, and bought a cheap, flip-up pay-as-you-go phone with twenty pounds worth of credit on it. This done, he grabbed a bottle of water from a sandwich shop and made his way onto the train, starting at the back and moving forward through the train until he saw Father Lawson sitting at a table seat near the other end of carriage D.

Settling down a suitable distance away, Declan pulled the phone out of the box, noting with relief that it came with an almost full charge. Inserting the SIM, starting the phone up and dialling a number, he waited.

Anjli Kapoor answered.

'It's me,' he said. 'I needed to contact you.'

'And we you,' Anjli replied, and Declan could tell the change in her voice wasn't good.

'What's happened?' he asked.

'They took Monroe and the kid,' Anjli replied. 'Looks like Macca did it. Killed a police detective in the process. Marcos and Bullman are working on it right now.'

'Any idea where they are?'

'No. And more importantly, we've learned that both George Byrne and Janelle Delcourt have disappeared, but both sides seem to be gathering forces, as if expecting a war.'

'Do me a favour,' Declan said, keeping his voice low. 'Go see The Twins. Find out what they know about this.'

'Why them?' It surprised Anjli that Declan would ask such a thing. Hell, it surprised Declan he'd asked such a thing.

'Because I've been following Father Lawson since he left them about thirty minutes ago.'

'Where are you now?'

'On a train from Euston,' Declan replied, looking up at the map of the route on the wall. 'Stops at Watford Junction and Bedford before I'm apparently getting off at Milton Keynes, because that's as far as Lawson's ticket goes.'

There was a pause as Anjli muffled the phone, and

Declan could hear her faintly shouting across to Billy, most likely passing on what Declan had said.

'Father Lawson has a church in Beachampton he attends,' she said. 'It's about a ... Come on, Billy ...' another pause. 'It's about an eight-mile drive from Milton Keynes, which is apparently the closest station.' There was a faint mumbling, and Declan assumed it was Billy passing more information. 'Apparently, it's smack bang in the middle between Birmingham and London.'

'Right,' Declan muttered. 'We need to find Monroe. Get Milton Keynes police to meet me at the station.'

'We can't,' Anjli replied. 'They want you for Derek Salmon's manslaughter.'

'You're kidding me!' Declan silently apologised to a lady across from him who glanced up at this. The train started to move.

'They found the DNA match to the skin cells. Salmon made an official complaint and Father Lawson gave a similar testimony when he left. We're using the fact that he's not who people thought he was as a defence, and Rajesh Khanna is checking the body right now, but until we clear you, you're a target. There's another thing, too.'

'What more?'

'George Byrne's right-hand man was stabbed this morning in Birmingham. The knife had the fingerprints on it of Dave Ewan, an enforcer for the Delcourts.'

'The one Macca's boys attacked?'

'The same. Apparently he was still a little pissed at that. Killed O'Brien and left a message saying Macca was next. We're picking him up now.'

Declan leaned back in the chair, considering this news.

'And all the players are in the wind, while Macca's taken Monroe?'

'Yes.'

'Something's happening and I mean right now,' Declan said. 'Copy this number I called you on, and if anything comes up, let me know.'

'What are you going to do?' Anjli asked, most likely concerned to what damn fool idea Declan was going to come up with next.

'I think I'm going to take confession,' he said, disconnecting the call and glancing up the train to Father Barry Lawson, currently reading a copy of *The Guardian.*

Something was going down, and Father Lawson was at the centre. Declan just knew it. And now, currently no longer a police officer, Declan found himself thinking like the soldier he'd been for twelve years before that.

A soldier who knew how to fight, and how to kill.

And if whatever Father Barry Lawson was involved in resulted in the death of Alexander Monroe, he'd kill every last one of them.

———

27

VISITATIONS

ANJLI KAPOOR HATED THAT BLOODY BOXING CLUB. IT WAS THE bane of her entire existence, a reminder of her past indiscretions and the smell of sweat and leather when she walked through the door always made her want to puke.

The club had been here since the seventies, and it didn't look like anyone had even attempted to decorate it or update the place since then. The off-green and tobacco-stained cream paint on the walls was cracking, covered over with aged boxing event posters of boxers who were in their prime then, but most likely dead now. The boxing ring in the middle had seen better days, the surrounding ropes slightly sagging with overuse, and the physical training equipment was held together with a mixture of leather straps, glue and duct tape. Glancing around the room, Anjli saw that only a couple of young boxers were training right now, one working on the heavy bags to the right while the other was utilising a knackered-looking skipping rope while the speakers played eighties rock music. However, as she entered the club one of the trainers, a meaty looking man in his forties, tracksuit over a tank top and his hair gelled back, walked out.

'No women allowed,' he said as he stormed towards her, jabbing his finger towards the door. 'Take your pretty little arse and turn around—'

He didn't finish as Anjli grabbed the finger, twisting it, sending the man to the floor in pain as she continued on. The two boxers, seeing this, stopped training and also moved in.

'Oi,' one of them said, the skipping rope still in his hand. Again, he wasn't able to continue as Anjli moved in fast, grabbing the rope, wrapping it around his hand in one quick motion and then, the rope over her shoulder, she pulled down, yanking hard at the arm, hearing an audible *pop* a split second before the boxer screamed, grabbing at his now dislocated arm.

And Anjli continued on, towards the back room and Johnny or Jackie Lucas.

It was Johnny that emerged though, his face a mixture of confusion and interest.

'What the hell are you doing!' he shouted, indicating the boxer on the floor, clutching his arm. 'Lenny has a fight in a week!'

'Not anymore,' Anjli replied. 'Send me some more, Johnny. I'll keep going all day.'

'Okay, so you're pissed at something,' Johnny said. 'Get on with it, spit it out.'

Anjli reached into her pocket and pulled out a flash drive. Waving it to gain Johnny's attention, she tossed it over to him.

'Photos,' she said. 'Declan's crime wall. All in high definition, all in close up. Every face, every name, every person. Taken when I was in his house. You can add that to the iMac you stole from him.'

Johnny looked down at the flash drive in his hand. 'As I said before, we didn't steal anything,' he said. 'But why bring these to me now, though?'

'They took Monroe,' Anjli replied. 'Macca Byrne kidnapped him. And George Byrne, Danny Martin, Mama Delcourt, they've all disappeared. Derek Salmon's dead. Declan's being blamed for it, but we know it's Father Lawson.'

Johnny stared at Anjli for a moment.

'So what you're saying is that things have moved on a little since we spoke?' he smiled.

'I'm saying that my DCI has been drugged and taken by a mental teenager who shot another copper in the face, and I think it's connected to wherever everyone has gone.'

She fell to her knees in front of Johnny.

'You want me to beg? I'll beg. But I need your help, and I've given you the photos you needed and more.'

'Get up,' Johnny waved, placing the flash drive on a table to the side. 'I don't exactly know where the meeting is, but I know that Father Lawson was here earlier trying to get us to go to it. I wasn't here though, Jackie was. I think he was quite rude to the priest.'

Anjli nodded. 'We think we know where he's going, but we need confirmation, because if we go to the wrong location, Monroe could die,' she said. 'We believe it's his church in Beachampton. What we can't work out is why.'

'Because he's a priest and they're God-bothering trouble-makers who want to put the world to rights,' Johnny suggested. Anjli shrugged.

'That would work if he was the Father Lawson you think he is, but he's not.'

'What?'

'Well current opinion is that Barry Lawson was framed as

Stephen Lawson, was sentenced to eighteen years, got out of prison six months ago and immediately went to Deptford to kill his brother. Since then he's been pretending to everyone that he's Barry, which is technically correct I suppose, and he seems to have been quite busy after he learned that his biological daughters were murdered.'

Johnny opened and shut his mouth for a moment.

'Okay, DS Kapoor, I wasn't expecting that,' he said. 'I'm guessing that he killed Salmon? It'd make sense, as the rumours are that Salmon killed her.'

'No, that was a smokescreen he told Declan—'

'I don't mean then,' Johnny interrupted. 'I mean that a year ago, my brother and I heard a tasty secret bouncing around, that Derek Salmon had killed Angie Martin on the orders of his overlord.'

'But which overlord?' Anjli asked. 'He's worked with all of them, I think.'

'Exactly,' Johnny smiled. 'All three of them. After meeting up and deciding that she had to go.'

Anjli stared at Johnny Lucas in shock. 'Are you saying that Janelle Delcourt, George Byrne and Danny Martin got together and decided to kill Angela Martin, keeping it from Macca and Moses?'

Johnny didn't reply. He didn't need to. Anjli already knew that this was true. And now, a year later, all three were driving to a secret location to meet each other once more.

But this time the Father Lawson in the meeting was different. And he wanted revenge.

'It's going to be a bloodbath,' she whispered. Johnny laughed.

'Oh Kapoor, it's already been a bloodbath,' he said. 'What with words being etched into men's chests and others being gutted like pigs and dumped into rivers. What happens today? It's going to be *biblical*.'

BILLY WAS ABOUT TO LEAVE TEMPLE INN WHEN HE HEARD THE iPad on his desk whirr into life.

Angela's iPad.

Using the silicone thumbprint that DC Davey had kindly made him, Billy opened the iPad up, glancing through it. There wasn't much on it, as many of the apps were out of date still and needed uploading, but the Photos app opened.

Billy scrolled through them quickly; they were mostly photos of Angela Martin, mostly safe for work selfies with her boyfriend, although as he scrolled through them, he found the more intimate images starting to appear.

Which was fine if it wasn't for one thing.

The boy she was with in these images wasn't Moses Delcourt. It wasn't Macca Byrne, either.

It was Harrison Fennel.

Grabbing his jacket and leaving the iPad on the table as he left the office in a dead sprint, Billy was already calling Anjli on his phone.

IT WAS EARLY AFTERNOON WHEN MACCA BYRNE PULLED THE car into the driveway of Hall House. He'd never been here before; hell, he'd never been to Beachampton before, but he'd already decided that he liked it.

After picking up the fed and the grass, Macca and Harrison had taken the M40 south from Birmingham. The police had a number plate recognition system on the motorway, but Macca didn't think they'd be looking for him just yet; Wesley's murder would already be aimed at the Delcourts, and the dead detective had no links to Macca, even if he'd worked for his dad. Even if they did look for him, an hour down the line was still early days for the speed that the police usually worked. Still, to ensure that they didn't risk too much, they came off the motorway at Banbury and headed across country, passing through villages with names like Brackley and Buckingham before coming up into Beachampton from the south, driving up the country lanes that led past the white metal sign that proclaimed:

WELCOME TO
BEACHAMPTON
PART OF AYLESBURY VALE
PLEASE DRIVE CAREFULLY

It impressed Macca that, as if by magic, the houses suddenly became more opulent and the walls became higher. Enormous hedgerows hid white bricked houses from view, wrought-iron gates the only way to see into the driveways, surrounded by wide open fields that stretched as far as the eye could see; these homes flanked him now as he drove north, Harrison leaning forward to give directions. Harrison had been here before, only once, but he was fantastic at remembering places.

There was a stream running alongside the road, and Macca had a momentary thought of stopping to look at it; he could see ducks on it. And there was a part of him, deep inside, that knew that this could be the last normal day he'd have for quite a while. But that idle thought disappeared as they continued through the village, passing the high-walled estates.

This was why Macca liked the village. They didn't like people observing them. Macca could relate to that.

Turning left at a junction, Macca found himself on another country road, this time with a church, The Immaculate Conception of St. Mary The Virgin visible on the right.

'That his church?' he asked. Harrison nodded.

'But that's not where we're meeting,' he said, waving Macca down the road. 'It's a little way up and on the right.'

And, just under a mile down the Thornton Road, no wider than a single lane country road, Macca saw the turning. A simple entrance, with twelve-foot-high hedgerows mixed with brick walls, it faced across at empty fields. Turning into it though, Macca saw a wrought-iron gate of its own blocking an avenue, about two hundred yards in length, with horse chestnut trees on either side of it. At the end was a red-brick building, half hidden by the trees.

'He got this for being a priest?' Macca said, impressed. Harrison climbed out of the car, walking to the gate. Rummaging under a stone, he found a large iron key and used it to open the gates, pushing them to the side so that Macca could drive through. Leaving the gates unlocked and open, Harrison climbed back into the back seat. Stripe, sitting quietly and in utter terror, looked at him. Harrison smiled at him before waving Macca on.

'This used to be Beachampton Hall, or at least part of it,' he said. 'It's almost four hundred years old, but it was a bit of a pit when Father Lawson first came here. Luckily, he had a secondary income, a drug-related and very lucrative one that built it all back up over the last twenty years.'

'Won't the police come here looking though?' Macca

wasn't stupid. He knew that eventually the police would come, and that the chances were they were already on their way. Harrison shook his head.

'This isn't in Lawson's or the Church's name,' he said. 'Nobody knows about this.'

They pulled into a driveway, staring up at the 17th century manor house. It was a two-storey red-brick house, half built with stone and with a tiled roof, the windows a mixture of both old and new, most likely from where Father Lawson had been repairing. It was larger than Macca had expected, the size of a small manor house, and he climbed out of the car to stare up at it.

'I want it,' he said. 'When we're done here, we're taking Lawson out too, and I'm moving in.'

'That's not how you get houses,' Harrison laughed. 'Besides, I got the impression that he doesn't really want it.'

Macca looked to the unconscious Monroe. 'So where do we put him?' he asked. Harrison pointed down the side of the house.

'You go past there, it's clear fields all the way to the River Great Ouse,' he said. 'But until we need them, he suggested we dump Monroe and the kid in the cellar. There's an entrance to it beside the gable wall there. The doors are all bolted from the outside and there's no signal here, so they'll have no way to get help.'

Macca turned and looked at Stripe, still in the car.

'Don't worry, buddy,' he said. 'You're just a witness. Nothing bad's gonna happen to you.'

Stripe scrambled back, as if trying to burrow into the back seat. 'Is that what you said when Harrison there buried Gabby?' he asked. 'Nothing bad happened to her either, right?'

'That wasn't Gabby,' Macca replied calmly. 'That was a back-up plan.'

He smiled.

'You, however, are the principal attraction.'

As Harrison reached into the car and grabbed at Stripe he bit at the larger man's hand, but Harrison was larger and stronger and, with one hard punch to the side of the skull, Harrison sent Stripe to the floor of the car unconscious. Pulling him out and slinging him over his shoulder, Harrison looked to Macca.

'So what, I have to take the fed?' Macca asked. Harrison shrugged.

'Should have punched the kid first,' he said, already walking to the west of the manor, and the entrance to the cellar. Macca smiled, pulling the unconscious Monroe out by his feet. He'd need to hide the car around the back before they all arrived.

He didn't want the surprise to be ruined, after all.

28

HIDEAWAY GATHERING

DECLAN HAD ALLOWED BARRY LAWSON TO PASS HIM WHEN THE train pulled up at Milton Keynes station, Sitting in his seat by the door, he'd watched as the priest rose, folded up his paper and left it on the train's table, following the other travellers as they left the train. Rising to follow, Declan ensured that he was keeping four or five people between himself and Father Lawson, still worried that he could be recognised at any moment.

Making his way through the ticket barriers, Declan exited Milton Keynes Station and looked around. He'd never been there before, and he wasn't sure what to expect. What he found was a built-up area in front of him with two traffic loops: the left-hand side for taxis, the right-hand side for pickups and drop offs, and two rows of bus stops in front of him.

He couldn't see Father Lawson, but he assumed that he would head to the taxis, as while on the train Declan had checked for public transport routes to Beachampton and found none.

This was where Declan was convinced that Father Lawson was going; his church, The Immaculate Conception of St. Mary The Virgin. Billy had sent the address to Declan by text, and it made the most sense. And, as Declan walked towards the taxi rank, he saw Father Lawson climbing into one of the black cars, a larger people carrier model with the white TAXI sign on the roof. Allowing it to drive past and noting the registration, Declan ran to the next available car, clambering into the back. The driver, a middle-aged Turkish man in a blue shirt looked over his shoulder. 'Where to?'

Declan resisted the urge to shout follow that car and instead leaned closer, showing the address that Billy had texted.

'Beachampton? Gotcha,' the driver said, pulling out from the taxi rank and following the road out of the station car park. Declan leaned back in the seat.

'How long?' he asked. The driver shrugged.

'About fifteen minutes, depending on traffic,' he said. 'The A5 is closed for roadworks, so we'll likely go via Watling Street. You in a hurry?'

'Meeting a friend.' Declan looked out of the window as the car moved onto a raised dual carriageway. 'I thought Watling Street was in London?'

'That's right,' the driver said. 'All the way from Kent, through London, past us and up to Wroxeter.'

Declan nodded, pulling out his phone. With a few minutes to spare, he dialled a number, waiting for it to answer.

'Hello?' Jess's voice answered.

'It's me,' Declan said. 'Borrowing a phone as mine's broken.'

'Mum was trying to call you,' Jess continued. 'Said some police officers called, were looking for you.'

'I'm man-hunting so off the grid,' Declan lied. Well, it was only a small lie. He was off the grid, and he was man-hunting. 'I just wanted to see how the date went?'

'Badly,' Jess admitted. 'I don't think we'll be seeing each other again.'

'Why?' this confused Declan. 'He seemed like a nice boy.'

'Too nice,' Jess replied. 'And even though we made a bet, I think he was intimidated a little by you.'

'Ah damn, sorry.'

'No, it's fine. I think we were just expecting different things. You know, moving at different speeds.'

'Was he going too fast for you?' Declan asked, his fatherly anger rising. Jess, however, laughed.

'Christ no, Dad,' she said. 'I was going too fast for him!'

'He sounds like a keeper,' Declan replied, smiling. 'You should marry him.'

'Nah, I think I'll give up on boys for a while,' Jess replied. 'They'd just interfere with my exams, anyway. Maybe I'll become a nun.'

'No nuns,' Declan said, perhaps a little too strongly. Jess paused on the line before replying.

'You okay, Dad?'

'I'm fine, really.' Declan watched the road. 'I just wanted to check in.'

'Dad, Mum's going on a date tonight,' Jess said. 'I don't know if I was supposed to keep it secret, but it felt wrong keeping it from you.'

Declan felt his insides tighten at this but forced himself to relax.

'I know, sweetheart,' he said. 'I told her to.'

'Oh,' this obviously surprised Jess. 'Does this mean you're going on dates too?'

Declan thought for a moment. 'Maybe soon,' he said. 'Look, I have to go now, so I'll call you back later, okay?'

'Love you, Dad.'

Declan finished the call, staring down at the phone. He hoped that the next time he spoke to Jess, it wouldn't be through a glass divider.

Reaching into his pocket, he pulled out his wallet. There, on a post it note was a phone number that he'd taken off his father's desk weeks earlier. It was a number on his phone's contact list, but he didn't have that phone, or that list around. Quickly, he typed in a text message:

> It's Declan. Don't ask. When things are calmer, let's have that drink. Let's discuss the future.

Sending it, he leaned back once more in the chair, looking around. They were deep in the country now, empty fields on either side. He went to dial the office but noted that there were no bars on his phone, and therefore no signal. Hoping that by the time they reached the church there would be, he relaxed and enjoyed the ride.

Declan didn't want to spook Father Lawson, so he had the driver stop the taxi a little way down the road from the church. Paying him and leaving the car, Declan kept to the hedges as he walked up to The Immaculate Conception of St. Mary The Virgin. It looked quiet.

Too quiet.

He was about to enter through the main gateway, trying to find a way through the churchyard that would give him cover, when he stopped.

Coming down the road towards him was the taxi that Father Lawson had caught in Milton Keynes. It was a people carrier, and the driver was a woman, the only one in the rank at the time that Declan saw. Pulling out his warrant card, he waved it at her as he walked into the road. Slowing down, she nodded as Declan made a "pull over" motion, pulling to a stop beside the church.

'What's the problem?' she asked, winding down her window. Declan pointed back up the road.

'The man you dropped off, the priest,' he said. 'Did you drop him here or somewhere up there?'

'About a mile back,' she pointed back up the country lane. 'Big old place, can't miss it. He in trouble?'

'Do you have another booking right now?' Declan asked, mentally kicking himself. He'd been so convinced that the church would be the target he hadn't even considered another location. The driver shook her head.

'On my way back to Milton Keynes now,' she replied. Declan pulled out a twenty-pound note, his last one.

'Can you take me back there?' he asked. 'To where you went?'

'Sure,' the driver said as Declan climbed in through the sliding side door. Using the side road to three-point turn the car, she started back up the country lane.

Declan stared at his phone with annoyance. It still didn't have a signal.

'Does your phone work?' he asked. 'Mine's a cheap one. Doesn't have a good connection.'

'It's not the phone, it's the network,' the woman

explained. 'All around here's shit. Passenham to Thornton is like a black hole for cell towers.'

Declan pulled out his notebook, scribbling down on it. Tearing the sheet out, he fed it through the small gap in the dividing glass between the back seats and the driver.

'When you hit a signal, call that number,' he asked. 'Tell them I sent you and pass that message on.'

Taking it with one hand while watching the road still, the driver pulled to the side.

'It's the next house on the right,' she indicated the tall wall and hedgerow that surrounded the estate. 'I'm guessing you don't want to go in from the front?'

'Probably not ideal,' Declan climbed out of the taxi, looking around. He could see a public footpath that seemed to follow the side wall. 'Do you know where that goes?'

'Yeah, that's the Ouse Valley Way path,' she replied. 'Thirteen miler. It'll pass through the fields at the back of the house. Or at least beside the back wall.'

She looked down at Declan's shoes.

'You'll ruin those though,' she said. 'It's a bridleway. The mud'll be thick.'

Declan almost laughed.

'That's okay,' he said. 'I was thinking of getting new shoes, anyway.' He nodded to the driver, crossing the road and climbing the stile that led to the footpath. Making his way down the path, he realised that the wall was going to be almost impossible to climb. Luckily, about a hundred yards down the path, there was a horse chestnut tree on the other side of the wall that had grown over it, the branches hanging over the path. Declan realised that by using two bricks in the wall he could gain enough height to grab the branch. He used it to pull himself over the wall, landing awkwardly on the other side, but still hidden by the horse chestnut tree.

The ground was bare all the way to the house, and Declan knew that the moment he began to make his way across, he was open to anyone looking out of the window. There was a path along the wall though, and so he decided that the best course of action would be to sidle along it, to see if there were any better options to gain a closer look at the building, to see if there was another entrance he could use. This was nowhere near the size of Devington Hall, but it was old. There were always old tunnels and passageways in these buildings.

Well, he hoped so.

He was about to move when a noise stopped him, forcing him to crouch low as, down the driveway, a charcoal grey BMW Type 2 made its way towards the house. Moving to get a better look at the front of the building, Declan saw Father Lawson emerge from it, waiting patiently. Stopping beside a white Bentley, the car doors opened and Moses Delcourt and a woman, most likely his mother, emerged. Father Lawson spoke to them softly; they were too far away for Declan to hear, so as they entered the house, Declan moved quickly along the wall, hunting for a secondary entrance. He guessed that the Bentley was owned either by George Byrne or Danny Martin, although as he hadn't seen it parked outside Danny's house in Cyprus Street when they visited him, he assumed that it was the former.

Now on the west side of the house, Declan saw that this side had fewer windows, but at the same time had another car parked on the drive that Declan could use for cover. And, against the wall, Declan could see a covered entrance to what was most likely to be a cellar, an iron bolt keeping it locked.

Looking around and ensuring that nobody was watching, Declan ran across, pulling the bolt, opening the door and quickly sliding through, closing it behind him.

Down the steps, Declan quickly and quietly made his way into a large under-croft. It was obviously the cellar to the house, but standing there, amongst the pillars, Declan could now see how large the house's foundations truly were.

There was a noise, and Declan grabbed a length of wrought iron that was resting against one wall, possibly from the front gate. Moving slowly, he saw what had made the sound and, dropping the length of metal, ran to the unconscious forms of Alexander Monroe and Stripe, dumped in the under-croft beside some stone steps that looked to go into the house.

They were both tied and gagged, although Stripe had been secured with zip ties while Monroe was handcuffed from behind. Sitting Monroe up, Declan took the gag off, pulling up one of Monroe's eyelids to check on him.

Stripe, now waking, was making a *mmph* noise through the gag, so Declan moved over and pulled the gag off.

'Don't shout,' Declan ordered. 'I'm police. I work for him.' He pointed at Monroe, and Stripe nodded.

'He's drugged,' he said. 'Dunno what with.'

'Who did it? Was it Macca?'

'Yeah, and Harrison.'

Declan nodded. 'Do you know what they plan to do?'

'Kill everyone,' Stripe said. 'They're planning something with the priest. And with Moses.'

'They plan to kill Moses?'

'Nah, man. They're working with Moses,' Stripe rubbed his arms, now freed by Declan, glancing at his watch. 'They said it in the car. I pretended to be asleep. They're planning to kill everyone.'

Declan looked to the door. The chances were that his message to Billy might not have got through yet, and even if he found a phone here, he'd likely not get the police from Milton Keynes here in time.

All he had to stop some kind of major coup, was an unconscious, drugged DCI and a terrified teenager.

Declan couldn't help it. He laughed.

'Plenty of time to sort this,' he said, trying his best to believe it.

———

29

PEACE TALKS, WAR ACTS

GEORGE BYRNE WAS ALREADY IN THE LIVING ROOM AS JANELLE Delcourt arrived, led in by Father Lawson. The room was a large living area; the walls wallpapered green with the bottom half layered with mahogany. There was an enormous stone fireplace against one wall, currently unlit, and on the opposite wall was a bay window that stared out at the driveway of the house. There was a side cabinet with some decanters of whisky and brandy on it, a painting of what looked to be a Georgian woman and a spaniel, and in the middle, on top of the hardwood floor was a large oak table: rectangular and with four chairs, one on either side of it. George had his back to the window while facing the door and saw them enter before Janelle saw him.

'You've got some nerve—' he started in anger, rising from his chair, but Father Lawson waved him back down.

'You know how this works, George,' he said. 'Only as long as all three of you agree to work together can peace work.'

'You bring your son?' George sat down. Janelle nodded,

finding a chair on the opposite side of the large, rectangular table and facing George.

'Of course,' she replied. 'The damn fool is the reason we're here after all. Him and your son. You bring your boy?'

George Byrne shook his head, pointing at his phone.

'I left a message and told my men to bring him if they found him,' he complained. 'But there's no bloody signal here, so I don't know if they did.'

'Sorry about that,' Father Lawson smiled benignly. 'We have an issue with cell tower coverage around here. It's why I like it so. No distractions.'

Through the window, Father Lawson saw a third car pull up at the front. A Mini Clubman, it was driven by Danny Martin who, getting out of the car nodded to Father Lawson and made his way towards the front door.

'You need to go welcome him?' Janelle asked. Father Lawson shook his head.

'Mister Martin has been here many times over the years,' he replied. 'He helped fund the rebuilding, after all.'

A moment later Danny Martin entered the room, nodding to Father Lawson and sitting down on one of the two remaining chairs, glancing at both Janelle and George.

'Where shall we three meet again,' he chuckled.

'You think this is funny?' Janelle hissed. 'This all started with your bitch of a daughter.'

Danny shook his head.

'Not my daughter, remember?'

George Byrne slammed his fist down on the table.

'*Dammit!*' he yelled. 'Shut up! My oldest friend was murdered today by you!' He pointed at Janelle. 'I want vengeance!'

'And we will gain vengeance today, one way or another,' Father Lawson replied. 'But first, let us pray.'

———

IN THE CELLAR BENEATH THE MEETING, MONROE OPENED ONE eye groggily, staring at Declan.

'Did you just slap me?' he asked.

Declan nodded.

'Several times,' he said. 'It was the only way to wake you.'

'You look way too happy about the prospect,' Monroe muttered, looking around the cellar. 'Did you get caught too?'

'I'm the rescue team,' Declan said, trying hard not to react to the absurdity of it. 'But it's just me, I don't know when or if the others are turning up and I'm only here because I was following Lawson.'

Woozily, Monroe nodded. 'Right then, we're in the shite,' he said. 'As ever. How do I help?'

'Try to shake off whatever they put into you,' Declan turned to Stripe. 'You were awake when they came in here, did you see what they did to get through the gate? Is it an electronic one?'

Stripe shook his head. 'There's a key under a stone,' he said. 'Harrison opened the gate and then left it open. They left the key in the lock.'

Declan nodded. 'How fast can you run?'

Stripe puffed out his chest. 'Pretty fast.'

'Good.' Declan led Stripe over to the steps that led outside. 'If you leave through here, it's a straight run past the car and into the bushes by the wall. Make your way around the wall, get to the gate, yeah?'

'I can do that,' Stripe replied. 'Then what?'

'Once you get out, turn left and run into the village. Find a phone. Call the police. Tell them that DCI Monroe and DI Walsh are in danger and give them this address. Can you do that?'

Stripe nodded, even though he looked terrified.

'I can do that,' he said. 'I'm Beorma.'

Declan patted Stripe on the back, unsure what the boy meant by that, and looked to Monroe.

'What's going on up there?' the older man asked. Declan looked up to the ceiling.

'Some kind of peace talks, trying to stop a war,' he explained. 'Dave Ewan, the Delcourt man who was beaten up? Well, it seems he stabbed Wesley O'Brien, who was George Byrne's right-hand man—'

'Was it a sheath knife?' Stripe asked. Declan turned to him.

'Yeah.'

'Then he didn't do it.'

'His fingerprints were on the sheath,' Declan started. 'And—'

'I saw him hold it,' Stripe continued. 'When Macca beat him up. He gave him this knife, told him to take a shot. Dave wouldn't. But he was holding the knife and the sheath it was in.'

Declan looked to Monroe. 'Macca's being clever,' he said. 'He's setting this up.'

'To kill Moses? Or are we missing something?' Monroe was still groggy, shaking his head.

'We'll work that out later,' Declan said, looking to Stripe. 'You need to go now, get to the village and call for help.'

Stripe nodded and ran up the stairs and out into the

garden. Monroe, now almost back to normal, looked to Declan.

'So now what?' he asked. Declan shrugged.

'Now we find a way into the house and stop whatever this is.'

'We'll need weapons,' Monroe mused. Declan looked out of the cellar entrance, over at the car parked to the side.

'I think that's Macca's car,' he said. 'It was the only one here when I arrived. We might be lucky. There could be something in there to use, and I think everyone's a little preoccupied right now.'

'Then let's go break into a car,' Monroe replied, already making his way slowly to the steps. 'If we make it out of this alive, I'm going to kill that DI White.'

'You won't be able to, I'm afraid, Guv,' Declan checked out of the entrance one last time, ensuring they weren't being watched. Along the wall, making his way to the gate, Declan could just about make out Stripe.

'Aye? And why's that exactly?'

'Because Macca Byrne shot him.'

Monroe was silent as they made their way over to the car. It was unlocked.

'What kind of bloody idiot criminal leaves a car unlocked?' Monroe hissed, rummaging fruitlessly through the empty glove compartment.

'Maybe they were more distracted by dragging you to the cellar?' Declan suggested, popping the boot of the car. Carefully moving around, they pushed the boot of the car open, careful to monitor the facing windows. Declan pulled up the base of the boot lining, where usually a spare wheel would be hidden away.

There was a spare wheel.

'Goddammit,' he muttered, picking up some cable ties, the only things worth taking in the vehicle, it seemed. 'Why don't gangsters hide weapons in cars anymore?'

Monroe, rummaging around his coat pockets, suddenly smiled.

'They didn't search me,' he said. 'They must have thought I'd be unconscious for longer.' Pulling out his hand, he showed Declan what had been in his pocket.

'Perfect,' Declan said.

———

IN HALL HOUSE'S LIVING ROOM, THE CONVERSATION AROUND the table was getting tense.

'Dave Ewan was a kiddie fiddler!' George Byrne was shouting. 'He deserved everything he got!'

'As did your boyfriend Wesley!' Janelle yelled back. 'But we didn't do it!'

'Your son did!' George was almost apoplectic with rage now, his face reddening. Danny Martin was chuckling, watching his two rivals attacking each other. Seeing this, Father Lawson rose, walking over to the drinks tray at the side of the room.

'As fun as this is watching you all shout at each other, the day moves on and so must we,' he said, opening a drawer and pulling out a rosary. Walking back to the table, he dropped it onto the surface. It was a black acrylic rosary, with paracord knots in between.

It was a familiar rosary.

'Where did you get that?' Danny Martin asked, reaching across and grabbing the rosary, turning it in his hands.

'Same person you gave it to,' Father Lawson replied. 'My brother. Right before I killed him.'

There was a silence to this comment.

'That's not funny,' Danny eventually replied.

Father Lawson sniffed.

'It wasn't supposed to be,' he said. 'But I suppose I should really explain the entire story, shouldn't I?' And with that he clapped his hands, shouting out loudly, 'Boys, I think it's time to come and say hello.'

The door to the room opened and Macca, Moses and Harrison entered the room. Each of them held a gun, and one by one they stood behind their parental figure, with Harrison instead standing behind Danny.

'What the hell is this—' George Byrne went to rise but was pistol-whipped back to the table by his son.

'Stay down, Dad.'

Father Lawson grabbed the rosary back from Danny and stared at the table.

'Let me quickly get through the introductions here,' he said. 'Your sons, you know. But me? Maybe not so much.'

'What are you talking about?' Danny said. 'I've known you since we were kids!'

'Are you sure?' Father Lawson asked. 'What's my name?'

'You're Stephen Lawson,' Danny replied, noting that George Byrne looked surprised at this.

'And how would I be Stephen?' Father Lawson asked.

Danny licked his lips, unsure whether to answer, but the muzzle of a gun, pushed into the back of his head by Harrison standing behind him, found his voice again.

'You took Barry's place after we framed him for murder,' he whispered.

Father Lawson clapped his hands. 'An inspired plan, too,' he said. 'Setting him up as Stephen meant that you could continue your drug trade without Barry's annoying morals kicking in.'

His face darkening, Father Lawson leaned onto the table.

'But here's the problem,' he said. 'Six months ago, the original Barry Lawson was released from Belmarsh. He went to find his brother. And, once he found him, he killed him.' Father Lawson frowned. 'Tell me, is it still identity theft when you kill someone to take back your *own* one?'

Danny froze.

'You're not Barry,' he whispered.

'Oh, I am, mate,' Father Lawson smiled. 'The same one who you set up and left to rot. The same one that strangled Stephen with his rosary, *this* rosary, and the same one that smothered Derek Salmon with a pillow.'

He leaned back, looking around the table, at the expressions of shock on the faces of the three crime bosses.

'And the same one that, after he learned that both of his daughters were dead, decided to *execute* the three people who killed them.'

And with that command, all three guns behind the heads were cocked and ready to fire.

30

MEXICAN STANDOFF

Now armed with the meagre pickings from Alexander Monroe's overcoat pocket, Declan and Monroe snuck around to the back of the house where the back door had been mercifully unlocked. Opening it slowly, Declan peered into the kitchen of the building; a long, tiled room with wooden counters and benches. It was empty.

'I thought this would have been a little more guarded,' Monroe whispered, moving behind one counter. Declan moved over to a knife rack, taking a wicked-looking carving knife for his own weapon. Pulling out his phone, he cursed.

'Still no signal,' he muttered. Monroe checked into his pockets with his free hand and sighed.

'I must have lost mine in the car,' he added.

Declan shrugged.

'All we can do is hope that the kid gets the message out,' he said as they moved into a hallway, making their way slowly towards the front of the house. As they reached a closed wooden door, though, Declan froze. He could hear voices through it.

'That's Danny Martin,' he whispered to Monroe. 'I think he's talking to Lawson.'

Monroe prepared himself. 'This is stupid, laddie.'

'Channel your inner Rosanna Marcos,' Declan hefted his knife and, with a silent three countdown to Monroe, he turned the door handle and moved into the room in one swift motion.

There were three people sitting at a table: Janelle Delcourt, Danny Martin and George Byrne. Behind each of them was their child, or protégé in Danny's case, and each of these held a gun that was aimed at the person sitting to their immediate left. At the fireplace stood Father Lawson, looking shocked at the new arrivals.

'Please don't do anything stupid,' Declan said, brandishing the carving knife at Macca as the teenage gangster spun the gun to face the two intruders. 'You may think you can probably take us out first, but you really won't.' He indicated Monroe, currently holding up an unpinned grenade. 'He drops that and this entire room goes up. No survivors.'

'You're bluffing,' Macca hissed.

Moses shook his head, nodding to Declan.

'I dunno, bruv,' he said. 'That crazy bastard had a gun to Kayas when he came to see us. I can see him doing this in his sleep.'

'You did that?' Monroe looked to Declan.

'Can we talk about that later?' Declan asked.

'Oh, we'll definitely be talking about that later,' Monroe replied, looking to the others. 'Only way to stop the death is to ensure all the deaths,' he stated. 'You were going to kill me anyway, so what do I have to lose?'

'You weren't gonna be killed, fed,' Macca *tch*ed. 'You were gonna be the witness to three crime lords offing themselves.'

Declan noted the other two guns, still aimed at their targets.

'I see that,' he said. 'Three gangland bosses meet in a room and shoot each other. Monroe wakes up, finds the bodies. Calls it in.' He looked to Lawson. 'I'm assuming you'll be playing the victim, the one that wakes the drugged DCI in the process?'

'Well, I was going to, until you spoiled the plan,' Father Lawson replied. 'I'm guessing that you're Declan? I thought you'd be shorter, from how Derek spoke about you.' He broke into a grin. 'Wait! I remember you! I saw you on the train!'

'Shouldn't have gone to see The Twins,' Declan replied. 'Only reason I found you.' He looked back to the others. 'Drop them, or we all die.'

'Some of us might want that,' Harrison hissed, gun unwavering. Monroe stepped forward.

'Would Angela have wanted that?' he asked. It seemed to do the trick, as Harrison reluctantly nodded, dropping the gun to the table. Macca wavered, gun in his hand.

'You don't know what this bastard did to me,' he said, indicating his father. 'He needs to die.'

'You don't have the guts,' George Byrne turned to Macca, who was now pulling out his butterfly knife, one-handedly opening it. 'Oh, you gonna slit my throat? Go on then.'

'I ain't gonna do that,' Macca replied. And then, before Declan could stop him, he rammed the blade down, spearing George's hand to the table.

As George screamed, reaching for the blade, Macca looked to Moses and nodded. Just like Harrison, Macca and Moses dropped the guns.

'You don't know what you're interrupting,' Moses said as Declan took the guns, passing one to Monroe who gratefully replaced the pin in the grenade and threw it to the side. Declan meanwhile placed the third gun in his trouser band while aiming the other at the people in the room while Monroe, pulling out a handkerchief passed it to George Byrne, taking the freshly pulled out and bloodied blade from him.

'I think I've worked it out,' Declan said to Father Lawson, pulling out some cable ties, throwing them onto the table. 'Indulge me, while your three accessories are secured?'

As George, Janelle and Danny rose, cable tying their progeny's hands behind their backs, Father Lawson walked over to the table and sat down.

'I'm all ears.'

'Let's start with the elephant in the room.' Declan walked to Father Lawson. 'Have you told them who you are yet?'

'I have,' Father Lawson replied. 'I didn't want them going to Satan without knowing. And yes, they also know that Angela and Gabrielle were my children.'

'Okay, so let me see if I can work everything out,' Declan smiled. 'You shared your role with your brother, and he was the one who worked with Danny. You did, after all, play with each other as kids. Stephen and Danny brought drugs in from Africa, and before you knew it, you'd found yourself in above your head.'

'He knew exactly what he was getting into,' Danny hissed.

Declan held up a hand.

'My story,' he said. 'So there you are, stuck in this situation, and then you find a small ray of hope. Sister Nadine. You consider leaving the priesthood, perhaps. You definitely conceive twins together.'

Father Lawson nodded silently.

'But this causes issues,' Declan continued. 'Nadine can't

keep a secret, and you can't tell her the truth. "Father Lawson" is supposed to be in Africa right then, and you're here, out of sight.'

'I had to see her,' Father Lawson admitted. 'It was stupid.'

'You're damn right,' Danny Martin hissed.

'So then we have the babies being born. You're told to go away, to stay here. Stephen takes over your duties.' Declan looked to Danny and George. 'And that's when you both come in.'

Danny folded his arms. 'I'm innocent here,' he protested.

'You have the drugs by now, but not the supply,' Declan suggested. 'The Twins aren't that interested in your plans, and you need a new distributor. Enter George Byrne. Craig Chapman now works with him, and there's an opportunity. Craig's wife is pregnant, Danny's wife is pregnant, the plan is made to have both men in the same Mission while their wives give birth, to hammer out a deal with Stephen Lawson where nobody sees it. But things go wrong.'

Danny nodded. 'Cheryl died.'

Declan paced around the room as he spoke. 'Now here's one bit I can't really confirm, but this is what I think,' he said. 'At the same time, Nadine gives birth. Twins. The nuns name them Gabrielle and Angela. The two babies from the two wives die from complications. Now the nuns have a dilemma. What do they do? They call in Father Lawson, who we all know as Stephen, and he speaks to Nadine alone, but tells the nuns that things were too stressful on Nadine, and she's passed away.'

'He killed her,' Father Lawson replied. 'He admitted it to me. He smothered her with a pillow.'

'So now the nuns need to decide what to do with the bairns,' Monroe continued. 'And they have these two convenient families there that don't know that their own babies are dead.'

'I'm guessing this was Stephen's idea. That you didn't know this,' Declan looked to Danny who nodded quietly. Declan continued.

'So Barry Lawson, the real one, returns from Beachampton and sees that Nadine and the babies are dead. He blames Stephen, blames everyone. He tells you he's not doing this anymore. That he's ending the incredibly lucrative deal you have going on. And you decide to remove him.'

'We didn't want to kill him' Danny replied. 'Just get him out of the way.'

'By setting me up!' Father Lawson snapped. 'You ended my life! Threw me into purgatory!'

Danny didn't reply.

'It was Derek, wasn't it?' Declan asked. 'He was the arresting officer. You had him falsify the fingerprints, prove without a doubt that Barry here was his brother.'

Danny nodded his head. Declan looked to the others in the room.

'And then Barry becomes a footnote,' he said. 'For the moment. Because meanwhile, in the years that follow, Gabrielle Chapman and Angela Martin grow up, unknowing of each other. And Danny here works out an alternative plan to take over everything.'

'He told me to introduce Angie to Macca,' Harrison, now sitting on the floor beside the sideboard, said. 'He wanted me to whore her out to him. But before that he'd already introduced her to Moses.'

'But by this point, she already knew that *he* wasn't her father,' Moses added, looking at Danny. 'She told me so.'

'Exactly,' Monroe took over the story now. 'She did this

DNA test and learned that Daddy Dearest wasn't. So, she went to the Mission and spoke to the nuns. She learned of the sister she didn't know that she had, and she went to Birmingham to find her. I never spoke to the nuns there, but I think I know what she found. Gabrielle Chapman was barely there. She'd suffered a debilitating brain injury when she was a child, maybe from when her parents died. With nobody to look after her, the nuns, feeling a sense of duty for the child of one of their own, took her in.'

'She was almost catatonic,' Harrison replied. 'Angie took me to see her once. She didn't even know when her own sister was in the room.'

'At this point, Angela wanted out of this world of crime,' Declan continued. 'She was in love. Wasn't she, Harrison?'

Harrison nodded. 'We were gonna run away together,' he said. 'We'd use Gabby as the way out. We weren't gonna kill her, just let everyone think that Angela had suffered some kind of stroke while we ran away with everything. We knew the nuns would have to help us, they were terrified of the truth coming out, and the police taking away their house. Angela ensured that she and Gabby were identical. We tattooed a rose on Gabby's shoulder, and Angela had to break her own forearm while on a school trip to mimic one that Gabby had gained somehow. And while we did this, Angela kept doing what Danny asked; she pretended to go out with both Macca and Moses. Danny thought she was building up his empire, but all the while we all worked together.'

Declan looked to Janelle Delcourt. 'At what point did you work out what was going on?' he asked. She shrugged noncommittally.

'Moses would never take over the Sisters,' she said. 'So he

thought that he could bring in that bitch, remove me and replace her as the Matriarch.'

'I didn't want to control your bloody sisters!' Moses shouted. 'I just wanted you to accept me!'

Janelle didn't look at her son.

'I should have spent more time with you,' she said. 'It would have strengthened you. Not led to this weak fool I see in front of me.'

'So, you got together?' Declan said, more a statement than a question.

It was George that replied.

'By this point Danny had learned that she wasn't his kid. She'd told Stephen in confession, thinking that he was her actual father, you see. So, we got together, here, a year or so back. We didn't know they were working together, just that the little cow was causing issues. She'd started taking drugs at this point. Lots of drugs. She was becoming a liability. We knew we'd be better off without her.'

'So you hired someone in this room a year ago to kill Angela Martin.' Monroe spoke now. Danny nodded.

'An old friend.'

'Derek Salmon,' Declan said. 'You hired Derek Salmon to do it.'

Janelle Delcourt nodded.

'Danny had used him before, but we had him on our books,' she said. 'We paid him to kill her, to make it look like an accident. But he killed the wrong girl.'

'He killed the idiot one,' Danny hissed. 'He was scared, thought he'd been spotted, didn't bother turning the light on when he found her. If he had he would have realised that although she was identical, she wasn't that identical, you know? He gave her a drug overdose, but it wasn't enough. She started to moan, to scream. Salmon realised about now that he'd done the wrong girl, and so the idiot strangled her with a rosary and then ran off, leaving us to clear the shit up.'

'That's when Harrison and you took the body and buried it. When Alfie Mullville saw you.'

'I thought Danny'd killed Angela,' Harrison said. 'I was gonna kill him and bury the body. I didn't realise until we got to the Lickeys that it was Gabby in the back. He wouldn't say who did it but hinted that it was Moses.'

'And what about Angela?' Monroe asked.

'Salmon again,' Danny replied. 'He found Angela in London but didn't have time to fake the death as an overdose. He killed her with the same rosary and then buried the body.'

'So Derek did do it,' Declan raised his eyebrows in surprise. 'And the Sisters told him to.'

'Sometimes the best misdirection is based in truth,' Monroe suggested.

'We let the boys think that the other one did it,' Janelle added. 'We wanted them suspicious of each other rather than helping each other against us. And at the start, it worked.'

'Until you came along.' Declan looked at Father Lawson, who beamed, nodding.

'Until I came along,' he repeated. 'About time we got to the good part.'

31

COUNTDOWN

Billy and Anjli stood outside The Immaculate Conception of St. Mary The Virgin, testing the door to the church, in case it opened. It didn't.

'This can't be right,' Billy backed away from the door, looking around. 'There's literally nobody here. And the ones that are, seem to be local and would have noticed something.'

Anjli nodded, walking back to the gate where several members of Milton Keynes finest stood ready to assist in the church's storming.

'I think we might be in the wrong place, guys,' she said reluctantly. She was angry at herself; time was running out. Declan should have been here by now, as the train he had been on had stopped at Milton Keynes a good half an hour earlier. She was worried that perhaps Father Lawson had carried on to Birmingham, and Alex Monroe was still in the West Midlands, or even dead by now.

'It has to be the right place,' Billy was holding his phone in the air as he turned in a slow circle, looking at it. 'We're almost literally between Birmingham and London. Is anyone else not getting a signal either?'

There was a sound from the village, a speeding car. The police officers with Anjli and Billy, all in heavy combat gear turned to face whatever was coming, but they didn't expect the furious forms of Doctor Marcos and DCI Bullman driving up to the church at speed, screeching to a handbrake skid mere yards from them as both Doctor and Detective bounded out of the car and ran to the constables.

'Are we too late?' Doctor Marcos said. 'Have we gone in yet?'

'No,' Anjli shook her head. 'There's no sign of anyone being in, and if Monroe had been brought here, there would have been people seeing it. That couple over there by the bench, for a start. They've been weeding the older graves for the last three hours.'

Bullman looked around the crossroads beside the church. 'Then which way do we go?' she asked. 'It has to be around here. I can't ...' she stopped as she stared up the Thornton Road.

'Is that Stripe Mullville?' she asked, pointing.

Doctor Marcos looked up the road and started running towards the approaching figure, Billy running beside her. A moment later they brought an obviously shaken and tired Stripe to the small gathering of police cars by the church.

'DCI Monroe and DI Walsh are in danger,' Stripe said. 'They told me to say that.'

'Who did?' Bullman asked. Stripe stared at her as if she was an idiot.

'DCI Monroe and DI Walsh did, obviously.'

'Where are they?' Doctor Marcos knelt before the boy now. 'You came from that direction. Is it that way?'

Stripe nodded. 'It's a house about a mile down there. Took me ages to run here.'

'Can you show us on a map?' Bullman asked as Anjli and Billy already ran for their car, the officers doing the same. Stripe nodded.

'I can do better than that,' he said. 'I'll take you there myself.'

———

'I SPENT SEVENTEEN YEARS IN BELMARSH PRISON,' FATHER Lawson explained. 'None of these old bastards came to visit. But I got visitors.' He pointed at Harrison. 'Angela, looking for answers and gaining none from my brother, came to see me with Harrison. They were the first people in over a decade that believed in me. She said she'd try to get me out, to prove my identity, but I never saw her again. I never knew why until I was released six months ago and learned of her disappearance.'

'Is that why you killed your brother?' Declan asked.

Father Lawson shook his head.

'No, I'd decided to kill him a long time earlier,' he explained. 'But my problem was I was thinking too literally. I killed him and regained my life way too fast. I should have tortured him, learned everything first.'

'That doesn't sound like a very priestly thing to do,' Monroe muttered. Father Lawson shrugged.

'I stopped being a priest the day I arrived in Belmarsh,' he said. 'Revenge kept me alive.'

'So how did you find out about the murders?' Declan asked.

'Derek Salmon,' Father Lawson chuckled. 'He'd been

trying to fight cancer, but they'd just given him the diagnosis that said, "pack your bags, buddy." He was scared, convinced he was going to Hell, which he was by the way, so he decided that a bit of confession wouldn't hurt. He thought I was Stephen, but I played dumb, said he needed to say everything as if I was a stranger. He got on his knees in the confessional and admitted to everything. The murders of my daughters. My incarceration. I almost killed him there and then, but I realised that he could be useful in bringing me to the people that truly deserved my wrath.' He indicated the three young men sitting on the floor. 'And I realised I wasn't the only one wanting vengeance. I gave him absolution and sent him on his way. I then passed a message to Harrison, proving that I was the Lawson he spoke to in prison, the real father, and that I wanted to gain revenge.'

'By taking everything from them, like they took it from you?' Declan suggested. Father Lawson laughed.

'That was the plan to start with,' he said. 'I worked with Macca and Moses, talking to them through confession, just like Angela had done before. We compared information. We worked out the best way to gain everything from this.'

'Gang war.' It was George Byrne who spoke. 'Use it to remove us all and replace us.'

'I never wanted to replace you,' Macca snapped in anger. 'I wanted you to accept me, and to lose something that *you* loved!'

'At least you had that opportunity,' Moses replied. 'My family wouldn't accept me because I was a man.' He looked to Declan. 'I loved Angela like a sister. But we were never lovers.'

'So, why the whole thing with Derek?' Declan asked Father Lawson. 'Why did he admit to the murder?'

'That was never part of the plan,' Father Lawson admitted. 'Derek was dying. It scared him that he might run out of time before he could end your career. He jumped the gun a little there. All I'd asked him to do was to reveal where he'd buried Angela. Not start some singular mission. And I hadn't expected the boy to have seen it.'

'So, why did you kill him?' Declan continued. 'When you gave him his Last Rites?'

'Because I'd promised to take his pain away,' Father Lawson said. 'I smothered him with his own pillow. Take that as a confession of my own.'

'So, you did all this to lead to today?' Monroe looked confused now.

'This wasn't the plan,' Father Lawson admitted. 'We wanted to take this longer, to make the families, all the families hurt more. But then Derek started getting impatient and got you involved, and the bodies appeared ... we realised quickly that we had to escalate this fast and end it quickly.'

'The parents all kill each other,' Monroe replied. 'The sons aren't here. They all have convenient alibis. I never saw Macca kill White; he drugged me before getting out of the car. Only Stripe saw, and I'm guessing that there was a deal to be made with him?'

'No,' Macca sighed. 'He was going to die too. He saw Harrison that night. We'd never know if he told anyone.'

'I would have untied the old man, not realising of course that they had brought him here,' Father Lawson explained. 'But that's a bit out of the window now.'

'You're rather calm for someone whose revenge plan just went out of the window,' Declan said, looking up at the window. At the gates to the house, police cars were swarming through.

'Not at all,' Father Lawson held his rosary. 'We're all going to prison. You can get a lot done in prison. I've made a lot of friends.'

'The hell we are!' George Byrne had been inching his hand towards his jacket slowly for the last two minutes and now, rising and pulling his hand out, his 1887 Webley Mark 1 revolver in his hand, he fired a shot at Father Lawson, spinning around to fire a second shot at Declan—

Who fired his own weapon at George Byrne. He hadn't meant to kill the gangster, but the movement was too fast to aim to wound, and he fired, aiming for the shoulder but catching George in the neck as he fell to the floor. There was chaos in the room, and as the police cars pulled up outside the house, Janelle Delcourt grabbed the grenade from the side, pulling the pin.

'I'm not going to prison!' she shouted, looking at Moses. 'You should have killed me when you had the chance!'

Declan and Monroe dived to the side as there was a loud bang and the simunition grenade that Doctor Marcos had stolen from SCO19 exploded over the room. Clutching at her paint covered eyes, Janelle screamed as she fell to the floor. Declan ran over to Father Lawson, only to find that the priest was already dead. The door behind Declan crashed open, and he spun around to see DCI Bullman, Billy and Anjli burst into the room, and then pause as they observed the chaos in front of them.

'You shot someone!' Doctor Marcos said from behind. 'And you said I was the reckless one!'

Declan and Monroe couldn't help it. They started laughing, holding each other up, unable to stop as the police entered, pulling up the survivors and dragging them out.

EPILOGUE

IT WAS ANOTHER HOUR BEFORE THE CRIME SCENE WAS TRULY examined, with Doctor Marcos complaining that the paint grenade had contaminated everything, while Monroe pointed out that it was her stolen grenade in the first place. Declan sat on the steps of the house, staring out at the garden, wiping some last flecks of paint from his cheek.

In the car was Alfie Mullville, staring sullenly at the chair in front of him. Declan nodded to the boy, gave him a thumbs up, but secretly he felt sorry for the kid. His parents were addicts and on the wrong side of the law most of the time; Alfie was better than that, but could never be *Beorma*, the mighty king of Birmingham that he wanted to be. Or maybe he would. Nobody knew what would happen now Macca and George Byrne were removed from power. At least with the Seven Sisters they'd just hire a new one, likewise The Twins replacing Danny Martin. But with the Byrnes gone, there were another series of battles about to start, with everyone vying for the crown. Declan looked over to Harrison Fennel, being placed into a car. His love for Angela had changed everything, and even from the grave, their plan to bring everything down was still happening, if not in the way that they had planned.

Anjli sat beside him on the steps, passing him a tea towel from the kitchen.

'You got some paint on your neck,' she said. Declan took the tea towel.

'I need to tell you something,' she continued. 'About The Twins.'

'Did you go to them like I asked?' Declan replied. Anjli nodded.

'Did you force them to say where we were?' he added. Anjli, once more, nodded.

'Then you don't have to tell me what you think you need to,' Declan said. 'You've done more than enough for me.'

'You need to know this, Guv,' Anjli continued. 'I owe The Twins. My mum, she has cancer. The NHS was going to take years, so she's on private healthcare. It's expensive, but Johnny Lucas sorted it for me while I worked at Mile End.'

Declan nodded. 'It's not the same as gambling debts,' he said. 'You did this to help someone else.'

'I gave Johnny photos of your dad's crime board,' Anjli continued. 'It was the only way to make a trade for the information.'

Declan didn't ask why Anjli had photos. He didn't have the strength to right now.

'Sometimes you do what you need to do to get what you want,' he replied softly. 'And he'd have got hold of them anyway, just like he got the iMac.'

'This is why I needed to tell you all of this,' Anjli turned to Declan. 'He claims he didn't burgle your house. Someone else took the iMac.'

There was a silence as Declan took that in. Anjli broke it.

'I just wanted you to know. I'll be handing my resignation in later today. I won't let Johnny or Jackie control me anymore.'

'You'll belay that order.' Declan placed a hand on Anjli's shoulder to stop her rising. 'If you quit, you get off lightly. I'm not having another DCI Ford moment here. You stay, and you fix things.'

'But what if I can't?'

'You fix things, Anjli.' Declan thought for a moment.

'Why did you get transferred to the Last Chance in the first place?'

'I'd rather not say.'

'Is it worse than this?'

'A little,' Anjli reluctantly admitted. Declan nodded.

'So, something worse than grassing on your fellow officers to organised crime.'

Anjli went to reply to contest this, but then stopped, lowering her head.

'Well, when you put it like that ...' she muttered.

'Whatever it was, you're living with it every day you come to work. And you still come to work. And now we know you're being forced to work for The Twins, we can make that work for us. Feed them information, see what we can gain from them.'

He leaned in.

'You're in debt to me now, DS Kapoor. And you'll work it off by being the best damn officer you can be.' He smiled. 'After all, you're not the first in the squad to find themselves in that spot, and we'll need to know who replaces Danny Martin and George Byrne.'

'You think they'll be replaced?' Anjli asked. 'I mean, we

don't really have a cast iron case here. It's mostly word against word. And we don't have more than Alfie Mullville and Mrs Baldwin's witness reports to Macca murdering White.'

'We don't need anything,' Declan smiled, a weary one. 'Mama Delcourt is already pushing for a deal. They'll all attack each other and give us the case in the meanwhile.'

Anjli smiled for the first time as Declan looked over to Monroe and Doctor Marcos, still arguing over simunition theft.

'Do you think they'll ever get it together?' Anjli asked. Declan looked to her in surprise, and she laughed. 'Come on, you must have seen how they act around each other. And Christ, she came like a bat out of hell to save him.'

'I can think of worse couples,' Declan smiled, rising to meet Bullman as she approached.

'Outstanding work, Walsh,' she said. 'You'll be happy to know that Lawson's statement about smothering Salmon has been proven truthful. Forensics at Tottenham North have confirmed Derek Salmon was murdered after you left. I still don't understand the fingernail scratch, but you skated through. I'll be watching you.'

And with a nod to Anjli, DCI Bullman walked back to her car.

Declan looked to Anjli. 'I need to stretch my legs,' he said. 'Catch you back at Temple Inn?'

'Later, Guv,' Anjli walked over to Billy, currently talking to a rather attractive male police officer. 'I need to stop DC Fitzwarren making a mistake he'll regret tomorrow.'

Declan pulled out his cheap little burner. There was still no signal, but at some point there must have been, as a text had come through:

My future doesn't involve Pete. Love that
drink. X

Declan smiled to himself. Monroe saw this and walked
over to him, nodding to Bullman as he passed.

'You okay, laddie?' he asked. 'I ask because you're such a
morose bugger at the best of times, but here you are, grinning
like a Cheshire Cat.'

'You know how you once told me to stop talking to Kendis
Taylor?' Declan asked.

'If I recall, I've repeatedly told you to stop talking to
Kendis Taylor,' Monroe replied. 'What about it?'

'I think I might go on a date with her.'

Monroe sighed, slapping Declan on the back. 'And you're
a romantic bloody fool for considering that.'

He looked around for a moment, noting that they were
currently alone.

'Has Billy spoken to you yet?' he asked. 'About his breakfast meeting?'

Declan shook his head. 'It's been a bit hectic, sir.'

Monroe pulled Declan to the side.

'He had a friend of his family, someone in the know call
him, telling him to get out of the Unit, keep his distance from
us,' Monroe said. 'Said that Charles Baker is gunning for us,
and you specifically.'

'Baker?' Declan frowned. 'I thought they finished his
career?'

'Apparently not,' Monroe tapped the side of his nose. 'So,
be aware, sonny. People are watching us, and not for our witty
personas and dynamic conversational skills.'

As Monroe walked off, Declan stared around the driveway; at Billy and Anjli, currently arguing following Anjli's

cock-blocking attempt and then at Monroe and Doctor Marcos, still fighting over paintball guns.

These were his family now.

Even DC Davey back in Temple Inn was family, although she was definitely a kind of distant stepsister; one that was often left in examination rooms and morgues way longer than a woman her age should be. And to hear from Monroe right now that someone wanted to break up that family?

Declan Walsh was going to have words.

DI Walsh and the team of the *Last Chance Saloon* will return in their next thriller

HUNTER HUNTED

Order Now at Amazon:

http://mybook.to/hunterhunted

And read on for a sneak preview…

PROLOGUE

Of all the Livery Companies in London, Charles Baker reckoned that the *Worshipful Company of Stationers and Newspaper Makers* was the most pointless.

Usually known as the *Stationer's Company*, they formed it way back in 1403, although it had to wait until 1557 for its Royal Patronage. Many people claimed it was an Elizabethan patronage, and this was the start of the Elizabethan "Golden Age", but the fact of the matter was that 1557 was still very much in the time of her sister, Mary I. She was better known as *Bloody Mary*, a nickname given mainly because of her persecution of Protestant heretics, burning hundreds at the stake during her reign, and therefore this long-established printing and stationer guild's "Royal Patronage" had been bathed in infamy from the very start.

Charles was a fan of the earlier versions of the guild; illuminated manuscripts were beautiful things, and Charles was very much a fan of beautiful things. It was just that once technology (in this case the simple printing press) replaced the art of calligraphy, a kind of crassness came into the industry. The stationers stopped non-members from having the right to copy texts; that's where the term *copyright* came from. Then from the printers came the publishers, and the publishers created the newspapers.

Charles Baker hated the newspapers.

Nowadays, though, the Stationer's Company represented more of the *content and communications* industries. This included digital media and software, and worse still, advertising and PR. Probably not what the poor buggers who created the guild over six hundred years ago had ever envisioned; that their beautiful, artistically designed manuscript guild would one day be filled with bloody Instagram influencers, science-fiction authors, and people like Rupert Murdoch and William sodding Hague.

But, as much as he despised many of the members, he couldn't fault the fact that they threw a damn good party.

In fact, it was a party that they threw that Charles Baker now found himself at, standing at the head table in the Livery Hall, with dozens of Freemen of the company and Liverymen watching him as he prepared to speak. It was an amazing location for a speech: deep mahogany wood panelling covered most of each wall, with a variety of hand-lettered members lists, portraits of liverymen, flags or even coats of honour adorning each one, with the top third of the wall (and the ornate ceiling above him) painted cream and gold, with guild flags hanging above heraldic shields. When the windows weren't looking out onto London, they were replaced with beautiful stained glass windows of ancient printers such as William Tyndale or William Caxton, given the same reverence that a church might give to a saint. It felt religious. It felt as if he was giving a sermon.

Which, in a way, he was.

'Thank you, Master of Company,' he said to the wizened old man in the tuxedo who now sat to his left, 'for that wonderful introduction, and thank you,' this was to the hall itself, 'for giving me such a warm welcome.'

There was a small smattering of applause at this. Charles forced a smile.

'As a Member of Parliament, I have had an interesting history with the Worshipful Company of Stationers and Newspaper Makers,' he said. 'In fact, I think that all Members of Parliament have, at times, had a similar situation.'

There was a low rumble of polite laughter. Charles allowed it to build and fall before he continued.

'When I was a child, printing fascinated me,' he continued. 'To be able to place words onto paper and change a single mind in the process was nothing short of a miracle to me, and it probably was the one thing that set me off on the career path that I chose.' He paused for a moment, allowing the silence to fill the room. 'But, although it set me on my journey, it hasn't been that kind to me.'

The room was still silent, but now the atmosphere had changed, as if the other invited guests had realised that this *wasn't* the speech that they had been expecting.

'As many of you know, a few weeks ago my beautiful, wonderful wife, Donna, passed away,' Charles continued, allowing a hint of emotion to creep into his voice. 'She had suffered from mental issues for much of her life, including clinical depression. So, when the national press started attacking me, started commenting on a child I'd had out of wedlock a life ago, before we even met, a child that I hadn't known that I was the father of, it proved too much for her, and she took her own life.'

There was a muttering in the hall after this. Charles had

never publicly spoken about how Donna had died. They had believed it was because of illness, not because of an overdose, or a noose in the underground garage of the Baker's house. Charles carried on.

'It's true,' he continued, 'and I will never forgive you, the ones that did this. I will hunt you down and I will destroy you.'

He was enjoying this.

'I look up and I see Caxton and Tyndale, the fathers of printing and I wonder, what would they say if they saw this travesty that sits here before them? Would they, like Doctor Frankenstein, be appalled at the monster they had created?'

The murmuring was building now, an angry rumble, as the people sitting at the tables now realised that this wasn't a simple after-dinner speech. This was a spanking.

'I may not be the Secretary of State for the Home Office anymore, but I still read the briefings,' Charles said. 'I've seen the rising gang war that is occurring between Birmingham and London, a war that you yourselves have given life to, after your reckless reporting of the murders of Angela Martin and Gabrielle Chapman in the national press. You cannot run unchecked—'

'But that was stopped!' A portly man at one of the closer tables shouted out. 'It was on the news tonight!'

Charles paused. The man spoke with such conviction that for a moment Charles wondered if he'd been mistaken. Glancing down at his phone, turned over on the table and switched to silent mode so as not to distract him, he picked it up, abandoning his speech for the moment as he turned the phone in his hands and saw the notifications of missed calls and left messages. Reading them, he nodded to himself.

'My apologies,' he continued. 'I was in session directly

before this, so I hadn't seen the news. And yes, it seems that both the Delcourt family and the Byrne family have been taken into custody following a police raid on a Beachampton residence earlier today.' He straightened his shoulders, giving the appearance of someone proud.

'I'm happy to say that the unit that solved this case comes from the City; in fact, their offices are less than a mile from here. Actually, the arresting Detective Inspector is the same one that saved my own life several weeks ago. Our police are a credit to us, if woefully understaffed. But that doesn't stop the fact that this wouldn't have escalated so fast if there had been some order, some regulatory aspect to your radical news agenda.' He was back on track now, casting aside the bad news as he pushed forward. 'If I ever get the chance to make such a change, I will ensure that all media, be it traditional press or digital, will follow the rule of law. I hereby put you on notice.'

With that, to a cacophony of complaints from guild members as they rose from their tables, Charles Baker placed his phone into his jacket pocket and, his work done here, turned to leave the table. However, blocking his way was the man who'd introduced him, the Right Reverend Doctor Reginald Walsingham, the current Master of Company.

'Interesting speech,' he whispered. 'If we'd known you were coming to tell us off, we would have called the current Home Secretary to replace you. I mean, we invited you when you still held the role, not when you became nothing more than a backbencher.'

'I'm far more than a backbencher,' Charles replied with a smile. 'You think these articles, these news reports hurt me? Things that I did when I was young and single, that I was never informed about. Follies of youth.'

'How about the reports of Devington Industries working with you on arms contracts? Or the rumours of illegal arms trades? Of Rattlestone?' Reginald raised an eyebrow. Charles laughed at this.

'Walk into the House of Commons on any Prime Minister's Question Time and throw a stone,' he said. 'I guarantee that whoever you hit on whatever side will have the same industry-related skeleton in their closet. Yes, I have made questionable choices in my career, but I have something better on my side.'

He leaned in.

'I have public sympathy.'

Reginald stared coldly at Charles for a long moment before speaking.

'You almost sound like you killed her deliberately to gain the widower vote,' he said.

'Old man, that's a very cynical view of life you have there,' Charles replied. 'But rumours are rumours and facts are facts.' He looked up to the stained window where a Latin phrase was emblazoned under the image of a man arguing with another over a proffered piece of parchment.

'*Verbum Domini Manet In Aeternum*', he said. 'Interesting motto.'

'The word of God remains forever,' Reginald translated.

Charles nodded. 'I know,' he said. 'I'm not a pleb. I did Latin at Harrow. I was just considering that you might think about changing it.'

'To what?'

Charles leaned in.

'The word of law remains forever,' he finished before patting the shoulder of the Master of Company, waving to the room of dinner guests and, with his Special Branch guards either side of him, marched determinedly out of the hall, the sound of angry diners rising behind him as he left.

'Where to, sir?' his bodyguard asked as Charles climbed into the back of his Ministerial car. He might have been nothing more than a backbencher to the public now, but that was for the masses to believe. He was destined for far greater things, and the party knew this; they had made concessions for him.

'The George,' he said, checking his watch. 'I'm running late.'

THE GEORGE INN WAS A PUB OFF SOUTHWARK HIGH STREET, just south of the Thames. It was an old medieval coaching inn where Charles Dickens had once drunk, although that debatable claim could probably be given to most of the pubs and taverns in London. A long, white-painted, galleried and timber-framed pub, it was mainly a series of interconnected bars with a restaurant and function room upstairs. It was to the latter of these that Charles, now in a thick coat, scarf and hat to disguise his identity, made his way up rickety stairs, opening the door on his left and entering a small, quiet room with windows along one wall.

In the room were four other people, all Members of Parliament. Malcolm Gladwell was the trouble-shooter of the Conservative Party, and the MP for some pokey little Berkshire dump that had been too stupid to vote him out in the last election. Stick-thin and with curly ginger hair, Gladwell was a sickeningly fit, bio-hacking ultra-runner in his late forties who looked a decade younger, thanks in part to the multitude of expensive supplements he sucked down every day. Like a cockroach, he'd most likely survive everyone.

Next to him sat Tamara Banks, one of Charles's rivals for the Conservative throne; in her early forties and resembling the bastard daughter of Cruella De Vil and Heinrich Himmler, Banks was a toxic Thatcherite, more right-wing than most of her party, a woman that had gained power and influence during the Vote Leave campaign, but was distanced enough to keep her reputation once Brexit polarised everyone.

Watching out of the window was Jerry Robinson, an Ulster Democrat. Squat both in stature and intellect, and patting down his greasy, dyed-black hair as he stared at the young, attractive women in the beer patio below, Jerry was a devout creationist who didn't believe in dinosaurs, believing that they were a test from God to see if humankind's faith was strong enough.

Charles thought that Jerry Robinson was a test from God. That, or a rather annoying joke.

The last person in the room was a Labour MP, one that Charles had known back when he was on the red side of the Commons. Norman Shipman was old, ancient even, nothing more than a well-dressed skeleton under stretched-tight skin. He'd been an MP back when Jim Callaghan was in charge in the seventies and every battle, every fight was etched into his face. He'd spent his entire political career on the back benches; but Charles knew from experience that this was where he did his best work.

In the shadows, in rooms like this, and with people just like the ones that Charles faced right now.

'You're late,' Tamara complained. Charles didn't bother to reply. Complaining about someone when they arrived was simply Tamara's way of saying hello to them.

'I see your man's in the news again,' Malcolm smiled. 'If he keeps this up, we might have to promote him to DCI.'

'He's not my man,' Charles poured himself a wine from a bottle on the side table before turning to face the others. 'Also to be honest, I'd have preferred it if he delayed a few days.'

'So where are we on these?' Straight to business, Jerry drank from his bottle of tonic water. He didn't use a glass, just the tiny bottle. It looked ludicrous.

'Do I have permission to move on with the target I informed you of during the last session?' Charles asked. Malcolm looked at Norman, as if waiting for guidance. Even though he was of a different political party, Norman Shipman was the obvious leading force in the room.

He nodded.

'I call this session of the *Star Chamber* open,' he said, his voice cracked with a mixture of age and far too many cigarettes.

Charles released his held breath as he leaned onto the table he sat beside.

'As I said last time, I put forward an extremist terrorist to include in the lists,' he spoke carefully, ensuring that he didn't mis-speak, or understate anything that he was revealing. 'We believe she was radicalised in Syria two years ago and, since returning to the UK, she's been running as part of a terrorist cell in South West London with a UK-born and radicalised, London-based handler.'

'Do we have any idea about what her plan is?' Tamara asked. Charles shook his head.

'All I know is that after we investigated her, she met with my wife the same day ... the same day that Donna killed herself.'

'You think this extremist caused your wife's death?'

Tamara seemed appalled, but Charles guessed it was a more mawkish curiosity.

'I do,' he nodded. 'I also believe she is a danger to our Government.'

'We shall put the name into the lists for consideration,' Norman nodded slowly, looking to the others. 'Any refusals?'

As the other MPs in the function room agreed to this decision one by one, Charles quickly tapped off a text on his phone under the table, sending it off before Norman looked back to him:

flick the switch

'What's the name to be added?' Norman asked, returning Charles to the conversation.

'Taylor,' Charles Baker replied. 'The extremist terrorist's name is *Kendis Taylor*.'

THE MAN WITH THE RIMLESS GLASSES SAT IN HIS CAR, PARKED on the pavement at Tudor Street, deep in the City of London. He'd been there for close to an hour now, watching the evening trade at the wine bar to his right as, ahead of him, he monitored the white-bricked, arched entrance into Temple Inn. There was a large, black gate and a yellow and black barrier blocking his way into the Inns of Temple, and the guard would be in the cabin to the side of it. That said, people walked in and out all the time with no issues, and the man with the rimless glasses knew the guards paid them no heed, especially when they dressed in overcoat, scarf and suit.

His phone beeped with a message; glancing down, he read it. The man with the rimless glasses didn't recognise the number, but he knew who the order had come from. He'd known ever since he'd moved allegiances, since they had freed him from custody under ministerial conduct subclauses, creating this new legend, this new identity of sorts for him.

He knew what the order meant.

Leaving the car, the man with the rimless glasses made his way through the entrance to the right of the arch, past the notice that stated that *only residents could bring their dogs through* and, keeping his head down he passed the guard who didn't even glance at him in passing, reading that night's edition of *The Evening Standard* and ignoring the suited man who continued down Temple Lane, and out into King's Bench Walk.

Turning right as he entered the large courtyard, the man with the rimless glasses carried on along King's Bench Walk, stopping when he reached a particular door. It was late in the evening, and he knew that nobody else would be in; the target was still there though, as his car was outside, parked in a bay opposite the entrance. Checking to ensure that nobody was watching, the man with the rimless glasses entered the City of London police's Temple Inn Crime Unit, otherwise known as the offices of the *Last Chance Saloon*.

———

DETECTIVE CHIEF INSPECTOR ALEXANDER MONROE WAS TIRED, but he didn't want to sleep, scratching at his short, white beard as he stared at his laptop screen, trying to will the words on it to stop swirling around the display as he tried to type. Earlier that day they had drugged him while in Birmingham; a nasty little bugger named Gamma Hydroxy butyric

Acid, better known as Liquid Ecstasy on the club scene, given to him by an equally nasty little bugger, the corrupt police officer Detective Inspector White, shortly before White himself had been killed like a dog in the street by Birmingham gangsters. Monroe had woken up in a basement in Beachampton, rescued by his *own* Detective Inspector, Declan Walsh. After wrapping up the case with the help of a large amount of bravado, bluff and a simunition grenade, Monroe was checked over by the Divisional Surgeon, Doctor Rosanna Marcos, who had fussed over him like a bloody mother hen before allowing his team to take him back to the office. He'd sent everyone else home, saying he just wanted to finish up before leaving, but the fact of the matter was that Monroe didn't want to go home. He didn't feel safe anywhere outside of his own office right now.

Also, when he closed his eyes, he had a fear, an irrational one, that he would wake up like last time.

Handcuffed and gagged in a basement.

So, Monroe had started this letter, trying to take his mind off the gnawing terror in the pit of his stomach. He'd already tried napping on the office sofa to see if that helped; it didn't.

However, the sound of someone walking up the stairs into the primary office stopped him.

Rising from his desk, he walked into the open-plan office, watching the door. Nobody was due back, and the steps were heavy. A man's shoes.

The man with the rimless glasses emerged through the entrance into the room, stopping when he saw Monroe watching him. Middle-aged with short, dark-brown hair, the man with the rimless glasses looked more like an accountant than an assassin.

'I know you,' Monroe intoned. 'We arrested you in Devington Hall.'

The man with the rimless glasses nodded, sauntering towards Monroe. He also knew that Monroe had been spiked earlier that day; he was relying on this to slow the old man's reactions, to make him an easier target to take down. Monroe however hadn't finished, still trying to clear his fuddled brain.

'You're the one that attacked Declan outside his apartment,' he continued. The man with the rimless glasses nodded once more, still continuing towards Monroe. He jerked his right wrist, and a vicious looking extendable baton flicked out.

'If this means anything to you, it's nothing personal,' he said as he raised it.

Alexander Monroe nodded, already realising that he wasn't fast enough to stop this attack, especially with the remnants of the GHB still in his system.

'So this is how it ends, eh laddie?' he asked calmly. The man with the rimless glasses thought for a moment, considering Monroe's last words.

'Yeah, pretty much,' he said.

Then he struck.

HUNTER HUNTED

Order Now at Amazon:

http://mybook.to/hunterhunted

ACKNOWLEDGEMENTS

Although I've been writing for three decades under my real name, these Declan Walsh novels are a first for me; a new name, a new medium and a new lead character.

There are people I need to thank, and they know who they are. To the ones who started me on this path over a coffee during a pandemic to the ones who zoom-called me and gave me advice, the ones on various Facebook groups who encouraged me when I didn't know if I could even do this, who gave advice on cover design and on book formatting all the way to my friends and family, who saw what I was doing not as mad folly, but as something good. Also, I couldn't have done this without my growing army of ARC readers who not only show me where I falter, but also raise awareness of me in the social media world, ensuring that other people learn of my books, and editors and problem catchers like Maureen Webb, Chris Lee, Edwina Townsend, Maryam Paulsen and Jacqueline Beard MBE, the latter of whom has copyedited all three books so far (including the prequel), line by line for me.

But mainly, I tip my hat and thank you. *The reader.* Who took a chance on an unknown author in a pile of Kindle books, and thought you'd give them a chance, whether it was with this book or with my first one.

I write Declan Walsh for you. He (and his team) solves crimes for you. And with luck, he'll keep on solving them for a very long time.

Jack Gatland / Tony Lee,
     London, January 2021

ABOUT THE AUTHOR

Jack Gatland is the pen name of *#1 New York Times Bestselling Author* Tony Lee, who has been writing in all media for over thirty years, including comics, graphic novels, middle grade books, audio drama, TV and film for *DC Comics, Marvel, BBC, ITV, Random House, Penguin USA, Hachette* and a ton of other publishers and broadcasters.

These have included licenses such as *Doctor Who, Spider Man, X-Men, Star Trek, Battlestar Galactica, MacGyver,* BBC's *Doctors, Wallace and Gromit* and *Shrek.*

As Tony, he's toured the world talking to reluctant readers with his 'Change The Channel' school tours, and lectures on screenwriting and comic scripting for *Raindance* in London.

An introvert West Londoner by heart, he lives with his wife Tracy and dog Fosco, just outside London.

Locations In The Book

The locations that I use in my books are real, if altered slightly for dramatic intent. Here's some more information about a few of them...

The Boxing Club near Meath Gardens that Johnny Lucas meets Anjli and Father Lawson in doesn't exist, and neither do the Twins - but the location used is the current **Globe Town Social Club**, within **Green Lens Studios**, a community centre formerly known as Eastbourne House, that I would pass occasionally in my 20s.

Hurley-Upon-Thames is a real village, and one that I visited many times from the age of 8 until 16, as my parents and I would spend our spring and summer weekends at the local campsite. It's a location that means a lot to me, my second home throughout my childhood, and so I've decided that this should be the 'home base' for Declan. And by the time book four comes out, I'll have completely destroyed its reputation!

The Gooch Street Bridge exists over the River Rea, as do the two decorative arches. I would pass it often when I lived in Birmingham.

Ambresbury Banks is indeed the name given to the remains of an Iron Age hill fort in Epping Forest in Essex, and is the north side of the **Jacks Hill** car parks. I would walk my dog often there when we lived in Epping, and the legends of Dick Turpin being in the area are all true. Although, as much as the rumours of various Kray Twin victims being buried there have been around for years, I've never seen one!

Saint Etheldreda's Mission House in Poplar doesn't exist, but is based on **St Frideswide's Mission House** in Lodore Street, which was the original Nonnatus House in 'Call the Midwife' (set in Poplar) and written by a midwife who worked there. In

1976 Mother Margaret Faith moved the Community to **Alum Rock** in Birmingham, where it remains today. This connection was one of the first things I considered when choosing Birmingham as a location.

Our Lady of the Sea Church in Deptford, however, is fictional. If there's any basis to it in reality, it'd be **St Nicholas's Church** in Deptford, where Christopher 'Kit' Marlowe is believed to be buried.

The Village of Beachampton exists, and is lovely. However, the Catholic Church **The Immaculate Conception of St. Mary The Virgin** does not, and is loosely based on the Church of England **Church of the Assumption of St Mary The Virgin**. In addition, **Beachampton Hall** did exist, and I use the estate to create Barry Lawson's country retreat, but the actual location doesn't exist. Also, Beachampton has a perfectly fine cellular service!

If you're interested in seeing what the *real* locations look like, I post 'behind the scenes' location images on my Instagram feed. This will continue through all the books, and I suggest you follow it.

In fact, feel free to follow me on all my social media, by following the links below. They're new, as *I'm* new - but over time it can be a place where we can engage, discuss Declan and put the world to rights.

www.jackgatland.com

Subscribe to my Readers List: **www.subscribepage.com/ jackgatland**

www.facebook.com/jackgatlandbooks
www.twitter.com/jackgatlandbook
ww.instagram.com/jackgatland

Want more books by Jack Gatland? Turn the page...

THE THEFT OF A **PRICELESS** PAINTING...
A GANGSTER WITH A **CRIPPLING DEBT**...
A **BODY COUNT** RISING BY THE HOUR...

AND ELLIE RECKLESS IS CAUGHT IN THE MIDDLE.

JACK GATLAND

PAINT
— THE —
DEAD

A 'COP FOR CRIMINALS' ELLIE RECKLESS NOVEL

A NEW PROCEDURAL CRIME SERIES WITH
A TWIST - FROM THE CREATOR OF THE
BESTSELLING 'DI DECLAN WALSH' SERIES

AVAILABLE ON AMAZON / KINDLE UNLIMITED

EIGHT PEOPLE. EIGHT SECRETS.
ONE SNIPER.

THE
BOARD
ROOM

HOW FAR WOULD YOU GO TO GAIN JUSTICE?

NEW YORK TIMES #1 BESTSELLER TONY LEE WRITING AS

JACK GATLAND

A NEW STANDALONE THRILLER WITH
A TWIST - FROM THE CREATOR OF THE
BESTSELLING 'DI DECLAN WALSH' SERIES

AVAILABLE ON AMAZON / KINDLE UNLIMITED

THEY TRIED TO KILL HIM...
NOW HE'S OUT FOR **REVENGE.**

NEW YORK TIMES #1 BESTSELLER **TONY LEE** WRITING AS

JACK GATLAND

THE MURDER OF AN **MI5 AGENT**...
A BURNED SPY **ON THE RUN** FROM HIS OWN PEOPLE...
AN ENEMY OUT TO **STOP HIM** AT ANY COST...
AND A **PRESIDENT** ABOUT TO BE **ASSASSINATED**...

SLEEPING SOLDIERS

A **TOM MARLOWE** THRILLER

BOOK 1 IN A NEW SERIES OF THRILLERS IN THE STYLE OF
JASON BOURNE, JOHN MILTON OR **BURN NOTICE,** AND
SPINNING OUT OF THE **DECLAN WALSH** SERIES OF BOOKS
AVAILABLE ON AMAZON / KINDLE UNLIMITED

JACK GATLAND

THE LIONHEART CURSE

HUNT THE GREATEST TREASURES
PAY THE GREATEST PRICE

BOOK 1 IN A NEW SERIES OF ADVENTURES
IN THE STYLE OF 'THE DA VINCI CODE'
FROM THE CREATOR OF DECLAN WALSH

Printed in Great Britain
by Amazon

40700425R00209